CONFESSIONS OF A HIGH SCHOOL GUIDANCE COUNSELOR

KELSIE HOSS

Copyright © 2021 by Kelsie Hoss

All rights reserved.

No part of this book may be reproduced in any form or by any electronic or mechanical means, including information storage and retrieval systems, without written permission from the author, except for the use of brief quotations in a book review.

This is a work of fiction. Names, characters, businesses, places, events, locales, and incidents are either the products of the author's imagination or used in a fictitious manner. Any resemblance to actual persons, living or dead, or actual events is purely coincidental.

Editing by Tricia Harden of Emerald Eyes Editing.

Cover design by Najla Qamber of Najla Qamber Designs.

Have questions? Email kelsie@kelsiehoss.com.

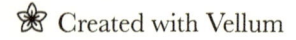

❋ Created with Vellum

For my boys.

CONTENTS

1. Birdie — 1
2. Cohen — 13
3. Birdie — 18
4. Birdie — 26
5. Cohen — 32
6. Birdie — 38
7. Cohen — 47
8. Birdie — 50
9. Cohen — 56
10. Birdie — 59
11. Birdie — 64
12. Cohen — 70
13. Birdie — 76
14. Cohen — 87
15. Birdie — 93
16. Birdie — 101
17. Cohen — 107
18. Birdie — 113
19. Birdie — 121
20. Birdie — 126
21. Cohen — 135
22. Birdie — 139
23. Cohen — 147
24. Birdie — 153
25. Cohen — 160
26. Birdie — 167
27. Cohen — 174
28. Birdie — 179
29. Cohen — 189
30. Birdie — 193

31.	Birdie	200
32.	Cohen	207
33.	Birdie	211
34.	Ollie	219
35.	Birdie	222
36.	Birdie	231
37.	Cohen	236
38.	Birdie	240
39.	Cohen	247
40.	Birdie	251
41.	Cohen	257
42.	Birdie	264
43.	Cohen	271
44.	Birdie	276
45.	Birdie	280
46.	Ollie	286
47.	Birdie	292
48.	Cohen	299
49.	Birdie	307
50.	Cohen	313
51.	Birdie	317
52.	Cohen	325
53.	Ollie	329
54.	Birdie	332
55.	Cohen	336
56.	Birdie	339
57.	Birdie	345
58.	Ollie	351
59.	Birdie	355
60.	Cohen	361
61.	Birdie	365
62.	Birdie	373
63.	Cohen	377
64.	Birdie	378
65.	Birdie	384

66. Birdie	390
67. Cohen	396
68. Birdie	397
69. Cohen	402
70. Birdie	405
71. Birdie	408
72. Birdie	411
73. Cohen	416
74. Chapter	420
Epilogue	425
Continue Reading!	429
Join the Party	431
Author's Note	433
Acknowledgements	435
About the Author	437

Dear Reader,

This book is full of humor, romance, and sexy scenes. Readers 18+ only, please!

Love,
Kelsie Hoss

1

BIRDIE

Confession: I don't have my life in order.

Nothing made me happier than early morning pancakes with my best friend. Except for maybe seeing a U-Haul on the street.

That *had* to mean Mrs. Cronckle was finally moving out to live with her daughter. With a smile on my face, I walked toward our townhome, ready to tell Dax we could say goodbye. No more senile neighbor who liked to comment on my weight, and no more of her creepy, winky cat.

I took the few steps into our front door and pushed it open. "Dax! You're not going to..." My heart stopped.

And that had nothing to do with the pound of bacon Mara and I had just consumed. Suitcases filled the living room. Among the bags, stood my fiancé.

Dax looked up from his phone, and very casually, slid it into his pocket.

"What's going on?" I asked, closing the door behind me, as though that simple latch would be enough to stop the inevitable from happening.

"It's not working out," he said flatly.

My mind was screaming, begging me to tell him that we were engaged. That only months ago he'd gotten on one knee and asked me forever. That even though I supplied most of the rent money, I couldn't afford this townhouse on my own. But all that came out was, "That's your U-haul?"

Dax glanced over his shoulder, just slightly, and that's when I realized we were not alone.

A petite brunette wearing a flowy dress and sky-high heels stood near our bedroom. The one Dax and I shared.

My brain short-circuited. "Dax? Who is she?"

"She's a friend," he said dismissively.

"Seriously?" I blinked quickly, fighting back tears and *rage*. It was the dumbest and most obvious lie. Couldn't he have come up with something more creative if he was going to thoroughly break my heart? He *was* an artist, after all.

He didn't reply, but that was all the confirmation I needed.

Now I knew why he was so hesitant to set the date for our wedding. But *why* did he have to cheat with someone like her?

Not only was she thinner than me, but she was *beautiful*, too, with stalk-straight hair that fell around her heart-shaped face and matched her doe-brown eyes. I couldn't help but feel self-conscious in my brunch leggings and T-shirt that showed just how much bigger I was than her. It was only seven in the morning. How did she look so perfect already?

Then a horrible thought crossed my mind. How long had this been going on?

But while I processed, he was already talking to *her*. "Can you take these to the truck?"

The truck. The one parked out front, ready to dismantle my life.

She carried two bags, then walked toward me where I stood in the doorway.

"Excuse me," she said.

And you know what I did? I fucking apologized for being in her way. What kind of masochist was I?

She walked outside, and I stepped farther into our living room. "So that's it?" I asked Dax, my voice shaking. "You're out?"

He sighed. "I haven't been feeling the connection, the fire that I should for someone I'm going to be spending the rest of my life with."

"And you're feeling the fire for her?" I didn't even

know her name. Shouldn't I know the name of a woman who helped dismantle my life?

"What about Ralphie?" Dex asked, sidestepping my question. "Don't you want to be with someone who won't mind you bringing that bird home?"

I almost rage-puked in his face. And yeah, that's a thing. "You're bringing up Ralphie?"

He threw his arms up. "What do you want me to say?"

I hated that question. It hurled all of his shitty behavior in my face and forced me to find a solution. "You could start with goodbye," I hissed and grabbed the bag closest to me, then threw it out the door, hitting his mistress. She cried out and stumbled backward.

It wasn't like I meant to hit her. I hadn't seen her coming. But considering she'd been in my house, helping break up my relationship, I didn't feel bad.

She looked at me like I was a monster and then to Dax like he was her savior.

"Go!" I yelled, then walked to *my* room, slamming the door behind me.

With tears streaming down my face, I slid down the door until I sat on the floor. Just an hour ago, I'd been laughing with my best friend at Waldo's Diner. And now? I was a mess.

I reached into my legging pocket for my phone, but when I clicked the button, it was dead. Deader than my relationship with my so-called fiancé who left me for a girl who couldn't tell a finch from a parakeet if she had an encyclopedia. Deader than encyclopedias.

With a groan, I crawled on my knees to plug it in and adjusted my frayed charging cord to get a little extra juice. And while I was at it, I had to get ready for work. Emerson Academy was just as strict on staff as it was on students, and showing up late was out of the question, regardless of broken bones, cars, and even hearts.

I walked to my closet and threw on a plain black dress. It looked like most of my others—professional, sleek, tailored. Just what you would expect of the person guiding high schoolers in decisions that would affect the rest of their lives.

Too bad I was obviously terrible at making decisions of my own.

My curly hair refused to behave, so I put it in a bun, sprayed down the flyaways, and grabbed my one-percent-charged phone.

I needed to leave or risk being late for work, but I couldn't bring myself to open the bedroom door. On one side was the bed I shared with Dax. And on the other side of the door?

I pressed my ear to the wood.

Nothing.

He was already gone.

My throat tightened, and my eyes stung, but I couldn't let myself keep crying. Not before work.

I left the bedroom and walked into the half-empty

living room. I folded my arms across my middle, taking it in. The home that I'd worked so hard to make ours had been dismantled in less than a day.

Knowing I'd fall apart if I stayed there any longer, I hurried to my car and got in. Except halfway down the road, I realized my skirt was trapped in the door. I had to wait for the next red light to open the door and give my legs some room.

I cursed Dax's name right along with this stupid skirt. Could it tell the kind of morning I'd had?

It was one thing to dump your fiancée and leave her with a townhouse rent that she can't afford on her salary. It was another thing altogether to make her late for work.

So, I sped as much as I could toward the school and ran in my sensible heels down the tile hallway. Faculty and staff were supposed to get to the school half an hour before the students, but I was closing in on fifteen minutes.

My office phone was already ringing when I reached my door. I fumbled with my keys, flipping past all of Dax's stupid studio keys, and shoved in the right one. The doorknob was as old as this fancy private school, so it took some jiggling before I burst into the office, making my bird squawk excitedly.

I rushed to the phone, yanking it out of its caddy. "Hello?" I gasped, trying not to breathe too hard.

"Miss Melrose," the secretary said in her sharp voice. "Why are you out of breath?"

I stifled my panting and said, "Chair yoga."

That earned me a harrumph. "A parent called this morning requesting a meeting with you first thing. I added it to your schedule but wanted to make sure you saw it in time. You didn't reply to my email when you should have arrived. Unless you were late..."

"Thanks for keeping track, Marge," I muttered, logging in to my computer. Very rarely did I have parents request last minute visits, and it was typically not the best of news. I could not handle any more trouble this morning.

"Mhmm," Marge said. The phone crackled as she hung up. At least it was Wednesday. Only two days left after today and then I could drown myself in a bottle or three of Cupcake wine.

I held the receiver to my ear until I clicked my way to my calendar, but it quickly clattered to the ground when I saw who requested the meeting.

"Pam Alexander," I muttered. "*Great.*"

Ralphie twittered at me, reminding me to fill his dish, so I hung the phone back up and opened the top drawer of my filing cabinet where I kept his specially formulated pellets and bottles of spring water.

Ralphie wasn't a spring chicken anymore—Grandma Karen got him for me as a high school graduation gift nearly ten years ago. Dax hated him, so when we moved in together, Ralphie found a new home in my office.

It was a win-win, really. I got to see Ralphie all day,

and most of my students loved him. Even the extra snobby ones.

I opened the cage, and Ralphie softly nipped my finger.

"How was your night?" I asked gently.

He tittered at me, then dipped his beak in the water dish.

"I had a rough morning. Dax left me."

Ralphie pinned his black eyes on me. Sometimes I really felt like he understood what I was saying. Either way, he was the best at keeping secrets.

"I don't really want to talk about it." I reached for the bag of seed and used a Dixie cup to grab a scoop. "What do you think Pam wants?"

As I poured the food into his dish, I wracked my brain for a reason she'd want to meet. As the cheer coach and a parent, there were several reasons I could imagine. Her child-actor son hadn't been in the office lately for bullying... Maybe I'd ruffled one of the cheerleaders' feathers.

I rolled my eyes toward the ceiling. Hopefully I could get out of this meeting with time to call my landlord before my next appointment. Dax should have paid this month's rent already, but I needed to make a plan for next month's rent.

With a few minutes to spare before eight, I went in the hall to get coffee from the teachers' lounge. The stuff they put through the machine tasted like dirty socks, but at least it had caffeine.

Students hung out around the hallways, and I tried to say hi to each one of them. Although most of the families were really wealthy, there were plenty of kids here who went weeks without a hug. Without someone saying they were proud of them. I knew because I'd been one of them once upon a time.

I smiled at a group of mean girls gathered around the lockers. There was a new ensemble of them each year, but they were always the same—with expensive handbags and glossy hair and pouty lips. Sometimes they were cheerleaders and sometimes not. But they always made life a little bit more difficult for everyone around them.

"Hi, girls," I said.

The queen bee, a girl named Oliva Nelson, flashed a smile faker than the frauda bag in my office. "Nice dress, Miss M. Heading to a funeral?"

I knew it wasn't a compliment, but I thanked her like it was. Giving her a wink, I said, "Always put your best foot forward, girls."

They giggled and whispered behind me as I made the last few steps to the teachers' lounge and filled my handmade ceramic cup to the brim.

One of my favorite students, Sierra Cook, had crafted this for me last year in art, and I used it every day. The intricate carvings of birds in the clay made me feel special. Like I was actually making a difference here, even if it was just in one student's life.

With my coffee still too hot to sip, I carefully carried it

back to my office and found Pam Alexander standing by the bench outside the door. She probably didn't want to get her pristine white pants dirty on a chair students used.

"Hi, Mrs. Alexander," I said, trying to sound chipper.

She glanced up from her phone, a look of annoyance on her face. "You're late."

I lifted my wrist to check my watch. 8:01. "Sorry about that. The extra minute must have been a *huge* inconvenience." I led her into the office, and Ralphie chirped loudly at her presence. Sometimes he thought he was a guard dog.

Pam gave his cage as wide of a berth as possible before sitting on the opposite side of my desk. At least she thought my chairs were clean enough.

"Marjorie said you called a meeting," I said, sitting across from her. "Is everything okay?"

"As a matter of fact, it's not." She flipped some blond hair over her shoulder and leaned forward. "My Ryde tells me that you have been pressuring him into applying for colleges."

So that's what this was about. "Are you referring to the guidance counseling meeting I had with him? Because I am required to meet with each of the seniors to help them with their post-graduation plans."

Her full lips pursed together. "He says you gave him applications to colleges."

"I did." And why did I suddenly feel on edge about it? "You know your son has amazing acting talents. I simply told him if he wants to explore a theatrical education at a school like Juilliard or Yale that—"

"He will do no such thing," she snapped.

My eyebrows drew together. "Excuse me?" Most Emerson Academy parents were set on their children attending the best universities. What was going on here?

"As we speak, major producers are considering him for roles in upcoming movies. He's not about to throw an opportunity like that away on something like college."

"Why does it have to be either/or?" I argued, getting fired up. My parents had told me the same thing—that I didn't need to go to college because my husband and family money would take care of me. Dax had proven how flawed that logic was. "You know, plenty of famous actors have attended college. Adam Driver, Natalie Portman—"

"Just because you're obsessed with the *Star Wars* franchise does not mean my son needs to become a trekkie."

I closed my eyes, wishing I had paid more attention in the yoga classes my mother forced me to attend with other rich white ladies when I was a teen. "A trekkie is someone who likes *Star Trek*," I explained. "They're not the same thing."

"Potato, tomato." She stood, hitching her purse in her elbow, then leaned over my desk. "You listen here, and you listen good. My husband and I donate so much to this school we could buy it if we wanted to. We have friends on the board of trustees, and my husband golfs with the headmaster. Do you understand?"

"Golf?" I asked innocently. "I've never taken much intere—"

"Don't be smart with me. I have friends in important places. Friends who could land your bargain-bin-wearing ass on the curb. Comprende?"

I stayed silent, keeping my gaze strong despite the tumult in my gut. She was right. And I couldn't afford rent as it was. I needed this job.

She stood. "That's what I thought." Then she walked to the door, and in the doorway, she smiled brightly and spoke loudly. "Thanks for such a productive meeting, Miss Melrose. Talk soon!"

As she walked away, I fell over my desk and hit my forehead on my arms.

The force was *not* with me today.

2

COHEN

I pulled along the curb at my son's school, Emerson Academy. The place always scared me a little. Probably because it was nothing like the public high school I'd attended in the next town over.

Ollie lifted his backpack into his lap as I drew to a stop, and his fingers were already on the door handle.

"Hey," I said. "I know we're running behind, but what about a 'see you later, Dad?' or 'have a nice day, Dad?'" He was only a sophomore in high school, but it seemed like yesterday I was his hero and all it took to earn a smile was an airplane ride or a piece of gum.

Ollie gave me a lopsided smile that looked so much like my own at that age. But where my hair was mostly straight, he'd gotten his mother's curls, and they grew out messy atop his head. "Bye, *father dearest*. I hope you have an astounding day enabling alcoholism."

"Sarcasm," I said. "Nice."

He pushed open the door and got out. "See you Monday. And water the plants, please."

"Will do. Love you," I said, wishing he wasn't too cool to hug me in front of all his friends walking past us in their navy-blue private school uniforms.

"Love you," he said quietly before shutting the door and walking away.

I stayed in the spot for a moment, watching him. Maybe it was teenage brain, but he'd been so up and down lately. Happy and chatty one moment and withdrawn in his room the next. Not for the first time, I wished I had a parent to call—provide some perspective—but that ship had long since sailed, crashed, and sank to the bottom of the ocean, never to be seen again. Maybe I'd call Gayle later—despite not having children, she was great with teens. I knew firsthand.

A horn behind me honked, and I looked in the rearview of my Tesla to see a soccer mom with bug-eye sunglasses pursing her lips at me. I went to drive forward but stopped just in time. Pam Alexander, venom in heels, was walking in front of my car. She gave me a mix between a glare and a grin, and I lifted my fingers at her in acknowledgement. I wasn't one to wish away time, but I couldn't wait until Ollie was out of this school.

The clock on my dash told me I was already late for

my next appointment, so I gunned it out of the parking lot and headed to meet my realtor. It had been two years since my wife and I split, which meant two years too long in an apartment.

I wanted to have a place for Ollie and me where we could make our mark—paint the walls, build displays for the houseplants he had all over our place, maybe even get a small yard for him to garden. The mild California weather meant he could have something growing all year long.

My GPS told me I was approaching the house, but I would have known anyway because of my realtor's small purple car. It had sparkles and a giant picture of her face on it. That car alone would have been reason enough to decline her services, but Steve, the manager at my bar, swore up and down she was the best.

As soon as I parked in the driveway behind her car, she stepped out, her hair and spiky pink heels making her almost as tall as I was. In the back of my mind, I could hear my ex's sure-fire criticisms. That made me like Linda even more.

"Hi, Linda," I said. "Tell me about it."

She gestured at the house. "Two bedrooms, one bathroom, galley kitchen, and a sizable backyard." The disappointment in her voice was apparent.

"What's wrong with it?" I asked. There wasn't any point wasting our time if this wasn't the one.

"You're going to love it."

"And?" I asked. "That's a bad thing? What about the commission?"

"I don't see you in this house!" She gestured at me, then the small home. "Don't you think you're going to get remarried someday? Your future missus will want space, maybe even an extra bedroom for a child-to-be?"

I snorted. "I'm a middle-aged man with gray hair and a sixteen-year-old kid. Yeah, I'm a real catch."

She shook her head as if she knew something I didn't. "Come on, Cohen. Let me show you around. It'll take about two seconds."

Chuckling, I followed her through the front gate. A chain-link fence surrounded the property, and I pictured Ollie and me getting a dog that would have run of the place. The "lawn" was mostly weeds, but I knew a guy who could help me handle that. And another who could help with the peeling paint on the exterior.

We walked through the antique front door, and I smiled at the hardwood beneath our feet. "These floors original to the house?"

She nodded. "So is the heater. But I think we could negotiate a credit for that."

I nodded, walking through the living room toward the dining room, which had a simple gray tile on the floor. The ceilings were a little low, but the house had plenty of character with built-in cabinets and antique fixtures. The kitchen was small—smaller than the one in our apartment even—but Ollie would be moving out soon, and it would be just me. I didn't need much.

Linda followed behind me, pointing out details about the house as I passed from the kitchen through the dining room to the small hall with the bedrooms and bathroom. Both small. But then I looked into the backyard and all that space. Ollie could have a garden *and* a greenhouse if he wanted. Maybe even campfires with his friends and a hammock strung between two trees.

"I like it," I said to Linda, who stood in the doorway behind me.

Her smile was wry. "I was afraid you'd say that."

I looked around the place, trying to see it from her perspective, but I couldn't see anything but potential here. "Is it really that bad?"

"I hope I'm not speaking out of turn," she said, "and you can ignore me if you think I am. But both of my kids are grown and gone. The house gets awfully quiet after they leave. Awfully lonely. And sometimes, that fear that keeps us from opening up to someone new can keep us from a lot of great things too."

My throat felt tight, but I cleared it and put a hand on her shoulder. "Thanks for the concern, Linda."

She nodded.

"Can you put an offer in tonight?" I asked.

With a petulant shake of her head, she said, "Alright, but I'm going to get you a hell of a deal."

"I'll count on it," I said.

3

BIRDIE

Confession: My best friend's a high school dropout.

Between meetings and getting called in to classrooms, I didn't have a spare minute all day to call my landlord. Or my best friend to tell her about the breakup.

Once I had a chance to collect my thoughts, I decided to start with the landlord. He was a douchy guy in his fifties who cared more about his frosted tips than anyone should, but there had to be a heart in there somewhere.

After I got out of the school parking lot, I hit dial on my phone and held it to my ear. Instead of a ring tone, an old rock song played, and I let out a sigh as I waited for him to answer.

Finally, his voice crackled across the receiver. "Go for Rob."

I cringed. "Hi, Rob. It's Birdie."

"Your ear ringing? I was about to call you."

I raised my eyebrows. "Oh?"

"Yeah, Mrs. Cronckle said Dax moved out this morning? That's a shame. I just wanted to make sure you were planning to pay this month's rent."

"You mean next month's?" I said, ignoring the dread pooling in my gut. That was just all the coffee I drank wearing a hole in my stomach, right? Not panic. Right.

The clicking of a mouse and clattering of keys sounded through the phone. "No, this month. He usually pays the first, but I haven't seen it yet."

"It's the ninth," I said, pulling my car to the side of the road. I jammed it into park, not caring how crooked my car was on the curb.

"Nine days late," he confirmed.

"Rob, he should have paid the rent." My hand shook on the phone. What had Dax done with the money I transferred to his account?

"He hasn't. So how would you like to go about making this month's payment?"

"I made the payment!" I cried. "I gave it to Dax to handle!"

He let out a pained sigh. "I hate to be this guy, Kitty, I do, but if you can't pay your rent, you can't stay there. You know there are tons of people lining up for a cute little townhouse on that part of town."

"I was going to call to ask for an extension for next month," I said, leaning against the steering wheel.

"I can give you until the end of this month to pay for last month's rent, and then of course you're on the line for next month's payment."

I sat back, blinking back tears. "And if I can't come up with it all?"

"Eviction may be on the table."

My lips parted. "*Eviction?*"

Voices came through on the other side of the phone, and he said, "Sorry, Kitty, I have another round of golf to get to. Bring the check by my office or get it in the mail asap."

The line went silent, and I stared at my phone.

There was only one thing left to do—call in reinforcements.

I couldn't bring myself to tell her about the most horrible of horrible days over the phone on my drive home, so I just asked her to come over.

Birdie: SOS. Can you come over? And bring wine? A lot of wine.

Mara: That bad? I'll be there as fast as I can.

Soon, Mara and I were sitting on the floor in my empty living room two glasses deep. Dax had even taken the couch after I left for work. Mara was on a deadline for her latest romance book, so her hair was in a messy topknot and she covered her ample curves with leggings and a tank top, but she still looked stunning with her full rosy cheeks and kind blue eyes.

Mara tapped her finger against the glass, pursing her lips. "You know, you could always ask your parents for money. They wouldn't miss it."

"I've told you three times. Not a chance." She opened her mouth to speak, and I raised my hands. "I will also not be taking money from you."

"Then move in with me," she said simply.

"What?" I asked, shocked. "You just got settled in the new house and you want me busting in?" Her online business writing romance novels had gone gangbusters, and she made triple what I did. Which was why she owned an adorable bungalow a few blocks from the beach in Brentwood and I couldn't afford to rent my townhouse in Emerson on my own.

"I don't know..." I said.

"Could you get a roommate? At least for a little while?"

I shook my head. "Rob doesn't seem like he's going to work with me. Especially since Dax didn't pay the last month *like he said he would*."

"I hate him."

"Same." But also... I missed him.

Evidence of our relationship was all over this house. It was the first one he and I lived in together, and we hadn't even made it a full year before he decided he was out.

I tried not to wonder if I was the problem. If I was too much for him.

If any of my students at school said something like that, I would say they're never too much for someone who can't get enough of them. I'm pretty sure I read that on Pinterest, but it was still true.

"Look." Mara leaned forward, her bun falling forward as well. "I have a guest bedroom. I have a two-car garage with only one car. You can keep your things in the garage until you find a place of your own." She smiled, tilting her head to the side. "You know it was fun living with me in LA."

"True," I agreed, finding a smile for the first time all day. "I wish we could go back there and I could enjoy grad school more instead of wasting all that time on Dax."

She shook her head sadly, taking another sip. "Someday, you'll see the lesson in the mess."

"I appreciate the advice," I said with a sardonic smile, "but I think your guest bed and half your garage are more than enough."

Instead of arguing, she hit my arm and took another drink of wine. I did the same.

"You know," she said, "why wait?"

"What do you mean?" I asked.

"Why hang out in this house when you could move in with me and get ready for your new life? Plus, an eviction on your record won't look good when you're trying to find your next place."

I looked toward the ceiling. "You know what? Fuck it. Let's do it."

She laughed and rubbed my arm. "That's how all the best decisions are made."

I stood from the floor. "Let's pack?"

"Save the packing for this weekend," she said, a devilish gleam in her eyes. "I have a different idea." She stood up and went to my bedroom, then to the closet. "Don't you have anything not-professional in here? It's about as neutral as it gets!"

I shook my head, leaning against the door frame. "I work at a private school, Mara. It doesn't exactly leave a lot of room for personal expression."

Her face lit up as she reached the back of my closet and pulled out a sexy sequin dress from our trip to Vegas for my twenty-first birthday.

"Look at this!" She held it out to me. "I bet you still fit in it."

I rolled my eyes. "I didn't keep it to wear again." I reached for the fabric, feeling the rough outside. I'm pretty sure it chafed my inner arms raw. "I kept it for the memories."

"Well, you're making new ones tonight," Mara argued, draining the rest of her wine.

"Like the memory of pathetically sleeping at my best friend's house until I can scrounge up a crappy studio apartment somewhere?"

She shook her head. "Like the memory of some hot guy's cock."

My cheeks instantly heated. Mara was always talking like that. "Just because you write smutty romance novels doesn't mean I'm going to be your next heroine."

Lifting her eyebrows, she said, "Try me. I bet by this time next year, you'll already be in love with Mr. Right and wondering why you ever wasted time or tears on that loser Dax. A night at the bar is the perfect jumping off point."

"I'll pass." I set the dress on a suitcase. "I'm already pathetic enough. I don't need to show up to school hungover *and* heartbroken."

"Like anyone will notice. Teenagers are too hung up on their own problems to care."

She had a point.

"And a rebound will help you feel better. No one's saying you have to date whoever it is."

"Whoever it is," I echoed. "Great start to the night."

She took both of my hands in hers, looking in my eyes. "Birdie. You have been dating or engaged for the last two years. One man. One penis. That's too long to be with one penis."

"I was about to marry the guy!" I protested.

"But you didn't. We both know that Dax wasn't good enough for you. He was terrible with money, constantly distracted by his 'art', and that wandering eye of his made me want to punch him in the face. And now you get the full buffet menu open again. Get a little palate cleanser in before you can enjoy all the options ahead of you... And wouldn't it be nice to go to bed with a guy who's really into you?"

I shook my head. Sometimes Mara was really convincing. "He just left me this morning."

"Did he?" she asked. "Because I think he checked out long before that. Especially considering he had a helper."

The words hit me straight in the gut.

"And I could do with a good lay myself. You know, for book research." She waggled her eyebrows. "Be my wingwoman?"

"Fine," I said. "But I need to pack an overnight bag first, and a box to bring some stuff by the school."

"Great." She winked. "We'll handle these boxes before we deal with yours."

4
BIRDIE

Confession: I steal from the student condom jar.

We loaded the bags into the back of her truck, and I got in the passenger side. Although the sky was barely darkening, I'd already had too much wine to be driving, and I didn't feel like being on my own anyway.

I realized that when I found another place, it would be the first time I'd actually lived by myself. In college, I lived in the dorms. Then I found Mara as a roommate on a Craigslist ad while I got my master's. And then Dax and I moved in together. Not to mention the eighteen years I lived in close proximity to the underside of my parents' thumbs.

She rolled the windows down, letting in the fall air, and

drove toward the beach. Her house was only a few blocks away, and we'd spent more than a few weekends laying out on beach towels with our Kindles.

"So what type of guy should we look for tonight?" she asked. "What are you into now that boring artist guy is out of the picture?"

I gave her a look. "Dax was not boring."

"He took you to a vegan restaurant for your birthday. You had wheatgrass shots."

I cringed, remembering the day. He wasn't even vegan, and neither was I. It was so pretentious. I much rather would have spent the day birdwatching or thrifting at a flea market.

"So you agree. I'm thinking you should try someone older. Maybe a silver fox?"

My chest constricted at the idea of being with someone new, but I reminded myself that Dax had done me a favor. Did I really want fifty more birthdays spent at vegan restaurants? Did I want to come in second to art for the rest of my life? Partner with someone who didn't care enough about me to follow through on his promise to marry me?

"You know," Mara said, mistaking my silence for hesitation, "older guys are often more knowledgeable. Could be just the thing to get you up to speed on what's new in the bedroom."

"How many new things can there be?" I asked, suddenly feeling self-conscious.

She shook her head. "You're in for a treat."

We soon reached her house, and I took in a water feature up front. "Is that new?" I asked.

She grinned. "Treated myself with the advance."

"That's amazing!" I said, trying to be the supportive friend I should have been. Mara dropped out of high school at sixteen, getting out of a truly crappy situation with her mom and an abusive stepdad. After years of working as a waitress and writing sexy stories for magazines for some extra cash, she self-published her first book online. And it took off—in a big way.

And here I was with my master's degree.

Irony sucked.

For me, not for Mara.

We got out of her truck and carried the bags to the garage, except for one I needed to bring by the school.

"Okay." Mara wiped her hands on her leggings. "Let's shower up and get dressed for your rebound."

I followed her into the house. "And how about you? Are we looking for Mr. Right?"

"You don't find Mr. Right at the club," she said. "You find Mr. Right Now, and that's ten times better."

I shook my head, going to her guest bathroom while she went to the master. It would take a special guy to settle Mara down. That much was for sure.

As I twisted the knob on the shower, hot water cascaded down. I stepped into the stream, wondering about Mr. Right Now and hoping my rebound would be good enough to clear my mind of Dax and maybe even land in a novel.

♥·♥·♥·♥

I adjusted the hem of my dress so my entire vagina wouldn't be on the seat of Mara's truck. "How did I wear this dress before?"

"It's hot on you!" she said, turning onto the highway that led toward Emerson Academy. Since it was on the way to the club, we were going to go ahead and drop off my box. "What are you worried about anyway?"

"First of all, my ass falling out of it. Second of all—"

She gave me a look. "It's not falling out. You'll be standing most of the night. Or lying down." She winked.

"You're taking this rebound thing pretty seriously," I said. "But there's a very good chance that no one will be remotely interested in all of this." I gestured at myself.

"And why is that?"

"I am pretty rusty," I reminded her. "Dax had about three moves, and they were mostly for his benefit."

"Ugh. Remind me why you dated him again?"

"He was so exciting," I said. "He showed me so many new spots in LA."

"Mhmm. Can we talk about the spot he couldn't find?"

I rolled my eyes. "Let's forget about him, okay? I don't want to think about him tonight."

"Happily. But speaking of dicks, I forgot to ask—do you have condoms in your purse?"

I blanched. "Shit, no." How had I forgotten to think about condoms? Half my job was to help make sure students didn't end up pregnant before graduation.

"I might have some extra. If not, we can stop by the store on the way."

"So sexy," I said. We reached the school and she whipped into an accessible parking spot close to the building. "Mara," I chided. "You can't park here."

She looked around the empty parking lot. "That's true. We're taking up all the spots for the people not at the football game."

I rolled my eyes and got out of the truck, thankful everyone would be too preoccupied with the game to see me going into the school. I shrugged on a massive cardigan I brought along and went up the steps to the front door. I had to hold the box against the door with my hip while I used my key to let me in, but finally I was inside.

The only lighting came from the dim emergency lights that stayed on all the time. Everything was silent, and it felt... peaceful. That is, until the heels I borrowed from Mara echoed on the tile floors and off the locker walls.

Thankfully, my office wasn't too far away. I jiggled the knob and got in. Ralphie chirped as I set the box down.

"Sorry, babe." I put my finger through the cage, and

he nipped at it. "I came back a little early. But I'll see you tomorrow morning!"

He cooed, seeming to understand, and I turned to leave the office. But then my eyes landed on something atop my filing cabinet: the clear glass jar filled with condoms.

I was supposed to discreetly give them to any student I suspected of being sexually active. Well, I was someone in the school, and I was asking...

I bit my bottom lip and walked to the cabinet, taking down the jar. There were several brands inside, and I took a few brightly colored ones, then tucked them in my cardigan pocket.

As I walked down the hallway, my pocket felt hot. But hopefully not as hot as the night I was about to have.

5

COHEN

Although most of the bar's business happened at night, I had paperwork and balancing the books to worry about during the day. Still, I tried to stay late on the weekends while Ollie was at his mom's to make sure everything was running smoothly. It was nice to get a feel for how the team worked together and step in as needed during busy times.

I stood behind the bar with the other bartenders, mixing drinks and serving customers, when my manager, Steve, patted me on the shoulder. "Cohen, how many times can I tell you? We've got this."

I shook my head. "Is it a crime for me to roll up my sleeves every now and then?"

He reached into the fridge by our legs, pulled out a

beer bottle and easily popped off the top. "You've been working nonstop. We're doing great and you're missing it." He handed the beer to me, then got another for himself.

"Drinking on the job?" I said with a sardonic grin.

"I like to call it quality analysis," Steve said, lifting the bottle. "Come on."

He walked from behind the bar, stepping out of the way of the bartenders, and went to one of the standing tables near the dance floor. There were two open seats, so he took one and I sat in the other, resting the soles of my leather shoes on the chair rail.

"Look at it," he said, gesturing at the bar.

As I watched people dancing, couples chatting, the bartenders and waitstaff working together, I couldn't help but feel a sense of pride. We'd hired some of the best, and they worked together like a well-oiled machine.

"Great work," I said.

He lifted his chin, taking another swig. "Same to you."

I grinned. "Looks like I'm not needed anymore."

"Good," he said. "Maybe you'll actually have time for a life."

"I do have a life," I said. "Ollie and I—"

"I mean outside of your kid and your job."

"Well, I did get my offer accepted on a house today," I said, grinning like a kid on Christmas morning. I couldn't believe I was going to have my own house for Ollie and me. Not one my in-laws had helped pay for. Not one my ex-wife constantly complained was too small. Something for me.

"That's awesome!" He lifted his beer toward me and drank again. "Where is it?"

"On the outskirts of Emerson. Twenty minutes from Ollie's school, ten from the bar. Nice sidewalks and easy access to the trails so I can run. And a massive backyard." I was getting a little close to bragging, so I shut my mouth and drank from my beer.

"So poker night's at your house? It's been a bummer having to be quiet with Millie sleeping."

He made a good point. Ever since becoming parents last year, he and his wife had shaken up poker night. None of the other guys had enough space, me included, but I could see fixing up the garage to be a good place for us. "You're on. Poker night at my new place next month—if inspections go well and Ollie's okay with it."

"Good deal." He gestured his chin toward the dance floor. "Don't you ever miss being with a woman?"

"Who says I haven't been with a woman?"

He lifted his eyebrows and took another drink.

Okay, so I'd been in a bit of a dry spell. After the divorce, yeah, I slept with some women. I met them at the bar, took them home when Ollie wasn't around, and had a hell of a time. But it didn't take too long to realize casual sex wasn't enough. I wanted more than that. But, like I'd told Linda earlier, I was a middle-aged man with a kid and an apartment and a business. Not exactly boyfriend material.

Maybe Linda was right though. My life would change once Ollie was gone. And as Steve had pointed out, I wasn't needed as much at the bar anymore. Would there be room in my life for something more?

I glanced toward the dance floor, and my eyes landed on the sexiest woman I'd seen in a long, long time. She wore a sequined dress, and her blond curly hair fell wild around her shoulders. With her full chest and hips, my mind went straight to what it would feel like to have her sitting on top of me, and my dick responded in agreement.

"Do you see that blond?" I said, nodding toward the woman and her friend.

Steve pointed at his wedding ring. "I see nothing."

More for me. She was hot as hell. And fuck. She was dancing. Even though she was clearly nervous, I couldn't help but watch the way her hips and her tits swayed in that dress. Or the way her smile lit up her entire face. A light sheen of sweat shone on her skin, and I imagined what it would be like to lick the salt off her shoulder, bite down on her neck... damn.

Hadn't I just told Linda I wasn't interested in dating? What was wrong with me? Steve was right' it had been a long time.

"Go talk to her," Steve said.

I looked at him. "She can't be more than thirty. What would she want with someone my age?"

"You're barely forty, and according to Tina's magazines, forty is the new thirty. Blondie might be too old for you."

I rolled my eyes. "Haha."

"You should get her a drink."

That was a good idea. But why couldn't I get my ass out of the chair? And why were my palms sweating? "I don't know, Steve. Ollie's been kind of off lately, and with the house hunt, I—"

"It doesn't have to be forever!" Steve said, exasperated. "Go have a conversation. You can do that, right?"

"Right," I repeated, mechanically pushing myself out of the chair. I walked toward the dance floor, but a crush of people passed in front of me—college students from the look of it. But by the time they passed, I'd come up with a million reasons why she wouldn't be interested in a guy like me.

Fuck.

I was a coward.

I drained my beer and went to the bar to get another one. Maybe three. Then I could bring her and her friend a drink.

I took my beer first, trying to work up the courage to talk to this girl. I'd never been this nervous before. Maybe because I was out of practice. Maybe because the way her curves filled out that dress had my body reacting in very inappropriate ways.

Either way, I promised myself I'd talk to her by the end of the night. And then I'd put the rest in her hands.

6

BIRDIE

Confession: I learned how to dance from Britney Spears music videos.

There are always those girls at the club. You know the ones. They're beautiful, but even more so, they're effortlessly sexy. When they hit the dance floor, the music takes over and somehow their body moves in a way that makes people look.

Me? I am *not* one of those people.

No, I could be wearing a corset and fishnet leggings and have all the sex appeal of a potato.

That was kind of how my body was shaped anyway. While Mara's curves came in all the right places, with an ample chest and wide hips, my weight was in my stomach.

Right in the middle. One time a student told me I was shaped like an Easter egg. And well, they weren't wrong.

Mara closed her eyes and ran her fingers through her hair, absolutely screaming sex with her dance moves.

I, on the other hand, had learned to dance from Britney Spears music videos (#FreeBritney). So I did the best I knew how and hoped no one was looking. I was getting too old for this anyway.

Wasn't there some type of club for fuddy-duddies looking for rebound sex? That's where I needed to go.

At the end of the song, my hair was sticking to the back of my neck and I had beads of sweat on my forehead. It was hot and humid, and I had never felt more unattractive in my life.

"I need to use the bathroom," I told Mara, which was really just code for "I need to cry in a bathroom stall while contemplating my existence."

As I walked toward the bathroom, I put my hand under my thick mane of curly dirty-blond hair so my neck would have a chance at drying off.

I ducked into the bathroom and dove into an empty stall, locking the door behind me. The entire place reeked of perfume and vomit, which just made my impending mental breakdown seem that much more fitting.

I leaned over my legs, wondering how on earth I'd gotten here.

I was nearly thirty. I had a graduate degree. I'd worked

at an amazing school for three years. Many of my students were already attending Ivy League universities.

But because Dax dumped me for someone else, I felt like the little shreds of toilet paper on the floor. Dirty and destined for the trash can.

Dax and I were engaged. Even though we hadn't set a date yet, marriage was on the horizon. But here I was, looking for a rebound instead. I rubbed my temples. What a mess.

My phone began ringing from its place in my purse, and I pulled it out, groaning at the sight of my mother's name on the screen. Instead of answering, I hit reject and resumed rubbing my temples, trying to breathe evenly.

My phone rang again. Frustration rising in my chest, I grabbed it and answered. "What, Mother?"

"That's not how you greet the woman who raised you," my mother said in a cold, emotionless voice she'd perfected over the years.

"I wasn't aware I was talking to my nanny," I said.

"You think you're so funny."

I let out a sigh. "I'm hanging up."

"That's interesting, because I heard the wedding's off and that you were getting evicted. I thought you might like some assistance."

Damn Mrs. Cronckle.

I don't know how, but I knew the gossip had started with her.

"I'm fine," I said. "I'm staying with Mara."

My mother's signature disappointed sigh came through the phone. "I don't understand why you insist on being difficult. You know Rex is open to a marriage between the two of you. He would take care of you. And if you're not interested in him, I could introduce you to Walter and—"

I rolled my eyes toward the ceiling. "I don't need anyone to take care of me." (Although this dress and my landlord's threat of eviction could make a strong case for the opposing side.)

"We raised you better than this," Mother said. "Always the best schools, one-on-one music and tennis lessons. We traveled on private jets and used proper etiquette at the dinner table. And you throw that away for what? To work with snot-nosed children as a teacher?"

"Not that you care, Mother, but I'm a guidance counselor. I help *high school* students make decisions that will impact the rest of their lives. I'm there for them, because there wasn't always someone there for me."

"Now hold on one minute—"

"I'd love to stay on and chat about what a disappointment I am to the Melrose family name, but I've got better things to do." Or people, for that matter.

I hung up and turned my phone to silent. Talking to my mother always made me so angry. They'd cut me off for my decision to go to college instead of simply learning how to manage a household and marrying well. Without their support to get me by, I'd worked extra jobs, I'd side hustled, I'd graduated summa cum laude. I could get over Dax, just like I got over my parents' lack of support.

Fueled by rage (and rum and Coke), I left the stall, washed my hands, and walked toward the dance floor, determined to have the rebound Mara thought I could have.

That was until I ran into a guy, who spilled his drink all over my dress.

I looked down at the beer covering my slutty Vegas dress, then up into the face of the most attractive man I'd ever laid eyes on.

Dax didn't have anything on him. Hell, Liam Hemsworth, the Australian god who used to hang on my wall and got covered in lipstick, didn't compare.

My mouth opened and closed like a fish as I took in this stranger. Holy Paul Rudd lookalike with fifty shades of gray in his dark brown hair.

"I'm so sorry," he said, touching my forearm. "I should have been more careful."

I would have spoken, you know, like a normal human being, if his hand hadn't been on my arm.

"You must be so frustrated."

Yeah, sexually.

Taking my silence for irritation, he apologized again and said, "Let me help you get cleaned up."

I nodded, still too tongue-tied to speak.

But instead of leading me back to the bathroom, he

took me behind closed doors to the kitchen area, which was devoid of cooks at such a late hour.

"Are we allowed to be back here?" I asked. Then I nearly hit myself. Here I was, in the presence of what had to be silver fox royalty, and I was asking him about the *rules*? How much more childish could I look? Thank god I hadn't worn Mara's disco ball earrings like she'd wanted me to.

"Yeah, I know the owner," he said.

Of course he did. Older people always knew people. Specifically, people who came in handy when a beer got spilled all over your dress.

We approached the sink, and he reached across me to the stack of rags on a shelf. As he did, I caught a whiff of his cologne, and my eyes practically rolled into the back of my head. Why did he smell so good?

Dax refused cologne, opting instead for essential oils, but my god, he never smelled like this. I finally understood what all the heroines in Mara's romance novels meant when they said their breasts perked up for a man. Because holy moly did the girls have a mind of their own right now.

With the wet rag in his large hand, he looked me over, an assessing air to his gaze.

I bit my lip, worried what he would think of me, and my body.

"This dress is ruined. Maybe we should get you out of

it," he said, his husky voice sending need pooling in my core.

"Wh-what?" I managed. I didn't know getting a rebound would be this easy.

He cracked his lips into an endearingly apologetic grin. "I might have an extra uniform back here."

He passed me and walked toward a closet in the back of the kitchen. As he bent into the closet, reaching for a box, I was acutely aware of the muscles of his back, of the way his shoulder muscles strained against his shirt.

God, I needed to get a grip. Wasn't I always telling kids to stop objectifying each other? Hadn't I been *engaged* that morning?

He reached deeper into the closet, and I forgot that thought altogether.

My lips parted. Now I *really* needed to get a grip. On him.

He came out with a black shirt. "It's four XL. Maybe you can wear it as a dress? It won't be a sexy as that one, but..." He shrugged and handed it to me.

My breath quickened. Had he just called me sexy? Silently, I thanked the stars that Mara had found the Vegas dress. It was already bringing me good luck.

"After you change, can I get you a drink, you know, to apologize?" he asked.

I smiled, giddy at the thought of spending more time with him. Hopefully time where I wouldn't be gaping and staring like an awestruck teenage girl. "That would be nice."

He nodded. "Meet me at the bar." He gave me a once over and a rueful smile. "It'll be a shame to see that dress go."

The kitchen door shut behind him and I danced, fanning myself with my hands. *Omigosh omigosh omigosh.*

Could this silver fox be my rebound?

Oh shit.

He couldn't be a rebound, right? Someone hot is not supposed to be the one you bounce back with. He's supposed to be the one you get with after the bounce back and then live happily ever after. Right?

Shit.

I got out my phone and dialed Mara, praying she would hear her phone over the music pounding outside.

"B!" she said. "Where have you been?"

"I just met a super-hot guy!" I cried. "He wants to get me a drink. But he's hot, Mar, like smoking hot. This isn't good."

"WHAT? Why not?"

"He's too hot!" I whined. "Like my-fragile-fucking-heart-will-never-get-over-him hot."

"Girl," Mara chided. "Enough with this nonsense. Get out of wherever you're hiding and have sex with the guy! And then tell me every detail after."

The wink in her voice made me smile. "Just in case I get murdered, I'm turning on the location on my phone."

"Smart. But hopefully the only thing getting murdered tonight will be any thoughts of Dax."

"I hope so too," I said. "I'll see you in the morning. I hope."

I hung up and shimmied out of the sequin dress. I held it in front of me, taking in all the memories we'd made together. Then I changed into the T-shirt and dropped the dress on the floor like I hoped the T-shirt would be in the morning.

7

COHEN

I was a fucking idiot.

A clumsy idiot.

I couldn't believe I'd gotten beer all over her. What was I? A stupid teenager with shaking hands and hormones controlling my every move? If I hadn't ruined my chances with my clumsiness, that stupid comment about getting her out of the dress would surely do the trick.

I tried to remember back to six months ago—that was about the last time I'd taken someone home. I used to be so smooth. So confident. What had changed?

The woman, that's what.

I didn't even know her name, but I was completely captivated by her. The way her eyes looked deep blue in the dimly lit kitchen. The fullness of her lips, parted in shock. The clear ring of her voice and the softness of her skin when I'd touched her arm.

I wanted to touch more of her. See if everything else was just as soft.

I shuddered. God, I was out of practice.

Clearing my mind, and subtly repositioning myself, I walked to the bar, ready to make good on my promise for a drink. I hated the way beer smelled after it had spilled and dried. Hopefully this would help make it up to her. Give me an excuse to get her talking.

As I waited for her to change, I ran through a list of potential questions in my mind. Something less mundane than the "what do you do" "where are you from" kind of thing. I wanted to know what was behind those pretty blue eyes. What made her smile that way when she and her friend were talking.

I wanted to make her smile too.

God, I was pathetic.

When there was a break in the line, I asked the bartender to get me another beer—one I'd be much more careful with—and leaned back to see her coming toward me.

Shit.

Damn.

Holy fucking hotness.

Even with her ample curves, the shirt was way too big on her, the sleeves falling almost to her elbows, but the hem was just as short on her as the tight dress had been.

My mind immediately imagined having her alone in the bar. Leaning her over the wood counters and pulling her curls and fucking her until she screamed my name.

If she could have heard my thoughts, she would have run away. Instead, she nervously tugged at the hem of the shirt and gave me a bashful smile.

So not only was she hot, she was also drop-dead fucking gorgeous.

I cleared my throat, trying to speak like I wasn't just eye-fucking the shit out of her. "You make my shirt look good. What can I get you to drink?"

"A mojito," she said, sliding into the chair next to me. My eyes traveled toward the spot where the flesh of her thighs pressed together, obscuring what I longed to discover. Then I realized how creepy my thoughts were getting and focused on her eyes instead.

She seemed confused. "Your shirt?"

I took a sip from my beer, trying to think about what she was asking. The shirt. I'd said it was mine. I took another drink, trying to think of a way to say I owned the place without looking like a pompous asshole. Damn, I really was out of practice. "It's my bar," I said lamely.

She looked down at the shirt, at the Collie logo on the front pocket. When she looked up at me, she blurted, "Your bathrooms are gross."

8

BIRDIE

Confession: I'm great at giving advice. Following it? Not so much.

WHAT THE HELL WAS THAT.

He chuckled. "They are?"

"The ladies' smells terrible. Vomit and urine everywhere." Why couldn't I stop talking?

He raised his eyebrows. "What? I mean, you can't help the piss in the men's, but the women's?"

I nodded. "I don't know how it happens, but it does."

He narrowed his eyes at me, a playful smile tugging at his lips. "I don't believe it."

The bartender slid a mojito onto the wet bar top, and I took it. "Come on." I got out of my chair. "I'll show you."

I could feel his presence behind me as we made our

way toward the bathroom I'd just locked myself into. I took a sip, if only to calm my nerves, but then I moaned and said over my shoulder, "This is the best mojito ever."

"Glad to hear it," he replied with a chuckle.

We reached the door, and I turned to him. "Are you sure you're ready for this?"

"Oh, I'm ready." The heat in his voice made me wonder what else he was ready for.

I pushed open the door, and he followed me inside. A few girls standing around the sinks glanced at him before getting back to their conversation. I could tell they'd just met—they were being so nice to each other. True friends in the bar used the b-word way more often.

His nose curled up. "This is bad."

"I told you," I said, folding my arms across my chest.

"No, this is really bad." He shook his head and took my hand. "We've got to leave."

His touch sent heat up my arm, and I imagined him touching me elsewhere. Him being the rebound of every girl's fantasy but my reality.

I followed him out of the restroom, and he stepped aside, breathing deeply.

I giggled. "Get some of that fresh bar air."

He laughed. "Good point. Want to get out of here?"

I bit my lip, holding back a smile. "Thought you'd never ask."

Instead of going out the front door, he led me to the back, reaching into his pocket for keys. Headlights flashed on a car that looked so expensive it could pay off the entirety of my student loan debts.

I stared at it, suddenly freaking out. He was rich. The kind of rich that could cover up my murder. And I'd taken a drink from him. What kind of adult was I? I didn't even know his name!

Noticing I'd stopped following, he turned toward me. "Everything okay?"

"Um... not really."

His dark brows drew together, and he stepped away from the car. "What's wrong?"

I bit my lip, taking him in. Not knowing his name didn't keep me from imagining his hands all over me. But first things first. "My name's Birdie Melrose. What's yours?"

He let out half a laugh and smiled. "Cohen Bardot."

Feeling better, I nodded and smiled, then got into his fancy car.

He pulled out of the club parking lot and started down the street.

"Where do you live?" I asked, gently tugging my shirt so it would hide the way my thighs pressed together when I sat down. My cellulite was on full display, even in the dim lighting. Something told me Cohen could have any girl he wanted, and I didn't want to get counted out because of my size.

"Downtown Emerson," he said simply.

My eyebrows drew together. "Are you going the wrong way?"

"Not quite."

"Does that mean you're going to murder me?" I asked. "Because downtown is that way and we're going this way."

He chuckled. "I have another stop to make first."

I closed my eyes, not wanting to hear his answer. "Where?"

"The store." He glanced at the dash. "If I drive fast enough, we'll get there before it closes."

It was almost ten o'clock now. "I have condoms," I blurted. Then I covered my mouth. How awkward could I be? "Not that we're going to need them—I mean, I hope we need them, and I always practice safe sex, but, just in case, you know, we do need them and you don't have them and that's why you're going to the store, I....have them."

My cheeks burned, and his profile revealed an amused smile, making my humiliation that much worse.

"You talk a lot when you're nervous, don't you?"

"To be fair, I talk a lot most of the time. It's kind of my job."

He lifted an eyebrow. "Talk show host?"

I snorted. "Hardly. I'm a guidance counselor."

"Doing important work. Not like the barkeep with the dirty bathrooms."

"Your work felt pretty important tonight," I admitted.

"Yeah?" he said, turning down another street.

"My friend practically dragged me out. She thought I needed...to meet new people."

He smirked, and God, that was sexier than all the other looks combined. "Remind me to thank her."

Did that mean there was going to be a time when he met my friends? A time past tonight?

Mara would have kicked me if she heard my train of thought. This was supposed to be a rebound. R-E-B-O-U-N-D. My chance to get back on the horse, not buy the horse and the cow and take them home to live happily ever after. Or whatever you do with a horse and cow. I'm not very ag savvy.

I had to get out of this mental funk. This thought that sex had to end in happily ever after. Or that I'd ever live happily ever after.

My eyes stung. "What store are we going to?" I asked, hoping for a good distraction and praying he wouldn't see my shining eyes.

"Marshall's," he said. "I know it's not anything fancy, but nothing else is open, and I owe you a new dress."

My eyes widened. He wanted to take me shopping for a new dress? He was good looking *and* kind? Okay, that was joint bank account material.

I closed my eyes again, forcing my mind away from forever. I just learned his name, after all.

His smile was sultry, but nowhere near as panty melting as his gaze trailing from my eyes to my bare legs.

Dax never looked at me with that kind of attraction.

No, he was always insisting on sex with the lights off or signing us up for gym memberships so I could get "healthier." Which really meant more attractive to him. But I was tired of that life, always trying to fit into an eight or smaller because that's what they carried at the fancy stores where my mother shopped. When I finally stopped watching myself in college, I gained weight and a freedom I'd never known before. I was a size sixteen now, and I didn't see that changing any time soon.

"You don't need to get me a new dress. You got me a shirt and..." Channel your inner Mara, Birdie. You can do it. "I thought it might look better on your floor anyway."

"We'll get to that."

9
COHEN

I didn't want to come on too strong, but judging by the flush in her cheeks and the way she shifted in her seat, the feeling was mutual. That was good because I had done just about everything I could to fuck it up.

I pulled into the store parking lot and glanced at the dash. Multiple trips here with Ollie had told me the place closed at ten. "Is five minutes enough time?" I asked nervously. I wanted to get her something new, replace the pretty dress I'd ruined. But if she was anything like my ex, finding the right item could take hours.

She responded with an endearing laugh. "You haven't seen me shop before."

God, she was perfect. "You're on," I said.

We got out of the car, and damn, I had to speed up just to keep up with her. If shopping was like this, I could get used to it. She went straight to a rack full of dresses at the back of the store and flicked through the hangers going toward the larger sizes.

I stood back, wondering what she'd pick, seeing if I could guess. There weren't many options in her size, which made me feel shitty, until she pulled out a dress printed with fruit. It looked soft. I wondered what it would feel like with my hands running over it. If I could hike it up and...

Why was she looking so wistfully at it? Like she wanted it but couldn't say yes? She bit her lip, flipping the tab.

I didn't care how much the dress cost. I'd pay it just to see her smile again. "Let's get it."

She looked from the dress to me, giving me that smile I longed to see. The dress was worth every damn penny.

Over the loudspeaker, a worker asked the remaining four people in the store to make their final decisions and check out. I offered to hold the dress for her, and we walked toward the front, paying and walking out through the sliding doors.

She held the plastic bag looped in her fingers, the bright colors occluded by the translucent plastic.

"So, the sequins aren't your typical style?" I asked as we reached the car. I opened the door for her, and she crossed in front of me to get in.

In her seat, I could see her cheeks flush pink again. "I usually don't get dresses that are so... loud."

"Yeah? Why not?"

She shrugged, not quite meeting my eyes. "I need to be professional, for my students."

I glanced at her legs in the seat. "Are you in?"

She nodded, and I shut the door for her, walking around to my side. I thought of Ollie and the clothes he liked to wear when he got home from school. Things with bright colors and crazy patterns that any one of my temporary daddies would have beat me up for. I would have killed to have at least one person in my life who wasn't trying to shove me into whatever box they'd expected me to be in.

I got in the car and glanced over at her. "I bet if you wore that dress to work, you'd be giving your students the permission they need to be exactly who they were made to be."

Her smile was the brightest thing for miles. "I knew I liked you."

My gut twisted, leapt for joy at that simple sentence. "I like you too," I said. Then I fingered the fabric poking out of the bag in her lap. It was now or never. "Want to come to my place so I can see it on?"

She bit her lip, bringing delicious color there, and nodded.

I couldn't put my car in drive fast enough. Hopefully, by the end of the night, I'd also see it off.

10

BIRDIE

Confession: I want to fall in love.

If I died and went to heaven, it would be in this apartment.

I hadn't been to any of the rooms other than the living room and the bathroom, where I was changing into the new dress, but I was already in love.

The whole place smelled like cinnamon. It was decorated simply with plants growing in kitschy hanging pots. I wanted to ask him where the decor came from, but I didn't want to find out it was an ex who had just moved out. Or would be back in a week or two.

My heart couldn't take it. Not least because I'd just lost a fiancé and gained an ex.

That's not what tonight's about, I reminded myself. It was about the rebound. But first, I had to show him this dress. He'd specifically requested it, and what came after would be a million times better; I could feel it in my bones. And maybe his boner. (Too soon? I'll see myself out.)

I slid the fabric over my chest, and it draped easily over my hips. It was the type of dress I always wanted to wear but would never in a billion years be brave enough to buy for myself. Much less wear in public.

I examined myself in the gilded mirror, taking it in. The fruity print was perfect for fall—a mix of peaches and pears and plums with a few bursts of bright green foliage thrown in. Plus, it nipped in around my waist, giving me at least the illusion of an hourglass shape.

An image of Cohen hiking my skirt to have me over his counter flashed through my mind. I shuddered and quickly left the bathroom in anticipation of making the fantasy real.

He stood in his kitchen, mixing something at the island. The smell of cinnamon was there, but something sweet too.

He held out a cup with a cinnamon stick and said, "Nightcap?"

I nodded and took a sip. "Oh my gosh, it's amazing." There was a hint of Fireball and cider, giving it the perfect blend of heat and flavor.

He smiled. "I used to bartend before I bought the bar. I still step in here and there if I need to."

My mother would be appalled if she knew I was in the same room as a bartender. It made me even happier to be there.

Then I realized I was thinking about my mom at Cohen's house. Yikes. This was *so* not the time.

As he sipped from his cup, he looked me up and down. "Do a spin."

The order uttered in the low timber of his voice made a shiver go up my spine, and I obliged.

"Slower."

It was one word. But it made electricity dance along my skin. I turned slowly, feeling his eyes on every inch of my body. And for once, I wasn't thinking about the size of my thighs or the stretchmarks on my stomach. No, I was thinking about what he was going to do with me—and what I wanted to do to him.

"That's it," he said. "You're beautiful no matter what you wear."

A smile grew on my face, unable to be restrained. "Thank you."

He leaned against the island. "I like that about you."

"What?"

"That you can take a compliment. Because you are. Beautiful. You should know that."

I let out a soft laugh. "I'm not sure I know that."

"Really?"

I nodded, leaning against the counter so we were standing across from each other. "My mom was pretty strict about my eating. And my ex wasn't exactly thrilled about my size."

Cohen's eyebrows rose. "What?"

"He never said anything outright fatphobic to me, but it was there. You know, in the way he kept the lights off in the bedroom or the gym memberships he sprang on me or the exercise equipment he bought so we could work on ourselves 'together.'" My eyes misted over, and I shook my head. How had I been so blind to his flaws? They seemed to be crashing at me now, assuring me of what a colossal mistake Dax had been. I didn't want to be that girl who let a guy tear her down. But I wasn't going to lie and say it didn't hurt. Feeling like you're not enough to the people you love most is the worst thing in the world.

"He's an idiot," Cohen said as simply as if he'd told me the sky was blue.

I gave him a grateful smile. "Thank you for that."

He nodded. "And your mom? Crazy. Although, I know a thing or two about difficult parents."

"Yeah?"

He took another drink and looked down at his cup. "That might be a story for another day." When he turned his sea-green eyes back on me, they seemed darker somehow. "I want to know more about Birdie Melrose."

I set my cup on the counter and looked at him, feeling more vulnerable than I had before. Less brave. "I just got out of a relationship. We were actually engaged. And I don't think I'm really ready to date right now."

His lips quirked slightly, and he pinned me with those eyes, making me feel more naked than I'd been in the bar's kitchen. Barer than I'd been in the skimpy dress.

"Tell me, Birdie," he said, his voice husky. "What is it you want?"

I want to fall in love.

The words popped in my mind faster than anything else.

I wanted the fairytale wedding and a house with a beautiful window to perch Ralphie's cage in and a husband to hug me from behind when he got off work. I wanted vacations on the beach and winters in the mountains and side-by-side headstones when we died. (Preferably, we'd go holding hands like they did in *The Notebook*.)

Okay, maybe that last bit was morbid, but you get the point.

I wanted love.

But for tonight, I steeled my heart and said, "I want you, in bed."

11

BIRDIE

Confession: I know way too much about sexually transmitted diseases.

His gaze on me heated, and he set his cup down on the counter. As he walked toward me, slow, purposeful, my heart pounded. If he couldn't hear the rush of blood, it would be a miracle.

He sensually ran his fingers over my arm and slipped his hand in mine, leading me toward the back of his apartment. My skin tingled as we walked, and nerves fired through my body, every cell on high alert.

Sex with Dax had never been earthshattering. And even though I'd read enough of Mara's romance novels to know my way around a metaphorical bedroom, I had no idea what would happen next.

Would I be bad in bed?

Did he have any STDs?

Oh god, what if I'd gotten an STD from Dax or his mistress? I hadn't noticed anything different down there, but now I was panicking, thinking I should make an appointment just in case.

But talking about that with Cohen wasn't sexy. How did one even bring that up? *Um, hi, I think you're hot and want to bang you, but my ex cheated on me and I haven't been checked and I'd like to see the paperwork from your latest doctor visit, please?*

This was a hot mess and *oh my gosh we were getting closer to his bedroom.*

I was supposed to be getting married to Dax this month! I was supposed to be a one-man woman for the rest of my life and here I was walking to a stranger's bedroom. What was wrong with me?

He opened the door to his bedroom, to the perfectly made bed and the glowing lamp and the abstract art canvas over the bed, and I nearly passed out.

"Are you okay?" he asked, examining me. "You're breathing hard."

"I—" I gasped for air, and my peripheral vision clouded. "I need to sit down."

Realization crossed his features, and he steered me to a chair by his bed, saying, "Sit. Put your head between your knees."

I leaned over my lap, spreading my legs to make room

for my stomach, and tried to breathe. But with my face against the dress, all I could smell was the store and new fabric and *dear god, had someone tried this dress on without underwear before I bought it?*

"Birdie, Birdie," Cohen hummed, rubbing my back. "It's okay. We don't need to do anything if you don't want to."

Tears stung my eyes as I gasped for air. This was *not* how tonight was supposed to go. I was supposed to be sexy, a free woman making a fresh entrance to the world. I was mad at Dax. How could he have done this to me? Taken up the last two years of my life and then toss them away like they meant nothing?

Angry tears poured from my eyes onto my dress, and my shoulders shook with sobs. I was so not getting laid tonight.

Or ever if I acted like this every time I got close to a man.

With tears streaming down my cheeks, I sat up and met Cohen's eyes. "I'm sorry. I thought I was ready for this, but I'm..."

"Not," he finished with a smile. "I'm not great at flings either. Maybe we should take it slow?"

My heart twisted at his patience. At his kindness. "Really? You don't have to. I'm a mess."

He smiled. "I'd love to take you on a date, get to know you without spilling beer on your dress."

"That sounds amazing." I bit my lip.

"But?"

I gestured at the tear stains on my new dress. "I'm clearly not ready to date."

"That's fine," he said. "I'll take you on a no-pressure not-date this week. Coffee or lunch—you do that with people you don't even like."

I mean, I ate lunch at the school every day, so he wasn't wrong.

"Do you want me to take you home?" he asked.

Oh crap. "I—my roommate is probably—" having hot wild sex with someone from the bar like I should have been "—occupied. Can I sleep on your couch?" It was that or going back to my apartment, and I was not doing that in this state.

"Of course," he said. "It's late anyway. I can sleep on the couch. It's not a big deal."

"You don't have to do that—I'd hate if you got a bad night's sleep because of me."

"One night won't kill me," he said. "But there is a movie on Netflix I've been wanting to watch... Maybe we could watch it in here together?"

I looked over at his bed. It was a king. "I'll stay on one side? I won't even roll over or anything."

He chuckled. "You have yourself a deal. Do you want an extra shirt to sleep in?"

"I can use the one from the bar." I put my hands on my knees to push myself up. "I'll go change. Again."

"I'll be here," he said, picking up the remote from his nightstand.

I made my way to the bathroom, kicking myself the entire way. Why couldn't I have just rebounded with the hot guy? Now he probably thought I was a spaz and was just ready to have me out of his house. Why was he being so nice to me?

With the bathroom door closed behind me, I got my phone out of the purse I'd left in there and sent Mara a text.

Birdie: You would be so ashamed of me.

Birdie: But enjoy your sexcapade. I'll just be here, NOT having sex. See you in the morning at Waldo's Diner. Bring my bag. We're going to need some breakfast before I can face work again.

I set my phone down and changed back into the 4XL shirt. I wished I had some shorts to wear or even underwear that covered more, because I knew the shirt would slip up as I slept, but I was a light sleeper. The second Cohen woke up, I could pull it down to cover more.

I picked up my purse and my new dress and carried them with me to his bedroom. Cohen had changed out of the jeans and button-down shirt he'd been wearing and now had on a pair of joggers and a thin white T-shirt that showed the muscles of his chest and shoulders. He lay back on the bed looking like sex on a... well, on a mattress.

Could I take back the whole taking-it-slow thing? This

man *radiated* sex. But here I was, watching a movie with him like some PG-13 teeny-bopper heroine. I could only imagine what Mara would say tomorrow at breakfast before school.

12

COHEN

This woman, in my room, just felt right. Yeah, it sucked I couldn't show her a good time tonight, but something about being around her electrified me in a way I hadn't felt for a long, long time. I didn't want her to think I was just some loser who wanted to hit it and quit it.

I wanted to get to know her. So I looked away from how adorable she was in that T-shirt and gestured at the TV. The home screen showed a comedy Ollie wouldn't watch with me because the actor was too old and lame. But he'd used a word I didn't even understand to call the actor lame. Maybe *I* was the lame one. "Are you okay with this one?" I asked.

"It's great."

She seemed honest, so I said, "Good."

I was about to press play when I noticed her hesitation.

She looked from me to the empty side of the bed and said, "Are you sure about this?"

How sure I was might have scared her. So I gave her what I hoped was an easy smile and said, "It's a movie, Bird. Watch it with me?" I hadn't meant to use a nickname for her, but it came so easily. I hoped it wasn't too familiar.

She smiled and lifted up the comforter. I wondered what she thought of the beige color Ollie had helped me pick. Or the extra pillows I kept on my bed so it wouldn't feel so empty at night.

She slid underneath the comforter, pulling it up over her chest, and situated herself on four of the pillows. She looked so at home it made my chest swell. "Comfortable?" I asked.

There was that shy smile again. She nodded, looking at the TV, and I took that as my sign to press play.

We were only a couple of feet away, but I wished we could cuddle. That might have been what I missed the most about a serious relationship—the time to just lie and be with each other.

Birdie giggled, and I realized I had missed the joke. I chuckled softly at myself and sat back, relaxing. Even though we weren't right next to each other, it felt good to have her here.

Ollie and I watched movies on the couch sometimes, but it had been a while. I made a mental note to ask him to hit Waldo's Diner with me for a milkshake this week and maybe catch an early movie one night if he had enough time with all that homework the Academy gave him.

I glanced over at the woman lying next to me and realized she had fallen asleep. It had been so long since a woman had slept over, but never had one this beautiful been in my bed. Her curly hair fanned around her heart-shaped face, and her luscious lips were slightly parted.

She seemed right at home amongst my many pillows, and the realization brought a smile to my face. When we woke up, I'd ask her out to breakfast, see if we could get to know each other better. Because even though the night started out looking like things would be hot and heavy, there was something natural about being around her. Something quirky about her that I wanted to know more about.

I had hoped we would watch the movie together, talking over the audio, but she was clearly exhausted. Maybe from work? Or her breakup. Why any guy would leave her, I had no idea. I hated her ex, and I didn't even know him. But I did know the way he made her cry, and it made me sick to my stomach. Not because I hadn't gotten laid, but because the pain had been so clear on her face.

She shifted, and I froze, not wanting to wake her up. She rolled in the pillows, her shirt riding up and the comforter slipping down, giving me a view of red lacy panties.

I bent at the force of my reaction. Holy fuck.

Feeling restless, and damn, I'll admit it, horny as hell, I rolled out of the bed and walked to the kitchen, cleaning up the drinks we'd had earlier and washing the cups in the sink. That distraction didn't quite work, so I grabbed the watering can and gave the multitudes of Ollie's houseplants a drink. He would take care of them Monday, but he'd asked me to water once over the weekend, and I promised I would.

As I looked around, I wondered what Birdie had thought of the place. There weren't too many personal effects in place—Ollie's mom had been the one who always printed and framed most of our photos.

Maybe I should see if Steve's wife knew a photographer, no matter how awkward just the thought of a photoshoot made me feel.

When I finished cleaning up, that mental picture of Birdie in my shirt and those panties sent my dick to attention.

I thought about going to the couch, but Birdie had said I could lie next to her. That she would stay on her side of the bed. And the couch... Ollie picked it out. He said it looked good, but damn was it a backbreaker.

I didn't want to be a creep though. With the way my dick responded to her, I'd be dry-humping her the second I fell asleep.

I couldn't stop thinking about her in my bed and the ways I wanted to make her scream.

My dick twitched.

A cold shower. That was what I needed.

I went to the bathroom, stripping out of my clothes and looking myself in the mirror. Thank fuck manscaping had become a habit because an ass like Birdie's deserved the best. My cock stood at attention, and instinctually, I took it in my fist, pumping once, twice.

It didn't come close to what she would feel like around my cock. But just the thought of thrusting into her thick folds made my dick throb.

Cold shower, I reminded myself. Cold fucking shower.

I reached over and turned the water on, adding only a little heat, and then I stepped in, not even waiting for the water to warm up.

The cold shocked my system, and I flexed against it.

But then all my fucking teenage brain could think about was what it would be like to have her in this shower, the water running down her body, dripping from her full breasts. I wanted to take a nipple in my mouth and suck until I heard her moan. Run my hands over her wet skin and take her here, water pouring over us as I did.

Cold water or not, I was hard, and this fucking boner wasn't going away.

I took my cock in my hand, closing my eyes and imagining the moisture there was hers. But I wouldn't go straight for her pussy. No, I'd make her feel good. I'd run my tongue along her slit and taste her. I'd lick her bud until she shuddered on my mouth.

Her head would fall back, that long curly hair grazing

the swell of her luscious ass. Eating her out from behind was sounding better by the fucking second.

But her ass wasn't the only thing I wanted. Her tits looked amazing in that dress, the fabric pulling them together and forming a deep cleavage I wanted rubbed against my cock.

And her lips, the thought of those lips on mine. On my dick. Going deeper down her throat.

I fisted myself harder, bracing myself against the cool shower tile.

Fuck cold showers.

I turned the knob hotter, pumping my cock as steam rose around me, imagining what her body would feel like pressed against mine. What her voice would sound like saying my name.

And I came.

I came so fucking hard just at the thought of her.

Completely spent, I washed away my come and another layer of skin, feeling a little guilty about fucking myself while she was in the next room. Someday, if I got a chance, I'd tell her how crazy she drove me just by being herself.

With my clothes on and my body completely spent, I went to the couch in the living room and lay down.

I couldn't wait until the morning when I could see her first smile of the day. And then I'd take her to breakfast and do what I could to give myself a chance with her. Because if I was being honest, I was tired of being alone.

13

BIRDIE

Confession: I made the walk of shame.

The first thing I noticed was how warm I felt, surrounded by thick blankets, cradled in a multitude of pillows.

But then I realized Mara's bed didn't feel like this. My heart beat quickly, realizing I had stayed at Cohen's house, in his bed. I listened to see if he was awake, but the house was dimly lit, pale light coming through the sheer curtains.

My shirt had hiked up overnight, so I carefully pulled it down in case he came in, then slid out of the bed. Part of me wanted to keep lying there to see where the morning took us, work be damned, but I couldn't face him. Not with how absolutely pathetic I'd been. Plus,

Headmaster Bradford would have my head (and my job) if I no-call/no-showed.

I tiptoed to the other side of the bed, grabbed my purse and moved toward the living room, where I'd left my shoes the night before.

He lay on his back on the couch, a small throw blanket around his feet. His face was so relaxed—peaceful instead of charged and chiseled like it had been the night before. I found I liked both versions a little too much.

My eyes trailed down his body, the strip of stomach visible where his shirt had ridden up and.... holy shit.

A morning erection tented his pants, and the tip of his cock pressed against the fabric, thicker than I ever could have imagined.

Holy shit.

I needed to leave. My head clearly was in cahoots with my vag because I was thinking far too much about staying and making both of our morning wishes come true.

I found my shoes by the island and slipped them on. In my heels and an old bar T-shirt, I left his apartment and came face to face with a mom and two children in the hallway. They were dressed for school with too-big backpacks on their backs.

"Good morning!" the little boy said.

The girl looked at me skeptically. "Why aren't you wearing pants? Is it no-pants day?"

With my cheeks turned on full blush mode, I straightened and said, "This is a T-shirt dress. Maybe your mommy has one..."

The mother's horrified look didn't help with my embarrassment. I wanted to say, *we didn't have sex!* But then again, there where children here. And also, was it any of her business if I had a fabulous one-night stand on a Wednesday? I mean, not really. Except for the fact that her children were offering hallway decorum lessons to me.

Ignoring the situation altogether, I turned and walked away, calling Mara on the phone instead of responding to her incensed texts.

When she answered, she said, "What do you mean you didn't have sex!"

A guy said something in the background, and she shushed him. "I saw you two leaving. He was a total silver fox."

I shook my head, squinting against the bright sunlight. "I had a panic attack in front of him! It was so humiliating. And then I didn't want to come home and interrupt you, so I stayed in his bed *by myself* until I snuck out! How much more pathetic can I get?"

"Do you really want me to answer that?"

I rolled my eyes. "I'm getting an Uber to Waldo's Diner. Come meet me with my bag? Please? I can't afford to miss work, and I need some sympathy syrup."

"I'll be there as soon as I can." She ended the call, surely to inform her partner there wouldn't be another round, and I continued down the sidewalk, my feet hurting just as much as my head.

That's the last time I go out with Mara. I was only closing in on thirty, but I was already too old for this. How Mara maintained her stamina was a mystery to me. Well, actually I knew. She took long walks on the beach while daydreaming up stories. But I wasn't crazy enough to try something like cardio.

Finally, an Uber picked me up and drove to Waldo's Diner, but I blanched when I saw the old car out front. My grandpa owned the place, but he usually didn't get here for another half hour! He couldn't see me in this state.

I slid down my seat and asked the driver, "Can you drive around for a bit?"

"Umm... you paid for the ride," he said.

I began digging through my purse. "I have a ten with your name on it if you pull around."

Just then, I saw Mara's truck pull in, and I breathed a sigh of relief. "Never mind."

"What about that ten?" he said as I reached for the door.

"Rule number one. Don't hesitate." I got out and scrambled to Mara's backseat, hoping Grandpa Chester didn't see me looking like this.

Mara was already laughing. "You're seriously that worried about your grandpa seeing you in some guy's T-shirt?"

I glared at her, reaching for my bag. "No need to add to the humiliation."

"That's fine," Mara said. "I'll tell you about my night."

While she went into detail about her hot and wild night, I got ready for work. Thankfully, I'd packed a dress that didn't need to be ironed. I struggled to pull on my shapewear, then slipped the gray knit dress over my head. My makeup bag was in there, so I used a makeup wipe to take off what I could, then hurriedly slathered on some foundation and added eyeliner and mascara.

"Too bad we can't swap stories," she said pointedly.

I ignored her, making sure I got a straight line along my lid. Once I capped my makeup and packed it up, we got out of her truck and walked into the diner.

It was decorated in a fifties theme with a boomerang pattern on the tabletops and chrome and pleather chairs. Sounds of sizzling food came from behind the bar, and delectable, greasy scents filled my nose.

But the person that made Waldo's Diner feel most like home sat a few rows down in his usual booth with a newspaper and a cup of coffee.

He grinned at me, deepening the wrinkles on his face, and pushed himself up. "There's my Birdie Girl."

"Hi, Grandpa," I said, going to give him a squeeze. He gave the best hugs. Just a second longer than you'd expect so you knew just how loved you were.

He stepped back and offered the same kind of hug to

Mara. Anyone who set foot in his diner became family, especially his granddaughter's friend.

"Join me," he said, scooting his newspaper over. As we sat with him, he said, "Is there a reason you were wearing a T-shirt earlier?"

My cheeks flushed bright red, and Mara burst out laughing.

"It's not what you think," I muttered.

Grandpa chuckled. "Does Dax have something to do with that?"

Mara aimed her eyes at the table, and I shook my head. "Dax and I... aren't together anymore."

He grinned big, then quickly hid his smile behind the newspaper. "I'm sorry to hear that."

I raised my eyebrows. "Are you?"

Mara chuckled quietly.

Grandpa shook his head at her and then slowly set the paper down again. "Well, I... might have imagined someone better for you."

"Better?" I said.

"You know, someone who actually makes a paycheck from time to time. And the guy has tattoos in languages he doesn't even speak! Who's to say he doesn't have 'asshole' tattooed on his neck in Vietnamese?"

Mara snorted with laughter, and I restrained a smile of my own.

"Tell me how you really feel," I said with a laugh.

He put his arm around me, kissing the top of my head. "I feel like you deserve the world. And Ralphie does too."

Mara nodded. "Here, here."

My favorite waitress, Betsy, came by the table and asked Mara and me what we'd like. Along with a black coffee, I ordered a big stack of pancakes and bacon for the hangover. Mara got close to the same.

"Hi, Ms. Melrose!"

My eyes widened, and I turned to see a middle schooler standing near the table with a woman who looked like her mom. Although I worked with the high school students, I went to the middle and elementary buildings from time to time to help their school psychologists.

I recognized Ginger because of her bright hair.

"Hi, Ginger," I said. "You can call me Birdie, you know." The girl was sweet, with curly red hair and a brace-filled smile. Judging by her mom's looks, she would grow up to be a beautiful woman.

Her mom said, "We were just grabbing a bite before school. Looks like she's going to have all As for this nine weeks!"

"That's amazing," I said, smiling despite my hangover.

Her mom agreed and excused herself to pay.

"Thank you." Ginger gripped her other arm with her hand. She was nervous.

"Come by my office any time," I said. "I'm sure Ralphie would like to see you too."

"Sure." She looked over her shoulder. "I better get back to my mom, so..."

"I'll see you at school."

She nodded and walked away, and I practically slumped in my chair out of relief. Thank god for semi-normal intereactions with students outside of school.

"So explain to me," Mara said. "Why didn't you have sex with Hottie McHotHot?!"

My cheeks heated, and I hissed, "Mara, one of my students is sitting over there, *with her mom*! And my grandpa's here!"

"And?" Mara glanced toward Ginger and her mom, waving. "They should know their counselor has a sex life and actually knows what she's teaching them about."

Grandpa nodded. "The world's a different place now."

I rubbed my temples. "The Academy isn't that progressive, Mara. And maybe neither am I. I kept thinking about Dax, and I don't think I could take disappointing yet another guy."

Her forehead creased, and she tilted her head to the side as she took my hands. "Honey, Dax left because he's an asshole."

"Exactly," Grandpa agreed, raising his mug.

I snorted softly. "I'm sure that's what the twenty-year-old he left me for thought too. You know, the one he chose over me."

She shook her head. "He did you a favor, B. Are you

seriously telling me you were happy with the way he ate spaghetti?"

Now I was confused. "What?"

"He slurped the noodles last time we were at La Belle. It was so disgusting. And I thought, my poor best friend has to listen to this for the rest of her life."

Grandpa nodded. "Those things will drive you crazy after a decade or two. You know it took a bit to get over the way your grandma left her teabags laying around when she was done steeping her tea."

I rolled my eyes. "Well, you two worked it out, and Mara, I'm sure you'll forgive spaghetti slurping for the guy you love someday."

"Of course not. The guy I love will be suave, debonair, rich, have neck tattoos, and probably a pierced tongue."

I made a side-eye at my grandpa, who was blushing and hiding his face behind his coffee cup. "I know Dax wasn't right for me," I said. "There were a lot of things I looked past, but Grandpa and Grandma are the only people I've ever seen in love like they are in your novels. My parents only slept in the same bed so the maids wouldn't gossip about them. My brother's at work all the time even though his wife is amazing. I thought what Dax and I had wasn't that bad."

"Not that bad?" She let out a sigh and faced Grandpa. "What's your advice then? What are we doing wrong?"

Grandpa finished sipping from his cup. "You're looking," he said. "Love isn't something you can find. It finds you, and usually when you least expect it."

Betsy came back, crowding our table with plates full of food before walking away. As we ate, the subject changed to the restaurant, to work, and eventually to goodbye. I needed to get to work, and Mara had writing to do.

Grandpa Chester gave Mara a hug, then held me tight. "You might not see it, Bird, but you deserve the best. Someone who would actually let you bring Ralphie home. Someone who loves you for you."

I smiled, thinking of Cohen and how he'd admired me the night before. "Thanks, Grandpa. I'll come back soon, okay?"

He waved. "Don't be a stranger."

Mara and I went to her car, and I buckled into the passenger seat, feeling much better than when I'd walked into the restaurant. I was still disappointed about how the night before had gone. I'd gotten in my own way with all that overthinking.

"What?" Mara asked as she drove toward the school. "What aren't you telling me?"

I shook my head and relayed the entire embarrassing night to her.

"Okay, that's definitely going in a book." She laughed. "And when is the not-date?"

"It's not happening."

"What?!" She leaned forward and turned toward me. "You're kidding! This was like the best foreplay ever."

"Oh my gosh, can we pause with the sex talk?" I said, blushing. "It's not going to happen because he never got my number. And he wouldn't call me even if he had it. He probably felt sorry for me."

Mara pulled into the school parking lot, putting the truck in park. "*I* feel sorry for you. Missing out on a silver fox like that."

I lifted a corner of my lips as I reached for the door. "Me too. I went to his house, and all I got was this stupid shirt."

14

COHEN

The next day, I picked Ollie up after school and took him to Waldo's Diner for milkshakes. It had been way too long since we'd had a chance to just sit and talk. I wanted to see how he felt about me dating. It was one thing for his mother to get remarried—which she had, a year after the divorce—but it was another for me to start dating when he spent five days out of the week with me.

But the second he got in the car, something seemed off. His lips tugged down at the edges and his shoulders were hunched like he was preparing himself for a blow.

"Are you okay?" I asked him.

He shrugged.

That was it? A shrug? I mean, he wasn't as wordy as Whitman, but I usually got at least a yes or a no. Maybe a grunt.

"Are you still good with Waldo's?" I asked.

Again, he shrugged.

God, it felt like being rejected. Fucking worse than waking up in my house alone to find that Birdie was gone. No note. No number. No nothing.

Instead of pulling out of the parking lot, I turned into an empty spot and parked. He didn't even look up from his phone. But his screen was black.

"Ollie, what's going on?" I asked. "Is everything okay?"

His jaw tensed. "I don't want to talk about it."

Everything in me wanted to pry. To see what prick upset him—student or teacher, I didn't care—but all the parenting books I'd ever read (and that was quite a few) said that digging for information was a bad idea. That good child-parent relationships were built on trust.

So instead, I said, "If you don't want to get shakes, that's fine. I actually have something to show you."

He didn't seem curious at all. Instead, he shrugged again.

I let out a sigh, as much frustration as I'd let myself show, and texted Linda. I was planning to take him by the house after going to Waldo's, but sitting across from a sulking Ollie for an hour didn't sound like a good time.

Cohen: Hey, can we meet at the house a little early?

Linda: Sure. Be there in 30.

I locked the phone and set it in the console, then backed out of the parking lot. It was mostly empty now, save a few cars I was sure belonged to student athletes. I hadn't played sports in high school—there had never been enough money—but I'd been so excited to have Ollie in all the things. Baseball. Football. Track. Any sport with or without a ball, I signed him up for.

It became very clear during his first (and last) t-ball season that sports were not for him. Although I had great footage of him running backward around the bases, he'd also acquired a black eye from overswinging, had sat in the outfield to play with the dirt, and only went to the last couple of games because we'd bribed him with candy. After that, I'd promptly signed him up for guitar lessons and acting classes and that was that.

As I drove toward the house I was hoping to make our own, Ollie sat slumped in his seat, staring at his phone. Thankfully now he had his earphones in and some video playing on YouTube.

A pit formed in my stomach—Ollie might have been a teenager, but his down days had never been this bad. What was going on?

I took another turn and saw the house through the windshield. It looked even more endearing now than it had before, with mature trees casting shade over the yard in the bright afternoon light.

The second my car was parked, Linda got out of her car and waved at us. And for the first time, Ollie said, "What are we doing here?"

"This is going to be our new house."

His mouth dropped open, and I grinned, excited to show him the surprise.

Wordlessly, he followed me out of the truck. Linda, of course, fawned over him, saying how beautiful his curls were and how much he "looked like his daddy."

Ollie managed a small smile, probably not used to someone like Linda.

"Let's go inside, shall we?" she said.

I nodded, clapping Ollie's back, and followed her toward the house. As we walked up, I hurriedly began talking, not wanting Ollie to be worried about all the updates it needed. "I'm going to have Jim's company paint the exterior, and Steve's brother does landscaping, so I'll have him get some good grass growing in the yard."

Linda unlocked front door, letting us inside.

"These are all hardwood floors, original to the house. Can you believe they're more than seventy years old?" I stepped into the kitchen. "I know you're not much for kitchen, but these appliances are actually pretty good. And let me show you the bedroom that'll be yours. It has a great view of the yard."

Ollie followed me silently, back to the room that would be his.

I pulled up the cordless blinds, showing him the expansive space we could make our own. "Isn't it amazing?" I said. "I think we could put a greenhouse in that back corner if you wanted one and plant a garden there, and then I was thinking between those two trees a hammock, and maybe I could even build a deck back there and get a gas fireplace set up. It could be really great for us, don't you think?"

He was being quiet. Really quiet. I turned to him, waiting to see his reaction, and my chest tightened. His lips were set in a line, and his shoulders were so tense they could crack a walnut.

Linda looked between the two of us and backed away slowly. "I'll give the two of you a minute."

"What the hell is this, Dad?" Ollie demanded.

I shook my head. "What do you mean?"

"You've been looking at houses?"

"Yeah, I wanted to surprise you." I was confused. "Did I do something wrong?"

"This house is forty minutes away from Mom's. Did you think about that?"

"Well, I—"

"You didn't think I'd want to see the place you settled on? Wouldn't want to have a say where I spent most of my time?"

Okay, now I was getting hurt. And angry. If I was a kid, I would have been damn thankful to have a place like this. I would have done fucking anything to have a dad who bought a place with me in mind, ready to make it my own.

"Watch it, Ollie," I snapped.

"Or what?" he said. "You'll buy this house without consulting me? Move me again?"

I could see the hurt in his face, and I immediately regretted taking him here. He'd been having a bad day before I ever even picked him up. The timing was wrong.

Still, I couldn't help my disappointment at yet another rejection as I said, "Let's go home."

15

BIRDIE

Confession: My real name is Beatrice.

I looked out the window of Mara's living room. "You have got to be kidding me."

"What?" She looked up from her computer as she sat in her big, cushy writing chair, her topknot bobbing as she did. Mara was on a deadline, and I was pretty sure she hadn't showered, or left that chair, since Wednesday night. It was Saturday afternoon.

I opened the curtain further so she could see the sleek black limo waiting in her driveway. "I just got a text from my mother insisting I go to their cocktail party for my sister-in-law's gender reveal party. Who does that anyway? Throws a cocktail party for someone who can't drink?"

Mara looked up thoughtfully. "Maybe they'll serve mocktails?"

"Mara, help me! The driver is walking to the door!"

"What?" she said. "It's not like he can come in here and drag you there."

I let the curtains fall back. "No, but he'll report back, and before you know it, my mother will be on your doorstep."

Mara frowned. "It's funny, because it's true."

We both knew it wasn't funny.

"May be best just to get it over with?" she said with a shrug. "The food's usually pretty good at those things anyway."

I sighed and walked to the door. The driver was midway down the sidewalk when I opened it and said, "I'll be out in ten."

I shut the door and went back to the guest room, digging through the suitcases I still hadn't unpacked. Friday night, Mara and I had cracked open two bottles of wine and finished packing up the townhouse. I was officially out of there, and Rob was thrilled he could get a new tenant on a longer lease and charge more than what I'd been paying.

Unfortunately, that meant all of my things were in boxes and bags—a visual reminder of my uprooted life. I found the dress that would make my mother complain the least and shrugged it on. My hair was still done from yesterday, so I just spritzed on some extra perfume and left.

When I made it back to the living room, Mara was already back in the flow and hardly noticed me walking out the door. I didn't recognize the driver waiting by the limo, but it had been years since I'd had to be "delivered" to my parents' house. After letting me in, he drove with the privacy window up, and I sat uncomfortably in the back.

Years away from rich living had changed me. My parents' entire lifestyle seemed so unnecessary now. I could have sat just as happily in the back seat of an Uber. Or, you know, driven my own vehicle if I actually wanted to go.

But I couldn't, so I sat back and looked at my phone. It was blank, free of any notifications that actually mattered. Dax hadn't reached out since he moved, and I was so mad and humiliated by it, I never wanted to hear from him again. I went ahead and deleted his number, the text thread between us. And while I was at it, I cleared out apps I didn't actually need or use anymore, wishing all the while I had given Cohen my number. Wondering what he was doing.

The longer I spent away from Dax, the more I realized how small my circle had become since moving back to Emerson and sharing a home with him. I used to go out with girlfriends in college. One friend worked as a waitress and gave the rest of us free fries. Another worked in the bowling alley and would let us play gratis when the manager wasn't around. We didn't have much, but we had each other.

Now we all lived in different areas and had drifted apart. I'd been fine, I thought, because I had Dax and Mara. But that was only a false sense of security. Mara was the closest person to a soulmate I actually had, but she probably felt the same way about her laptop. I needed to put myself out there, make new friends.

Maybe meeting the person my mother had lined up for me wouldn't be the worst thing in the world. Maybe I'd feel less lonely than I did now. And who knew? Maybe he felt the same way about wealth that I did—that it was meant to be shared instead of exalted and hoarded.

Although I knew my students would go on to do great things and likely accumulate wealth, I always stressed the importance of using money to do the right thing, not always the fun thing.

The limo slowed, and I brought my face closer to the tinted window so I could see where we were. My parents' mansion appeared, so large, so intimidating. How had I called it home for eighteen years? How had I ever been just another prep school student at Brentwood Academy, the rival to the school I now served?

As the car came to a stop, I scooted over and went to the door, opening it before the driver could get to me. He seemed perturbed by that, but was sure to shut it behind me.

No one else was entering the party, so I assumed

Mother really had waited to see if I'd show before dragging me here.

I used the knocker to announce my presence, and a maid I didn't recognize let me in.

"Where's Elsa?" I asked her. Elsa had worked for my parents for as long as I could remember and probably even longer than that.

"Retired," the maid answered simply, taking my coat. Maids were to be seen and not heard in my parents' world, but Elsa had been like family to me, and I was done living by their rules.

"What's your name?" I asked.

She seemed taken aback by the question and stuttered, "Elaine?" She said it like a question, like she wasn't even confident in her own name.

"Nice to meet you, Elaine," I said with a bright smile and extended my hand.

She shook it timidly.

"Are you from around here?"

Shaking her head, she said, "I'm actually from Nevada. My husband's family lives here."

My mother's tsking sounded like nails on a chalkboard. "Elaine, how many times have I told you that you are to be seen and not heard?"

See? I'm not making this stuff up.

"Yes, ma'am," Elaine whispered and scurried away.

I glared at my mother. "We were having a conversation."

That seemed to disappoint her just as much as my career choice. She grabbed my arm and steered me toward the backyard, where guests were sure to be congregating around the pool and bar. "Honestly, I don't know why you insist on treating them like you're on the same level."

"Mother." I stopped, and she paused, glancing around like she worried someone would see us.

"What are you doing?" she hissed. "You're already late."

"Why did you want me to come here? We obviously don't have the same ideals. And you *clearly* don't like who I am now."

"Regardless of what you think, or how you behave"—she frowned and continued walking forward—"we are still family. You can't just decide not to be a Melrose anymore. Especially since you won't be marrying that vagrant."

"Vagrant?" I said.

I hadn't meant to be defensive of him; he certainly didn't deserve my defense. Maybe I just didn't want to admit to my mom how bad of a mistake I had made by placing my trust, and my heart, in Dax's hands.

Instead of responding, she continued toward the backyard, whispering, "Now, when you see Anthea, don't act surprised. She's gotten so big, and she's self-conscious about it."

I followed her, knowing it was easier to do what Mara said—get it over with. She opened the door to the backyard and led me through. "She's pregnant," I said back. "Isn't growing another human supposed to take up some extra space?"

"Not in your ass." She winked, then turned toward the cabana and waved. "Donald, she made it!"

My eyes flicked from my dad to the pool, which was colored a bright pink. "Anthea's having a girl?"

Mom nodded happily.

Dad lifted his martini glass at me from across the pool. "Want a drink?"

Did I ever. "Rum and Coke?"

"Great," he said, turning back toward the bartender. If that was the best greeting he could offer, I'd take it.

Despite myself, I looked around, trying to see who had come. There was the usual crowd from Brentwood and some of the wealthier families from Emerson. The Academies might have been rivals, but networking amongst the wealthy knew no bounds.

Mother was always trying to schmooze the richest of the rich at these parties. I noticed the Rush family, who were well-known in the gaming industry; the Bhattas, who owned a production company, and... *great*.

Pam Alexander stood next to her husband, chatting up another couple. She looked up, noticing us, and flashed a falsely warm smile.

Mother fell into the hostess role, walking us closer so she and Pam could exchange kisses on the cheek. I decided

I would be professional, even if she acted like she'd melt if a drop of water landed on her.

"How are you, Pam?" Mother asked.

"Wonderful." She held up a fruity drink with an umbrella sticking out. "This is delicious. You must tell me the name of the service you use."

Mother put her hands out for Pam to take. "If I told you, I'd have to kill you."

They both cackled.

My ears were seconds from bleeding.

"*Beatrice*, is that you?"

I cringed. Only my mother and father and their colleagues called me that. I turned to see who it was and found a much more pleasant surprise.

16

BIRDIE

Confession: I hate cats.

"Hi, Anthea," I said, leaving Mom and Pam talking, and went to meet her where she stood by the pool. She looked absolutely adorable in a strapless white sundress that clung to her growing stomach. Her hair had clearly benefited from the pregnancy, as it fell in thick and lustrous auburn waves.

When I reached her, I gave her a hug. "You look beautiful."

She rolled her eyes. "Your mother told you to say that, didn't she?"

"Like she told you to call me Beatrice?" I quipped.

She winked. "I had to tease you a little bit, *sister*."

I shook my head. Anthea had a sharp wit about her that made me both like her and fear here a little bit. "How's the pregnancy going?"

"Terrible. Morning sickness every hour of the day. Swollen ankles. And all I want is a freaking vodka shot. Why did your mother think this cocktail party would be a good idea?"

"Hey, I'm not claiming her," I said. "Look at Doug."

She frowned. "I heard about Dax and your apartment. I'm so sorry. Are you sure you don't want to come stay with us?"

Fucking Mrs. Cronckle.

"It would be weird," I said. "And besides, you're about to have a new baby. You hardly need me in your way while you're preparing."

As though instinctively, she put her arms over her growing stomach. "You're using the baby as a cover. You just don't want to see your mom more than you have to."

"That too." I laughed. Right now, I really could have used that rum and Coke, but I looked toward the bar and saw Dad deep in conversation with one of his business associates. It would be hours before I got my drink—if he even remembered.

"You know," Anthea said, "Doug still loves you, even though you two went different directions."

I sighed. "I know." But he resented me too. While I went to college and shirked what our parents saw as a family obligation, Doug was being trained to take over my father's insurance company.

He didn't need to say it out loud for me to know he felt like I'd gotten a life of freedom while he was chained with golden handcuffs. He just didn't know that he could take them off. But I couldn't talk with his wife about that. "Let's talk about someone else."

"Someone?" Anthea asked.

Under her investigator-lamp gaze, my cheeks felt hot. "I meant something," I said quickly, shifting my gaze toward the pristine pool.

"Who's the guy?"

I would have said no one, if I weren't already smiling. I reached up and scratched my neck. "It's nothing, really. I met this guy, but I was a complete spaz and can't show my face in public ever again."

Now she was interested. "Who is it? Maybe I know him."

"Probably." I shrugged. "You know everyone."

"So..."

I narrowed my eyes but couldn't keep up the gaze for long without smiling. "Okay, promise if I tell you his name, you won't get involved?"

She crossed her finger over her chest. "Who?"

"Cohen Bardot? He owns that club on Watercrest."

Her mouth fell open. "Seriously? He is so *hot*."

My brother came up behind Anthea and wrapped his arms around her. "Who's hot?"

"No one," I said before Anthea could tell him. I gave her a look, asking her to keep it a secret.

"Some actor," she said. "How are you, babe?"

"Good. Need another mocktail?"

Anthea rolled her eyes toward the sky. "That's *exactly* what I need. Another Shirley Temple to make this heartburn even worse."

Doug cringed, and sensing the danger zone, changed the subject to me. "Sorry about Dax, sis." In the same breath, he added, "You know this guy just started at the firm that Mom wants to introduce you to. Maybe you two will hit it off?"

I frowned. "I think I'm swearing off men forever."

"In that case, perhaps the new CFO. She's pretty hot."

Anthea elbowed him in the gut.

Doug recoiled, rubbing his middle. "Well, maybe it's too late for the CFO. Look who Mom's bringing this way."

I looked over my shoulder to see Mom walking toward me with a stiff in a suit, and I turned back to beg Doug and Anthea to hide me.

Of course they were walking the other direction.

"Beatrice!" Mom said. "I'm happy I found you. I wanted to introduce you to Walter Walters."

Keep your face straight, Birdie. Keep your face straight.

"Hi there," he said, extending his hand.

His sweaty hand, I discovered as I shook it. He extended a rum and Coke, and I glared toward the bar at

Dad. So he was in on the setup too. Now I knew why Mother was so adamant I come to the party.

Mom smiled between the two of us like we were the Sistine chapel and she was Michelangelo. "I'll let you two get to know each other."

She walked away, and I took a long drink of the rum and Coke. Strong, just like I needed.

Walter cleared his throat. "So, you teach?"

"I'm a guidance counselor."

"Oh."

I closed my eyes. Maybe if I couldn't see this awkward encounter it would cease to exist. But when I opened my eyes, there he was, thinning hairline and all. How old was he? Forty?

But then I remembered someone else who was older and realized age didn't matter at all. No, it was just Walter. We were a minute in and had about as much chemistry as water and oil.

"You work with my dad," I said.

"I'm an executive account director."

"Oh. Nice." I only knew what that meant from many boring family dinners. It was a position Dad gave people to test them before moving up to a higher position. They must really want me to marry this guy if he was doing that well in the company.

"What do you do for fun, Beatrice?"

"Actually, it's Birdie," I said. "I like to bird watch. Go to the beach."

He shuddered. "I hate sand. It gets everywhere."

"And I'm assuming you don't like birds either."

"Birds?" he said. "Have you ever seen the movie?"

I rolled my eyes so hard I could see my brain. I *hated* that movie. Gave birds a bad name. "And I'm assuming you like cats?"

"In fact, I am more of a cat person." He smiled like he'd passed some sort of a test. He couldn't have been more wrong.

"You know house cats have more than halved the bird population?"

"No, I—"

"Sorry, Walter, I'm not feeling well." I lifted my glass. "Thanks for the drink," I said and walked away, hoping the driver was ready to take me away from this place that never felt like home.

17

COHEN

The bar closed early on Sunday nights, so I went straight from Collie's to Seaton Bakery, hoping my surrogate parents would have some advice on what to do with Ollie.

He'd hardly talked to me after seeing the house, and even though I'd texted him a couple of times over the weekend, he hadn't replied. I even tried texting and calling his mom but only received short answers like Ollie was busy. I had to think it wasn't just about me and the house. There was something going on, but I didn't know what.

The bakery was closed too, but I could see the lights on in the kitchen. Gayle and Chris always stayed late on Sundays to prepare dough for the week and deep clean the dining area. I loved that they saved the late, dirty work for themselves, even though they easily could have hired someone.

I knocked on the door, making the hanging bells rattle, and Gayle looked up from the chairs she was scrubbing. As soon as she saw me, her face broke into a grin, making lines form around her eyes and lips. She may have been getting older, but she'd always be beautiful to me.

She yelled something over her shoulder, probably letting Chris know I was there. Grabbing a ring of keys from her apron pocket, she unlocked the door and pulled me into a hug. "How are you doing, honey?"

"I'm okay," I said, taking in the smell of this place—like cleaner and sugar and flour. Like home. "Mind if I crash for a while?"

"Of course not," she said.

Her husband, Chris, came through the kitchen and said, "Hey, buddy. How are ya?" He clasped my hand and pulled me into a hug. I could barely believe I was almost his height now. When I'd met him as a teen, he'd seemed to tower over me.

"I was actually hoping I could pick your brains," I said.

Gayle nodded. "Of course. Grab a rag. We'll work and talk."

Chris went to the kitchen and retrieved a couple more rags, and soon we were all in the dining area, scrubbing down chairs and scraping gum from under the tables. While we worked, I told them about Ollie, how he'd been quiet all week and the blowup he'd had when I showed him the house.

"Well, first of all, congrats on the house," Gayle said, sending me a genuine smile.

I nodded my thanks.

"Do you think it could be something with his mom?" she asked.

I shrugged. "I wouldn't know. He won't talk to me at all."

Chris's gray eyebrows were drawn together. He'd gone gray early, but it looked like he was at least keeping all of his hair. "How are his grades?"

"I have no idea... but I can check." I got out my phone and went to my login screen. I tried to check in on his grades every month or so, but Ollie was a good student. Usually all I saw were As, Bs and the occasional C. But this time, the screen showed me something completely different.

There were several red 0s showing missing assignments in multiple classes. What was going on?

"How is it?" Gayle asked.

I shook my head, raking my free hand through my hair. "It's looking bad—for the last week or so he's missed almost every assignment."

Concern filled both of their faces, and emotion nearly clogged my throat. I'd never get used to having someone care for me like they did.

"Maybe you can talk to his teachers?" Gayle suggested.

Chris nodded. "I bet there's something going on at school. Bullying or something."

I nodded slowly. "That's a good idea. I'll head in there Monday. Maybe speak with the counselor."

I felt better, knowing at least I had a plan for how to help my son. I refocused my energy on a particularly pesky stain on a booth, trying to scrub it off.

"How about you?" Gayle asked. "How are you doing? Are you seeing anyone?" I couldn't miss the hope in her voice. Or the exasperation in Chris's when he added, "Not that you have to be seeing anyone. You could be a bachelor for life and we'd still love you."

I would have laughed, but Birdie's rejection still stung. "I met this woman the other night, and she was amazing. Like no one else. But she left before I could get her number or even her last name."

"And by left…" Gayle said.

I rolled my eyes. "We had a very wholesome dinner and then she hailed a cab."

Chris chuckled silently while she gave me the side-eye. But I wasn't about to tell her I jerked off to a woman who clearly didn't want anything to do with me.

"That's a shame," he said.

Gayle nodded. "Wasn't meant to be."

"What?" I said. "Why wouldn't it be? I don't want to go too far in detail, but I haven't reacted to a woman that way… ever."

Chris laughed out loud, but Gayle shook her head. "Spare me the details."

"Can do," I said.

"What I meant," she said, "was if it's meant to be, it will work out. You'll see her again and get another chance. If not, you won't and someone even better will come along."

I wished I believed her. But I didn't have time to worry about that. No, I had to take care of my son.

❤·❤·❤·❤

I went farther than usual on my morning run, pushing myself hard to clear my head, then I showered and got ready to go into the Academy. My plan was to get there before most of the students so I could have time to speak with the guidance counselor without Ollie seeing me.

My ex dropped him off at the school Monday mornings, so I didn't have to worry about explaining to him why I was going inside. Yeah, I wanted to know why he'd been dodging his homework, but this was so out of character for him. More than anything, I wanted to know if he was okay.

When I parked in the lot, the building was just as intimidating as ever—large and imposing with Latin engravings and gothic statues staring at me.

I took the stairs up to the front doors, looking at the

inscription. *Ad Meliora*. Ollie had told me once what it meant, but I always forgot.

Maybe I'd ask his guidance counselor when we were done talking about Ollie.

Right inside the doors was the front office, so I opened the door to see an older woman with short red hair behind the desk. Her name tag said Marjorie Bellows. She looked up at me like she was already disappointed.

"Hi, Ms. Bellows," I said. "Could you point me in the direction of the guidance counselor's office?"

"Sure," she said. "Ms. Melrose's office is down this hall on the right. It has a bench outside."

I nodded, getting out of there and taking deep breaths as I went down the tiled hallways. I nodded at a few of the teachers I saw as I walked, said hello to a couple, but I kept my gaze ahead. I needed to get in and out of here before Ollie did.

Ahead on my right, I saw an old wooden bench, and it looked like the door was already open. As I got closer, I heard the most beautiful voice, and my jaw dropped.

18
BIRDIE

Confession: My bird is my therapist.

"It was awful, Ralphie," I said, preparing his food and water the next morning. "You wouldn't believe the dolt my parents tried to set me up with. And the party?" I finished pouring the seed into his dish, then shut the cage door. "An airplane wrote 'It's a Girl' in the sky. I'm surprised Anthea didn't divorce Doug and our family right then and there."

"Sounds like a pretty bad party," a smooth voice said from the doorway.

I turned to see who was there and backed into Ralphie's cage.

He squawked and flapped his wings in protest, but this

was not a time for outrage. It was a time for shock. Pure and utter panic. And maybe a *hint* of sexual attraction.

"Co-Cohen, what are you doing here?" I stuttered.

He smiled. "I could ask you the same thing."

"I work here," I said, turning to straighten Ralphie's cage and gather myself.

"Who's this guy?" Cohen asked, peering around me.

"This is Ralphie." I smiled affectionately at my bird, then back to Cohen. "He's basically my best friend." And therapist, I didn't say.

Cohen chuckled, bringing his finger close to the cage. "I used to have a pet parakeet."

"What was its name?" I asked.

"General Feathers."

I giggled.

"Hey, I was only seven when I named him."

"That's cute," I said, admiring him interacting with my bird. Ralphie came closer to Cohen, curiously taking him in, then he gently nipped his finger with his beak. He approved. And my heart melted to a puddle.

Cohen smiled. "That's a good boy."

"He usually doesn't like men," I said. Dax might have had something to do with that.

"Well, he's a sweetheart."

"I think so." I folded my arms over my chest. "So, what are you doing here?" I laughed nervously. "You didn't find every school in the area and search for me, did you?"

"No," he chuckled. "Actually, this was a happy coincidence, considering you never gave me your number... or a goodbye."

My cheeks flushed with embarrassment. "I thought I'd spare you the inconvenience of turning me down."

"Why would I do that?" he asked, stepping away from Ralphie.

I rubbed my arm. This really was awkward. "Because I have about all the grace and charisma of a watermelon?"

He shook his head, an amused smile making him look that much more attractive. "You are one of a kind, Birdie. I never would have turned you down."

His husky voice made my insides shiver the way they had that night. Part of me still wished I had taken him up on a one-night stand. Or at least stayed for breakfast. "I still don't understand, though. The Academy doesn't usually do intern placement with bars." I laughed nervously. Something about this man made me giddy and scared and horny all at once.

"No, I'm here to talk about my son."

It was like he'd dumped a bucket of ice water on my head. "Wh-what?"

"Ollie Bardot is my son," he said.

My eyes widened as my head caught up to the words I was hearing. This man. This very sexy man who had spilled a beer on me and seen me in an oversized T-shirt and had his boner pressed into my hip was ONE OF MY STUDENT'S FATHERS?

Holy shit.

This really couldn't get any worse.

Not only was I a chicken and a tease who tiptoed out of his apartment. I was his kid's unprofessional guidance counselor.

I covered my face with my hands. "You're Ollie's father."

"I am," he said calmly. There was a slight frown on his perfect features as he said, "I'm worried about him, and I didn't want him to know I'm meeting with his guidance counselor, so... here I am."

"Sit," I said, gesturing at one of my chairs. I sat behind my desk, getting Ollie's file from where it had been atop my stack. "I actually had it on my list to call his parents today." If only I'd looked at the file before being surprised like this, maybe I could have worn something other than my long-sleeved top and plain dress pants. Maybe even worn my hair down instead of this slicked-back bun.

But I couldn't focus on how I looked, not now when we had a student to take care of. Ollie was much more important than me or my crush on his father. "What has he told you?"

"Nothing," Cohen said. "That's the problem. Usually he talks to me after school, but the last couple of weeks, he hasn't been speaking at all when he comes home."

"And has he said anything to your wife?" I asked, terrified of the answer—that he would have cheated on his spouse with me.

"His mother hasn't been speaking to me lately, especially since we don't have to meet to get Ollie to our places."

"That must be so hard." My heart hurt for Cohen, even though a tiny spark of happiness lit at his answer. I'd seen how hard it was for divorced couples to co-parent high school students. Judging by his answer, Cohen and Ollie's mom were clearly separated and I hadn't almost committed adultery.

Cohen nodded sadly. "Ollie's adjusted so well since he came out his freshman year, and the divorce two years back, and he seems to like his new stepdad, but this silent treatment is so not him."

I kept my face even, taking in the new information about Ollie's orientation. As far as I knew, he wasn't out at school, but kids were mean. If someone had found out, or even guessed, maybe that was a contributing factor.

I flipped open the file and took out emails I'd gotten from a couple of his teachers and printed out. "Mr. Davis, his videography teacher, says he's been very withdrawn in class the last two weeks. And Mr. Aris, the math teacher, says Ollie's missing five assignments. He's worried if Ollie doesn't start submitting his work soon, he'll really hurt his GPA."

Worry covered Cohen's face, etching into every handsome inch, and he rubbed the short stubble along his jaw. "Has he been getting picked on by any of the kids? Have you seen anything different at lunch?"

"I haven't noticed anything," I said, "but that doesn't mean nothing's happening. Maybe even online. How about his relationships outside of the home? Has he stopped speaking to friends? Broken up with a boyfriend?"

He shook his head. "He hasn't told us about a boyfriend, and his friends haven't come over lately, but he usually spends more time with them on the weekends when he's with his mom."

I frowned and looked back down at my files. "None of the notes mention anything happening here at school. Let me call his mom, and hopefully we can figure something out."

"Thank you," he said. "Really, I just didn't know what to do."

"This was a great first step." I reached across the table, putting my hand atop his to comfort him, but just the contact made my stomach swoop. I pulled my hand away and straightened my shoulders. "Thanks for coming in."

He smiled, not moving to stand. "I'm glad I did. And now that I know how to get a hold of you... maybe we can plan that lunch?"

"I-I—" My heart fell. "I can't."

His eyebrows drew together. "Why not? I really thought we hit it off."

"We did." Ugh, I so did not want to say this, but I had

to. "It's just that dating parents is strictly against the rules at the Academy."

"You're not serious," he said.

"It's in the bylaws. The concern is that it would lead to unfair treatment of the students."

Cohen shook his head in disbelief. "So the only way we're allowed to get Ollie special treatment is through extra donations?"

My rueful smile came easily. "Seems like it. Money talks."

"But..." He tapped his fingers on my desk, the pattern mesmerizing. "What exactly constitutes dating?" he asked.

I refocused my gaze on his face. "What?"

"Are parents not allowed to meet with teachers outside of school?" he asked with a neutral expression. "For instance, if you were a man, would I be allowed to have dinner with you?"

"Well, there's nothing in the handbook against it."

He lifted his eyebrows. "So it's only kissing that's off limits?"

My cheeks heated. "Amongst other things."

"Then have dinner with me."

"Cohen..."

"You said you didn't want to date. And I don't either. As a concerned parent, I'd like to speak with you more about possible solutions... And as a friend, I'd like to get to know you better."

I fought my growing smile. "I'd like that too. As a friend."

"Friday?" he asked.

"In Brentwood," I said, writing my number on a sticky note and handing it to him.

He took it and winked. "Crossing into the enemy's territory, are we?"

I smiled. "Perhaps."

With a smile of his own, he waved at Ralphie. "Bye, Ralph." Then he turned to me and said, "I'll see you Friday, Ms. Melrose."

"Goodbye, Mr. Bardot."

19

BIRDIE

Confession: I try to help other people solve their problems, but I have no idea what to do with my own.

I kept a closer watch on Ollie that day. Meandering the halls was part of my job, so I made sure to do a couple of rounds past his locker, but I saw nothing out of the ordinary. At lunchtime, he sat with a couple other girls and guys from the school orchestra, but he seemed reserved, his eyes slipping out of focus when his friends didn't notice.

After school let out, I closed my door and dialed his mom's number. Audrey Howard. She was no longer in our system as a Bardot, which made talking to her while having feelings for her ex-husband a little easier.

She picked up the phone, and I said, "Hi, Ms. Howard. I'm Birdie Melrose, the guidance counselor at Ollie's school."

"Hi there," she said. "Is everything okay?"

"I'm not sure. Ollie's missing several assignments, and we've noticed he's been a bit withdrawn lately. I was wondering if everything is okay at home?"

"Oh no," she said, seeming concerned. (I couldn't say that for all the parents I called with this kind of news. Half of them got frustrated by the inconvenience and half didn't even care.) "We went out of town last weekend and he was okay then. Spent most of the time on his phone, although that's not completely abnormal. My ex has him during the week, so he deals with most of the homework, and I usually don't have to remind Ollie about it on the weekends, but I'll give him an extra nudge on Saturday."

"Okay," I said, disappointed there wasn't a clear problem with a solution I could find. "Will you let me know if you think of something?"

"Of course," she said. "Hopefully we can fix whatever it is soon."

I hung up, feeling dissatisfied. I hated it when my students were hurting. Especially hated when I didn't know why or how to fix it.

With the call over, I got up and began gathering my things to go. I had an appointment to look at some apartments in Seaton. They were well under my budget, and if I liked them alright, I hoped I could even save some extra money to put toward a down payment on a home like Mara had.

As I drove across town, I pictured myself on this commute. It was about thirty minutes. Not too bad, but I'd definitely like living closer if I could.

The farther I got from the school, the shabbier the buildings looked. No doubt about it, Seaton was the poorest town in the area. We had a few students on scholarship from there, but other than that, I never thought about Seaton much, and I'd only been there a couple of times to look at the pier. But Mara and I had shared a postage stamp of an apartment in LA. I could make this work.

But even the apartment complex parking lot made me reconsider. Shards of broken glass littered the asphalt, glinting in the sunlight. Ripped up furniture sat haphazardly by the dumpster. And beyond that, there was a deadly silence to the area that was unsettling. Even the children outside were quiet, nervous, like they were waiting for something bad to happen.

I pulled in front of the main office and turned off my car, breathing deeply. Maybe this was just my upbringing rearing its ugly head. I'd been conditioned to think of poor as bad, and that wasn't always true. I owed it to myself, and my budget, to give this place a chance.

I got out of my car and locked the door, then walked a few steps into the lobby. A fly strip hung over the reception desk, dotted with black carcasses, and a girl with inch-long fingernails sat at the desk, clacking on old computer keys.

"Hi there," I said. "I have an appointment to tour an apartment."

"Right." She clicked on the mouse and stood up. "Come with me."

I followed behind her, carrying my purse in front of me with both hands, as we walked toward the U building.

"Laundry is in the D and Z buildings. So you'll have to walk to wash it. I recommend staying there until it's done. If you have pets, you gotta pick up after them or you get a fine. Utilities aren't included. Gotta set them up with the city..." She reached the building and swung open the door. The hallways were dimly lit with what looked like emergency lighting and painted a shade of lime green I'd never seen inside a building before. As we passed other tenants' doors, I could hear the sounds of life—barking dogs, crying children, televisions turned too loud.

All the noises assailed my senses, making me feel overwhelmed and claustrophobic. Just the fact that I was here was a strong reminder of all I'd lost when Dax decided to walk away.

Dax and I had a plan—spend a couple years in the townhouse, buy an historic home in poor condition, and fix it up to be the one-of-a-kind home of our dreams where we'd live happily ever after. But that future was fiction, and I had to keep my mind in reality.

I took a deep breath, trying to calm myself, and paused

behind her as she took a key from her ring and shoved it in the lock. Just like at my office, she had to jiggle and shake it to get it to turn, but the door opened, and she led me into an apartment.

Believe it or not, the shade of dingy yellow on the walls was worse than the green in the hallway. The carpet had been stained and rubbed raw in places where an animal clearly used to scratch, a cat by the look (and smell) of it.

The kitchen was small with basic cabinets and black and white appliances. Stained laminate countertops. And the single bedroom was small with a simple closet. The bathroom had a pedestal sink and no room for storage.

But it was just me, right? I could make do with this. Plenty of people did.

Tears pricked at my eyes. This wasn't the life I wanted, but I was starting to wonder if I actually had a choice.

20

BIRDIE

Confession: I've never had this many inappropriate thoughts about a man in my life.

"I've told you that you can stay here as long as you like," Mara reminded me as she handed me lipstick for my not-date with Cohen. We were in the bathroom as I tried to get ready and not panic at the same time.

I took the tube and examined the shade of pink. "Is this not too young? I don't want him to think I'm a child."

"It's fun," Mara said. "And you're going on a date, not a business meeting."

With a shrug, I began spreading the makeup on my lips, then reached for a tissue to blot it off. "I know you said I could stay, but I don't want to impose. Wasn't that the point of buying your own home anyway? That you could live on your own, by your own rules?"

"I mean, there was some stuff about building equity in there, but also, you're like a sister to me. More than my own flesh and blood. If that place is half as bad as you're trying to make it out not to be, then I don't want you living there."

"It really wasn't that bad—" I began.

"'Not that bad' and 'good' are two different things," she quipped.

I let out a sigh and handed her lipstick back. "I don't like feeling like an imposition."

She shook her head. "If you keep doing my dishes, you can live here forever."

I giggled. "Now that's a rent payment I can afford."

"Exactly. Now look at me."

I turned toward her, squaring my shoulders. I'd decided to wear the dress he bought me that first night, especially since I wouldn't run in to anyone I knew. Maybe just to see him smile. Maybe to show him I wasn't always a complete mess who went to bars in skimpy dresses and talked to birds.

"You look absolutely beautiful," she said with a small smile. "And whatever happens on this not-date, I want you to enjoy it." She cupped my cheek with her hand. "You are the very best friend I've ever had, and you deserve the best."

My eyes stung at the emotion in her voice. Mara

always knew the right words to say to me. With the knowledge that, no matter what, she was in my corner, I felt more confident than I had all day.

We left the bathroom, and I gave Mara a wave before picking up my purse and going to my car. Cohen had texted me the address of a restaurant in Brentwood I'd never been to before. Most people from Emerson stayed on their side of town unless there was a new client or a large sum of money involved.

On the way there, I listened to one of my favorite podcasters since the breakup. Sure, it was sappy self-help stuff, but how do you think I got over eighteen years of living with my parents? I constantly tried to learn better ways to cope and connect, neither of which my parents taught me. My self-help podcasts annoyed Dax though—he would rather listen to indie artists or NPR.

I had terrible taste in men. I could see that now. Would my judgement be clearer with Cohen?

Part of me wondered if I should just turn around now. If getting to know another man would even be worth it. But Mara's voice telling me I deserved to be loved played in the back of my mind until I arrived at the restaurant and parked outside.

As I walked to the front door with the big sign saying View House, Cohen stepped outside, his smile just as attractive as the outfit he wore. His eyes scanned my body, making my cheeks heat, and he said, "You are a vision in that dress."

I sheepishly looked toward the ground and back to him. "If you compliment me too much, you're going to cross the line into date territory."

He chuckled. "Is that in the Academy handbook as well?"

"Maybe we should ask the headmaster," I teased.

"Hard pass." Opening the door, he stepped back to let me in, and I was immediately chilled by the air conditioning. The host asked us if we were ready to be seated, but I turned to Cohen. "Is it okay if we sit outside?" Dax never wanted to be around the flies or even a hint of humidity or sunlight. He preferred to be indoors, to say the least.

"Of course," he said, and the host led us to a patio table on an expansive wooden deck. As I sat down and looked over the railing, I realized where the restaurant had gotten its name. We were high enough up that we could see the city and the greenery of its trees splayed before us. I could even see a line of ocean blending with the sky.

"It's beautiful out here," I said.

He nodded. "One of my favorite places to eat. They don't have bad craft beers either."

My eyes widened with delight. "I want one of those."

"That can be arranged." He passed me the drink menu, then his face disappeared behind his own menu. I felt a twinge of sadness that his eyes were obscured. The blue green color seemed to change each time I met him. Today, in the evening light, they looked a lighter green compared to the darker teal I'd seen earlier in the week.

I decided on a drink, then turned my gaze toward my own menu and found a crab cake sandwich that looked good. Once the waiter had taken our orders, I felt strangely vulnerable. Like all the distractions that had existed before were suddenly gone. Now there was only us and this beautiful view.

"Tell me about yourself, friend to friend." Cohen winked. "Did you always want to be a guidance counselor?"

We were getting right into it then. I looked toward my hands in my lap, then back to him. "Actually, I wanted to be a fashion designer."

His eyebrows rose. "That would have been my last guess."

"Because I dress badly?"

He nearly choked on his water. "No-I-I just-I. You seem to be—"

I laughed, holding up my hand. "I'm picking on you."

His nerves quickly melted into a smile, which I returned.

"I was a different person in high school," I said shortly.

"How so?"

I looked over the view, wondering how much to tell him. How much of the past I really wanted to dig up and remember today. Finally, I let out a quiet breath and said, "High school was such a hard time for me; I figured it probably was for other people too."

He nodded. "High school was the worst."

Now it was my turn to be surprised. "Seriously? With that jawline? I bet you cruised through the halls on a white horse."

He chuckled. "Hardly. I barely passed any of my classes, and everyone thought I was stupid and headed toward jail time as soon as I graduated."

"What?" I asked. That wasn't the vibe I was getting from him at all. Had I really misread him that badly? And if I had, did that mean I had bad taste in men that went beyond just Dax?

"I didn't have the best role models, and I was angry," he continued. "Angry people do stupid things."

"That's the truth," I agreed, feeling like I understood him on a whole new level.

The waiter came back with our drinks, and I took in the dark fizzing beer in front of me.

Cohen held up his glass and said, "To friendship."

"And nothing more," I added, to remind both him and me, then moved to clink my glass with his.

Or tried to, before he said, "Hey!" and pulled his glass back.

"What did I do?" I asked, looking around. "Is there a bee?"

"No," he chuckled. "I went on a trip to Germany last year—sourcing some new drafts for the bar—and my German friend told me if you don't look each other in the eyes when you say cheers, it's seven years of bad sex."

My cheeks flushed at the places my mind went. "We can't have that, now can we?"

His eyes held mine, turning my stomach into a puddle in their heat. "Cheers," he said again, his voice low and smooth.

"Cheers," I repeated, my hand barely steady on the glass as I clinked my cup to his.

I was in trouble.

The waiter soon returned with our food, and for the rest of the meal, we drank and ate and talked. He told me about Ollie and how he had a natural green thumb. How he'd first come to realize he might want to open a bar. And he asked me about myself too, learning about my hobbies like birdwatching and beta reading Mara's smutty romance novels. I couldn't help but notice how easy it was to be around him. Or how his words and the way he spoke them sent butterflies dancing in my stomach.

The bill came, and Cohen reached for it.

"No way," I said, extending my hand for the leather folder. "We're splitting the check. Friends split checks."

"Apparently you have bad friends. I like to treat my friends from time to time, especially when I was the one who asked them to meet up."

I looked toward the expansive view for a moment, then back to him. "Well, I'm learning something else about you."

"Yeah?" he asked as he stuffed his credit card into the slot. "What's that?"

"You're stubborn."

He chuckled. "I just know what I want." His eyes narrowed slightly, like he was seeing me and no one else, and it made my skin sizzle.

Being his friend and nothing more was going to be hard. I *had* to have more self-control than this. Simply the sight of a hot guy had me all off-kilter and thinking about things I shouldn't have been thinking about in a very public place.

The waiter came and got the card, and Cohen said, "Do you want to get some ice cream after this? There's a stand nearby, and it has a four-star rating online."

I giggled. "You check ratings?"

"You don't?"

I shook my head. "Everyone's either getting paid to leave a good review or having a bad day and leaves a one-star."

His eyebrows rose. "So if you saw a review that said someone found a finger in their chili, you would just ignore it."

"I wouldn't see it in the first place." I reached for my drink and finished the last of it. "Take this beer for instance. I never looked at the reviews before I came here, and I'm a very satisfied customer."

He snorted. "That's because *I* took you here, and *I* looked at the reviews."

"But if you hadn't looked at the reviews, it still would have been good."

With an exasperated smile, he shook his head. "You like to roll the dice, don't you?"

"When the stakes are small?" I shrugged. "Sure."

"That's where we disagree." He leaned forward and rested his elbows on the table, which had been cleared except for our drinks. "See, today, this, wasn't a small-stake event to me."

My heart sped. "What do you mean?"

"What's the one thing you can't get back?"

I bit my lip, waiting for his answer.

"Time," he said, his eyes flicking to my mouth. "I knew I'd never get another chance at a first not-date with you. No way was I going to blow it."

My lips lifted into a smile of their own accord. "Rest assured, you did not 'blow it.'"

"That's good to hear."

The waiter came back, and Cohen scribbled his signature, along with a tip, on the receipt. Twenty-five percent. As a former waitress, *swoon*.

Standing, he extended his hand and said, "Ice cream?"

Despite the voice in the back of my head telling me holding hands was a bad idea, I slipped my fingers through his.

Best bad decision ever.

21

COHEN

I don't care if it made me sound like a simp; our hands were fucking made for each other.

Over the course of our meal, I'd learned a few things about Birdie—she was stubborn, funny, her eyes looked up and to the left when she was deep in thought, down and to the right when she said something sad.

We walked down the sidewalk, our fingers linked, talking about our surroundings. Just easy conversation. She liked the antique shop we passed and even pointed out an old painted washtub I'm pretty sure Ollie would have gone gaga over as a planter.

A couple passed by us on the sidewalk, making Birdie and me walk closer together. Our clasped hands brushed against her curvy hips, and my mind went blank for a moment.

Think, Cohen. I had to come up with something intelligent to say. This woman worked at one of the best high schools in the country, for crying out loud.

"So, how is the apartment search going?" That was a pretty neutral topic, right? It would give her a chance to talk. Maybe me a chance to offer support.

She let out a heavy sigh, and I instantly regretted my decision to open my stupid mouth.

"You don't have to talk about it if you don't want to," I said.

"It's not that." She let out another sigh. "I'm just having a hard time finding something close enough to the school but also in my budget."

"I had a hell of a time finding mine," I admitted.

"I bet. There's a three-year waitlist on it now." Her smile quickly turned mortified. "Not that I'm a stalker or anything. It's just really pretty there."

The nervous way she smiled was endearing as hell. I chuckled and said, "Can't say I blame you. I only got in because one of my friends bought a house and was moving out."

"Lucky," she said.

I wondered if I should tell her about the house I was buying, offer my place, but it was too soon. The inspection was next week, and I needed to keep the cart behind the horse, so to speak.

"Where did you go to college?" I asked instead.

She smiled and shrugged. "UCLA. It was a great education, in more ways than one."

"How so?"

Her laugh was infectious. "Well, you know, the usual."

An uncomfortable sensation swirled in my gut because I really didn't. How bad would it be to admit that I'd never gone to college? That I'd only gotten my GED a few years after Ollie was born and that was only because I needed it to work on the construction crew that paid the best.

Since then, I'd audited a few business classes at Brentwood U—sitting in for free and doing the homework on my own time—so I could learn the basics for my bar. That was a far cry from the experience Birdie had and the one I hoped Ollie would have.

"Like what?" I decided to ask.

She shrugged, her shoulders lifting until they touched her curls. "The basics. Alcohol tolerance. How few hours of sleep I could survive on. The amount of classes I could skip without hurting my grades."

I raised my eyebrows. "Someone employed at the Academy skipped classes?"

Her cheeks flushed. "Just the gen eds. AP English at the Academy was way more difficult than my freshman composition class."

"I can imagine."

"How about you? Where did you go?"

This was it. The moment she'd find out what a catch I

really was. "I dropped out at seventeen. Got my GED at twenty-three."

I watched her carefully, waiting for that hint of judgement I always felt when spending time around Academy teachers or parents. Instead, she grinned and said, "It figures, doesn't it?"

"I don't understand," I said.

She laughed, shaking her head. "My best friend doesn't even have her GED, and she makes three times what I do. Clearly, I took the wrong path in life."

"You're making a difference," I said. "That's worth more than money."

Her eyes warmed on me, and she slipped her fingers from mine, holding on to my arm with both of her own. "Thank you, Cohen."

"Any time." Everything in me wanted to kiss the top of her head, let her know how truly I meant those words, but I held back, focusing my gaze instead on the ice cream shop ahead of us. It was painted aqua blue with bright white trim, and a line extended all the way to the street. It must have lived up to its 4.5-star reputation.

I lifted my arm, pointing. "That's our place."

22

BIRDIE

Confession: Want to get on my bad side? Waste perfectly good ice cream.

The ice cream stand was cute, and it had plenty of flavors to choose from. I watched with anticipation as Cohen ordered. A double scoop of mint chocolate chip in a chocolate waffle cone.

"Nice," I said. "I'll have that too."

"Easy peasy," the woman behind the counter said. Cohen paid, again, and we stepped to the side to wait. This area didn't have as nice of a view, but there were picnic tables scattered about a gravel lot. Couples and families sat enjoying the beautiful fall weather and each other's company.

It was one of those days, one of those spaces, that made you feel like all was right in the world.

Or maybe that was just Cohen.

He said, "Why don't you find a seat? I'll get the cones when they're ready."

What a gentleman. With a nod, I began walking and found an open space for us to sit. As I waited for Cohen, I looked around to see who was there. In my world, people watching was more of a sport than football. And I could have been an Olympic "athlete" at it.

For example, the couple just a table over were clearly in a fight. She had her shoulders away from him, wasn't even making eye contact as she toyed with her spoon in the paper bowl. Her partner had his eyebrows furrowed, legs crossed like he was protecting himself.

Dax and I had been in plenty of those fights before. Usually about money—the time our electricity got shut off because he forgot the bill had been a giant blowout. I'd never, never had that happen in my life before, even when Mara and I were scraping together pennies to pay our expenses at the apartment.

I turned my head away from the couple, away from the reminder of what my life could have been like had Dax not walked out on me, and my eyes boggled at what I saw. Headmaster Bradford sat with his wife and their grandchildren only a few tables away.

I got up so fast I fell over the picnic bench, making rocks dig into my hands and knees. My skirt had flown up, falling over my stomach, and I yanked it down to cover my underwear. A few people looked my way, but Bradford was preoccupied with a dollop of ice cream that had been dumped into his lap.

I hurried toward the back exit, keeping my head down and my faithful black purse clutched in front of me. If Bradford saw me here looking like I was dressed for the circus, with a student's father no less, my career could be on the line. And breaking a major policy like the no-dating rule didn't look good on a resume when applying to other schools.

As soon as I was on the opposite side of the building, I got out my phone and dialed Cohen's number.

When he answered, he asked, "Where did you run off to? I don't see you, and I have ice cream dripping down my hand."

If I wasn't completely panicked, I might have laughed. "*Headmaster Bradford* is there with his family!"

"Oh. *Oh*. Walk down the block toward the screen-printing place. I'll drive the car to meet you."

The steady tone of his voice had me nodding and following his instructions. Maybe even calming down a bit. "Okay. Right. And if he sees us, it's not a big deal. Friends can get ice cream together."

"Friends getting ice cream wouldn't run away from their bosses."

I cringed. "So I'm not the best at playing it cool."

"Understatement of the year."

"I wish you could see me glaring at you."

"Turn to the left and I will."

I looked over and saw him in his sexy car with the window rolled down.

"Show me your ankle, and I'll give you a ride," he said.

"Oh mercy me." I covered my chest with my hands. "What will my father say when he finds out?"

With a chuckle, he reached across the console and pushed the door open. "Get in."

"So forceful," I said in the same breathy voice as I climbed into the car. "Where's the ice cream?"

"I threw it away."

My mouth fell open. "You threw away *four-and-a-half-star* ice cream? How could you?"

"I wasn't about to get it in my car!"

"Uh huh. Well, now this not-date has been ruined."

With a sexy smile, he said, "Luckily for you, I know a few places with mint chocolate chip. And plenty of napkins."

"My hero." I folded my hands over my chest again and let out a dreamy sigh.

"Happy to be of service, ma'am."

He stopped at a fast-food place and got us mint chocolate chip shakes. "Much less messy," he said, handing my cup and straw to me.

The lined paper cup was cold and moist under my fingertips, the perfect contrast to the evening sun hitting me through the tinted window. "Where's Ollie tonight?" I asked as he pulled into a parking spot so we could sit together in the privacy of his car.

"With his mom."

I noticed how he called her Ollie's mom instead of his ex. The difference may have seemed subtle to most, but to me, it was massive. Calling her "Ollie's mom" was like honoring her role in their child's life instead of her part in his past.

I took a sip of my shake and said, "She told me she didn't know what was going on with him, but she'll keep an eye out. I can't tell what's going on at school, but he does seem withdrawn."

Cohen nodded slowly and took another pull from his shake. "I'm worried about him."

My heart wrenched for him. I could feel his worry in every word. "We'll figure it out," I said, although I had no idea how.

"I hope so." He turned his gaze on me. "You know, when Ollie told us he was interested in men, my first thought was what the kids at school would think of him." He shook his head, looking back at his drink and adjusting the straw. "I never even worried about what Ollie thought of himself."

Maybe it was the tone in his voice or how close we were sitting, but I reached out and put my hand atop his thigh. I wanted to comfort him, erase the lines forming on his forehead and the worry in his darkening eyes. "You're a good dad, Cohen."

He lifted his eyebrows. "How can you tell?"

"I can hear it in your voice."

His lips turned up slightly. "What about you? Have you ever thought of having kids?"

"I used to," I said, deciding to lay it all out there. "My fiancé left me right before I met you, and I thought I'd do the whole thing, you know, house, car, 2.5 kids. But now that we've been apart, I keep wondering if I actually wanted that or if I just thought I should want that."

He nodded. "I never thought I'd have kids. Ollie was a surprise, and his mom and I got married as soon as we found out. But, as it turns out, when you get married, you need to be in love with your spouse and not just your child. The second I saw him, I knew I was meant to be a father. Meant to be *his* father."

I smiled softly. "And what about when Ollie leaves for college?"

"I'll have all his plants to take care of," Cohen said. "And my house will be a lot messier. I thought teens were supposed to be gross, but he makes me feel bad about my cleaning habits."

Laughing, I said, "I can relate. When I moved out of my parents' house, I had no idea how to manage a house without a maid."

"Seriously?"

"Yep. Ripped that silver spoon right out of my mouth." I held up the disposable cup of ice cream. "Been dining on plastic ever since."

He chuckled. "You, Birdie Melrose, are funny."

What was really funny was the way my body reacted to the sound of my name on his lips.

"Why didn't your parents pay for a maid? Wasn't allowed in the dorm room?"

I gave a wry smile, shaking my head. "Not exactly. When I told them I was going to college—with a plan to work in a school—they were disappointed. To say the least. They cut me off and said my trust fund would be waiting for me when I changed my mind. And well... you saw where I work."

"Wow," Cohen said. "That must have been hard."

"Not as hard as living someone else's life," I said, taking a final sip from my cup. "Empty."

"Let me take it—I'll throw them away," Cohen offered. He took my cup and got out of the car, walking toward a trash can near the drive-through. And man, the way he walked away...

He got back in and started the car. "Since it's our first not-date, I should probably take you home."

Why did the sentence make me so sad? Instead of thinking on it, I nodded and said, "Probably." I sobered as we drove a little farther down the road, back toward View House where my car waited. "That was a close one, with the headmaster."

Cohen frowned and nodded. "Maybe it would be better to meet somewhere more private."

"For what?" I asked. "We can't date." The three words

hit me in the chest as I realized how much I wanted to continue getting to know this amazing specimen of a man. I was pretty sure I liked him more than Dax already, and that was a terrifying thought for someone who was completely off limits. Especially so soon after my last relationship. Maybe it was better to get some space—to guard my heart.

He was quiet as he slowed and turned into the lot, stopping next to my car. He put his own vehicle in park and turned to me. "Tell me you don't want to see me. Tell me you're not having just as much fun as I am. Tell me"—he hesitated and reached to brush a strand of hair behind my ear, sending shivers over my skin—"tell me you don't want to kiss me as much as I want to kiss you."

My eyes landed on his mouth, on his full lips and the slight cleft in his chin with a dusting of shadow. "I...can't."

I couldn't be honest with him. The truth was, each second that passed made me want to kiss him even more. He was funny, kind, attentive, easy to talk to...everything I wanted in a man but didn't dare dream I could have.

"You can't kiss me, or you can't tell me you want to kiss me too?" he asked.

"Both," I answered, then I opened the door and got out of the car.

23

COHEN

The guys and I sat around a table in the bar Saturday morning after the staff had cleaned up from the night before. Yeah, it was a weird time to drink beer and play cards, but Steve's wife did yoga and drank mimosas Sunday mornings, so how weird was it really?

Until my house sold, we decided mornings were best. We had the all-clear to bullshit as loud and as long as we wanted to.

Chris frowned at his cards and said, "Fold."

Steve folded too, leaving it between my accountant and me. Despite making good money and having a lot of high-paying clients, Jonas was down to earth and didn't bid us out of the competition.

He eyed his cards, then me. "I'll raise you ten."

Jonas didn't know I had a flush in my hands. "I'll take your ten and raise you twenty more."

Jonas swore. "Fuck, I'm in." He shoved a big portion of his chips to the middle of the table and said, "Let's see what you have."

Everyone leaned in as I flipped my cards over, revealing the set of spades.

The other two laughed, but Jonas let another swear fly as he showed me his hand with three tens, an ace and a two.

"Lucky son of a bitch," Steve said, laughing.

As I swept the chips toward me, I replied, "We'll find out whether or not I'm lucky today. But so far, it's not looking great."

Chris raised his gray eyebrows. "Seriously? You just won."

"And last night, I got shut down by Birdie yet again."

"That blond?" Steve asked.

"Wait, wait, which blond?" Jonas asked, which led to an explanation of Birdie and why she didn't want to date me. They were all good reasons.

"I don't know," I said. "I should just back off. Try again in a couple years."

Steve snorted. "A girl like that's not going to be free in a couple years."

He had a point. But I gave him a look and said, "I thought you didn't see anything since you were married."

"Bingo," Chris said.

Steve ignored me.

Jonas was a little quieter than the rest of us, but he said, "Maybe she just doesn't understand how much it matters to you."

All of our heads swiveled toward him.

Looking a little hesitant, he explained, "Well, you met her at a bar. She probably doesn't want to risk anything on a fling."

"How do I show her that? If I ask her to be my girlfriend, she'll run," I said.

Jonas shrugged. "Hell if I know. I'm not the one with a ring. Or a divorce for that matter."

I turned to Chris and Steve.

Chris leaned forward. "Do something special for the girl. Show her you've been paying attention to more than her body."

I thought for a second, then took the deck and shuffled. "I'll figured something out."

I didn't want to lose a chance with Birdie Melrose.

♥•♥•♥•♥

Linda had called in a favor with an inspector who worked on the weekends, so I cut myself off after one beer and grabbed lunch after poker. I kept hoping that the inspection went well. Despite Ollie's reaction to the house, I had to believe he was reacting that way because of whatever was going on in his personal life. At least, I hoped so.

On my drive from the bar to the house, I imagined what my commute would be like. Now I was pretty close—just fifteen minutes, so it would be adding time. But I found I didn't mind. When I had a million things to think about, it seemed to fly by.

The grass and weeds had been mowed since the last time I was here, and the sight made me grin. Growing up without much and then having a house practically bought by my ex's parents made the idea of owning something that was really, truly mine even better. Sure, I owned the bar, but tons of us had come together to make it work. This would be something all my own.

Linda pulled in behind me and got out of her purple car. "How's it going, honey? Did you and Ollie work things out?"

I shrugged, turning away from the house and the yard. "He's not talking to me much lately."

"Ah, the teenage years." She winced and shook her head. "Can't say I miss that."

"Your kids behaved like that?" I asked.

"Oh yeah. If we went a day in my house without a yelling match, it was a miracle."

"I'd take that over the silent treatment," I replied. "I have no idea what's going on with him."

She patted my back. "It'll be over before you know it and he'll be inviting you to his first crappy apartment, wondering why he ever complained about a good home."

As the inspector's truck pulled in, I couldn't help but hope she was right.

The guy—he introduced himself as Bill—got straight to work, walking the perimeter of the house and pointing out things like guttering that wasn't quite connected right or areas that needed to be caulked. Linda gave me a thumbs up as we went to the front door.

Everything he brought up, I'd expected, but I wouldn't be able to breathe right until I knew there wasn't anything structurally wrong. She brought the key out of the lockbox and then unlocked the front door.

The work was slow, testing outlets and plugging in each appliance. I paced back and forth, praying nothing was wrong, and Linda touched my arm. I must have been making her nervous too.

Bill got up from the sink, cringing. "I'm going to need to see the crawl space."

My brows drew together. "Everything okay?"

"The water pressure's awfully low. I'm worried there might be a leak somewhere."

A million cuss words flew through my mind, but I tried to take deep breaths. Tried to keep the disappointment from hijacking my heartbeats.

We went back outside and found a false window on the back side of the house. He pushed it open, and my heart sank. I could hear the hiss of water. It was running, and that was never good.

There was no way to describe the next hour as

anything other than a clusterfuck of epic fucking shitastic proportions.

Not only were the pipes under the house original to when it was built and completely fucking rusted out, but the foundation had shifted so severely the house would probably have to be mud jacked to correct it. The wiring wasn't up to code inside, and climbing onto the roof revealed it would need to be replaced as well.

I could have bought another fucking house with two extra rooms for all it would have cost.

With a sympathetic look lining her face, Linda said, "Don't worry, honey. I'll come back to the owners and see what they can get fixed—or what discounts and credits they can offer."

I left the inspection dejected as hell and hoping with all I had that I could make at least one thing go right.

24

BIRDIE

Confession: I read smutty romance.

Mara and I sat in folding chairs behind a table at a craft fair. She was trying something new—selling her romance novels in person as well as online and in bookstores—and I'd agreed to come along because if I was alone, I'd call Cohen in a second and let him kiss me breathless like I'd so desperately wanted to do Friday night.

We'd gotten to the fair early Sunday morning, and there was basically no one there aside from other vendors who took one look at Mara's man-chest covers and turned their noses in the air. As though their existence wasn't a product of sex.

"How did you not kiss him?" Mara said. "Do you have a will of steel or did you swear off men after Dax?"

"Mara, I could get *fired*."

"And?" she argued, looking perplexed. "Do you really want to work for a school that polices your private life?"

"I like working there. I love my students, I have great resources, I'm making good connections with colleges. My whole life is at that school."

Mara shook her head. "But at what cost, B? Your heart?"

I let out a sigh. She was only saying everything I had been thinking. But I'd also been arguing with myself and had plenty of rebuttals. Argument number one? "My heart's led me astray before."

She gave me a look. "Tell me truly. Did you love Dax?"

I looked ahead at the jars of salsa atop the table across from us. "I think I loved the idea of him."

"What do you mean?" she said.

"I liked that he was a rebel at heart. You know I spent my whole life living the way my parents wanted me to, going on diets to please them, touring the colleges *they* wanted me to attend. But he didn't worry about what anyone else thought. Part of me wishes I could be that way too."

"Look at you!" Mara cried. "You are that way! You went to the college of your choice, no matter how much it cost you. I haven't seen you buy diet food since the first year we lived together. You're working the job you always wanted to, to hell with what your parents thought."

I lifted a corner of my lips. "I think part of me felt like maybe Dax was the best I could do. He wouldn't even keep the lights on, Mara. If my own fiancé didn't want to see me, who am I to think that anyone else would?"

Mara gave me a side hug, and I hugged her back, wishing I could undo all the years of dieting my mother had put me through, all the times I'd accepted Dax's silent dismissal of my size.

"What does it say about me that I'd rather be with someone I felt lukewarm about than be by myself?" I asked. I knew it couldn't be anything good.

"Um, maybe that you grew up with frigid WASPy parents and you're trying to make up for lost time and affection?"

"Okay." I held up a hand. "When did you get your therapy degree?"

"I write romance; it's *basically* the same thing."

I giggled, feeling a little bit lighter, and took a sip of my coffee.

"So are you going to see him again?" she asked.

With a small smile, I took another sip and said, "Of course."

How could I not?

Soon, the crowd picked up and Mara chatted with guests while I ran the cashbox and helped them purchase books. By the end of the day, she'd sold a couple dozen copies (and handmade book sleeves to go with them) and I was completely exhausted.

The evening passed by quickly after that, with a visit to Ralphie and another couple apartment tours that turned out to be busts as well. One was well over my budget with all the added fees, and the other had clearly falsely advertised on their website. I hated it when apartment complexes showed off pictures of the "clubhouse" and forgot to show that the actual units looked like they had been inhabited by squatters for the last five years.

On Monday, I went to school, ready to spend some more time with Ralphie and get to the bottom of what was going on with Ollie. Between first and second period, I caught him in the hallway and asked him to come to my office.

Ollie was a sweet kid, with a pile of curly hair atop his head and wide green eyes that looked so much like his father's. But I noticed the shadows under his eyes and the way his shoulders seemed to hunch forward dejectedly.

When we reached my office, he sat in the open chair and said, "I thought my planning meeting wasn't until next semester."

He was right. We spoke to juniors in the spring semester about their plans for the fall so they could get a jump-start over the summer. "Actually, I called you in to talk about something else."

He looked toward the ground. "My mom made me work on my missing assignments over the weekend, and my dad set a homework time for when I get home every day. It won't happen again."

"I'm glad to hear that," I said, waiting for him to meet my eyes. When he didn't, I said, "Ollie?"

He looked at me, and said, "Yeah?"

"Is everything okay? Is there anything I can help you with?"

He blinked slowly, looking down again. "I'm fine. Can I get back to class?"

Clearly, he wasn't fine, but prodding him would only make him throw up his walls even harder. And he needed to talk to someone—withdraw from social life and schoolwork for no apparent reason could indicate any number of scary things to come.

So instead, I stood with him and said, "Sure. But I want you to know, this office is a safe place. And I'm here for you, no matter what it is."

With a nod, he pushed the door open and left.

I sighed and shut the door behind him, then got my cell out of my purse. I pulled up Cohen's number and sent him a text.

Birdie: I talked to Ollie today. He said he's all caught up on homework, but still no word about what is going on.

Cohen: Thanks for checking in on him. It means a lot.

Birdie: Of course... but I'm wondering if speaking with a therapist in a private setting might be helpful for him? I can give you some referrals if you want.

I cringed, waiting for his response. My parents thought

therapy was self-indulgent—an excuse to sit around for an hour a week and cry when you could easily replace that time with work or cocktails. I hoped Cohen was different, because whatever was causing Ollie's behavior wasn't likely to go away on its own.

Cohen: Please. I'm at a loss.

My heart melted, and I immediately reached into my file where I kept business cards of the best therapists I knew in the area. Over the last couple of years, I'd gotten feedback from students on which counselors were the best and which should be avoided at all costs.

I snapped photos of a few of the ones I knew did well with LGBTQ+ teens and set my phone down.

Shortly after, another message came.

Cohen: Thank you.

Birdie: Of course.

A student knocked on the door for a scheduled planning meeting, and we sat and explored her options for the next hour. It was one of my favorite parts of my jobs—talking to students about what they hoped for their lives and finding a strategy to make their dreams come true.

When she walked out of my office, I took my coffee cup to the teachers' lounge for an afternoon pick-me-up.

The videography teacher, Mr. Davis, had just replaced the pot and said, "How's it going?"

"Good," I said with a shrug. "You?"

"Just got in some new equipment. Feels like Christmas."

I chuckled. "I feel the same way when recruiters bring all their tchotchkes. Is it bad that I save the best ones for myself?"

"Considering the work you do? I'd say you earned it." He smiled and lifted his cup. "I started a new pot, by the way. Enjoy."

I smiled and looked down at my own cup. Mr. Davis was probably one of my favorite teachers to work with. Dax had always thought double dates were lame, but I wondered if someday, when I had someone to take me, I could ask Mr. Davis and his wife out to dinner.

Thinking of the only person I wanted to date, I checked my phone and found a new message.

Cohen: How's Ralphie?

I smiled at the text and sent him a picture of Ralphie I'd taken this morning.

Birdie: Chipper, as always.

Cohen: He's adorable.

Birdie: I think so.

I filled my cup with coffee and walked toward the door, nudging it open with my hip.

Cohen: I found something I think you'd enjoy. Are you free Saturday?

Before I could talk myself out of it, I sent my reply.

Birdie: I am. What do you have planned?

25

COHEN

I sent a noncommittal text about my plans for the weekend—I was hoping to surprise her—and clicked back to the picture of the business cards she sent me. All three had heart-shaped rainbow stickers on them, I assumed meaning the therapists were good for the LGBTQ+ community.

Despite the fact that I was looking at counselors for my kid because I couldn't help him, I felt relieved. When Ollie's grandparents learned about his sexual orientation, their first suggestion was to send him to conversion therapy. An idea my ex had entertained.

I didn't put my foot down on much, but that was one thing I would never allow my son to go through. I knew what it felt like to be considered bad just because of who you were or where you came from. I'd never allow Ollie to be put through the same experience if I could help it.

Sure, the world could be a mean place. There were a few friends I had to set straight when it came to homophobic slurs, and there were a few shows I couldn't stand watching anymore because now I understood just how hurtful dialogue was. But I would make our lives as safe as possible for Ollie's sake.

I typed the number from the first card into my phone and called. That therapist didn't have an opening for months.

The next number I called went to voicemail. But on the third, someone picked up. By the time the call was over, I had an appointment made for four o'clock on Thursday afternoon. I wasn't sure how Ollie would react, but I had to make him see that I was only doing this because I cared for him. I wanted him to talk to someone... even if that someone wasn't me.

With that done, I got back to work. I needed to prepare my books before sending them to Jonas. Even though I'd hired him for accounting services, I still liked to take a hands-on approach to finances at the bar and make sure everything ran smoothly.

Time seemed to fly by. I could have worked like this for hours if it weren't for my phone ringing.

Linda's name was on the screen, so I snatched it up and answered as quickly as possible. "Hey, Linda. Any word from the owners?"

"Not great," she said. "With all the repairs they have to do, they'll be taking a loss selling it at this price. It's looking like they're going to keep it as a rental property."

My heart sank, puddling in the bottom of my stomach. I'd been so sure that house was the one. And honestly, I was tired of looking. Tired of getting my hopes up only to be let down.

"We'll find the house that's right for you and Ollie," she said. "Maybe it'll be helpful if he gets to come to the showings."

"He has school and homework. There's not a lot of free time for us in the afternoons."

"Weekends?" she suggested.

"He's with his mom." My eyes prickled, and I pinched the bridge of my nose. That basically left me two choices. Keep looking on my own and piss off my son, who was already struggling, or put extra pressure on him to finish his schoolwork.

"We can keep going with just the two of us?"

I let out a sigh. From the tone of her voice, we both knew that wasn't a good idea. "Let's start looking again in the summer. Sorry, Linda."

"Don't apologize," she said, as sweet as ever. "Take this time for you and Ollie to figure out what you really want. And come the end of May, I'll be calling again."

"Thanks, Linda," I said and hung up the phone.

♥•♥•♥•♥

It took a little compromise and negotiating from both me and his mom to get Ollie to agree to see a therapist. In the end, Audrey and I both swore we would keep the therapy between the three of us—even though we both told him it was nothing to be ashamed of—and that after three months of weekly therapy he could stop going if he wanted to.

Still, I could tell he was nervous when he got into my car Thursday after school.

"Are you ready for this?" I asked.

He shrugged, not meeting my eyes.

"I'll be with you for the first appointment and every one after if you want me," I reminded him. "But I think it'll be great. Birdie said this gal's one of the best."

"Birdie?" Ollie said.

"Ms. Melrose," I corrected myself. "She was the one who sent me the recommendations."

"So she knows I'm crazy. Great," Ollie muttered. "What happened to the three of us being the only ones to know?"

I frowned. "I didn't tell her I made you an appointment. I only asked who she thought was best. You know you're not the only one who's ever needed to talk to someone."

Ollie met my frown with a scowl. "Who said I needed to talk to someone? Huh? You're the one who forced this on me."

Yet another ding in my dad suit of armor.

"I'm not arguing with you," I said, gripping the wheel tighter. "Especially right before therapy."

This might have been hard for him, but I also knew his childhood would likely come up in session. And that scared the hell out of me. I knew I had never been a perfect parent—hell, I had a lot of shitty examples growing up—but I loved him with all I had. With the mother I had, I knew love didn't make up for every sin.

She had loved me. I believed that. It just wasn't enough.

We pulled into the parking lot of a simple brick business complex and got out of the car, not saying a word to each other. The receptionist checked us in, and soon we were sitting on a couch—as far away from each other as possible.

The room was nice, dimly lit with a small, soothing water feature in the corner. I couldn't help but notice the tissue box within reach or the diffuser making the scent of eucalyptus fill the small space.

Cecilia Johnson sat across from us in a plush chair, holding a notebook. "Tell me," she said, "why are you here and what are you hoping to accomplish?"

Ollie sent me a withering look. "Ask my dad."

I leaned forward, wringing my hands. I felt just as nervous as I had on my wedding day. As nervous as I had filing for divorce at the courthouse. "I'm worried about Ollie, and I want to make sure he has someone to talk to."

Cecilia nodded, making a note in her legal pad. "And what worried you, Cohen?"

"A few weeks ago, he really shut down, and when I checked his grades, those were slipping too."

Cecilia nodded. "Do you have anything to add, Ollie?"

His lips pressed together, and I could practically feel anger radiating off him. "Why do I have to tell my dad every feeling? Maybe I wasn't talking because I didn't want to."

"And why didn't you want to?" Cecilia asked, cutting straight to the quick. I liked her already.

Ollie paused, looking at his hands. He kept picking at loose skin with his nail, making a soft clicking sound. "Because I was embarrassed."

I'd expected anything but that. I thought he'd tell her he hated me. That he wanted nothing to do with me. That he would stay with his mom full-time and see me on the weekends instead.

But this was an even worse punch in the gut. Why would Ollie be embarrassed about something? Especially when it came to me?

Cecilia leaned in, a caring expression on her face. "Ollie, if you're willing to, you can speak privately with me. I am only required to share information if you ask or if there's a threat of harm to you or someone else or if I'm subpoenaed by the court on a criminal case."

Ollie looked from me to Cecilia and let out a sigh. "I promised my parents I'd try."

Cecilia's small smile matched my own. Taking my cue, I stood and told Ollie I'd be outside whenever he was ready. For the first time in a while, I felt like I had a win.

26

BIRDIE

Confession: I'm a better sister-in-law than I am a sister.

Doug called me Friday night.

Doug never called me.

Fear seizing my chest, I immediately left the living room where Mara and I were watching TV and went to the guest room to answer.

"Doug? Is everything okay?"

"Er-kind of," he said. "Can you come over? I have a business dinner I need to get to, and Anthea is trying to paint the nursery."

I raised my eyebrows. "She's thirty weeks pregnant."

"Try telling her that. She's wearing two N-95s, and she looks absolutely feral."

"I'll be there in half an hour."

We hung up, and I went to tell Mara what was going on.

Giggling, she said, "I want you to tell me everything when you get back."

"Promise," I replied, reaching for my purse. I got in the car and drove to the richer part of Emerson, thinking Anthea must be nesting for the new baby. Her baby shower was still a few weeks away, but that was just an excuse to eat sugar cookies at this point. Everyone knew she and Doug could afford everything their baby needed and more.

I approached their multi-story home just a few minutes away from where Doug and I grew up. The yard was perfectly manicured and the path to the door lit with solar lights. It was already dark outside, and I wondered how long it would take Anthea to get tired and give up.

I was about the ring the doorbell when the garage door opened and Doug came out, dressed to the nines in a designer suit and brightly colored pocket square.

"Thank you, Birdie."

I waved my hand at him. "I'm happy to help. No big deal."

He nodded. "Well, she's back in the nursery. Come on."

He led me through the garage, which was perfectly clean and organized, then let me in the kitchen. "Third door on the left. If you can't find it, just follow the psychotic breathing and brushing."

I saluted him like I used to when we were teens and our parents let us take the sailboat out on our own. "Aye, aye, Cap'n."

He smiled for a moment, then a look of worry quickly darkened his features. "Take care of her, will you?"

"Of course."

He turned back to his car, and I walked through their house. I hadn't been here since the housewarming party a couple years ago, but it looked every bit as clean and put together as it had then.

Just as Doug had promised, I could hear furious brush strokes against the wall, and I peeked my head in to see Anthea double masked and angrily painting clouds onto a light blue wall. Feral might not have been the wrong word to describe her.

"Whatcha doing?" I asked.

She looked at me, a splotch of paint on her cheek. "Painting. Obviously." She turned back at the wall and continued painting. "I can't believe Doug didn't do this weeks ago."

"You could have asked me to come help. Or, you know, hired someone."

"I'm not turning into your mother," she said. "Wealth calcifies people. You just sit on your throne and forget how to lift your fingers, much less anything else."

"You're telling me." I went to the window and opened

it so at least she'd have some ventilation. Whether or not it would get through her masks was another story. "Do you have an extra brush?"

"Just this one," she said slowly.

"Then why don't you let me paint and you can start sorting clothes?"

"How do you know I need to do that?"

I lifted my eyebrows. "You may not be calcified yet, but I guarantee you've bought every cute baby outfit you've walked past since you found out you were pregnant."

Her cheeks turned slightly pink. "They're so cute though."

"I've bought a few myself," I said. "Which you will have to fold after the baby shower. So hand over the brush."

Reluctantly, she gave me the brush, but she still held on to it tightly. "I'll text you a tutorial video I found. Watch it before you get started."

"Sure," I said.

She finally let go, and I held it in my hand as I waited for the message. As soon as my phone dinged and I began playing the video, Anthea seemed satisfied and left the room. The directions seemed simple enough, and soon, I was at work getting lost in the mindless strokes of my brush.

Within a couple hours, I had finished what Anthea had started. I stepped back and took a picture of the cloudy walls, smiling.

"It looks amazing," Anthea breathed behind me.

I turned toward her, smiling. "She's the luckiest little girl in the world." My niece would have the best life. I already knew Anthea wouldn't love her conditionally like my parents had me.

Anthea circled her arms around her middle. "Want to have some Rice Krispie Treats? I made some earlier."

"Is that a rhetorical question?" I said. "Where should I put the brush?"

"Just throw it away. I have a feeling Doug won't deal with another nesting episode involving paint past thirty weeks."

"You're not wrong." I tossed the paintbrush in a wastebasket and followed her to the kitchen.

The dish of Rice Krispie Treats had already been cut into once, but she got out a couple of oversized squares for us and set them on paper towels.

"What, no fine china?" I teased.

She half-glared, half-smiled at me. "We only do that for the guests who haven't been cut off by the Melroses."

"Fair," I said, picking up the treat and eating a bite. It was heavenly.

"Are you... doing okay?" she asked hesitantly.

I nodded, knowing she was referring to the called-off engagement. "I've had a few good leads on apartments. I'll make it."

She frowned. "Are you sure you don't want us to set

you up? I know Walter is a dud, but there's this other guy in accounting—"

"Not interested."

"You don't even know him!" she argued.

"I know he's in accounting."

She giggled and licked some marshmallow off her fingertip. "True."

My phone dinged, and I looked at the screen, seeing a new message from Cohen.

Cohen: Can I pick you up at eleven tomorrow? Can't wait to see you and show you what I have planned. I think you'll like it.

"You're smiling!" Anthea accused. "Who is he?"

My cheeks warmed as I typed back a message. "No one." I hadn't even realized I'd been smiling. Or distracted for that long.

Birdie: That sounds great. Important question. Will food be involved?

Cohen: Of course. Four stars or better. See you then.

When I set my phone down and looked back at Anthea, her expression told me she didn't believe my previous lie. Not one bit.

"So you just smile all goofy when your girlfriends text you?" Her mouth fell open. "Please tell me you're not talking to Dax again. That guy is such a douche canoe."

My eyebrows raised. "Douche canoe?"

"Well, now that you're not dating, I can say what I really think of him."

"And that would be?"

She shrugged, taking another bite of Rice Krispie. "That his eyes wandered a little too much for my liking. And he has a stupid laugh. And his art was derivative and trying too hard."

Although it hurt to hear other people had noticed how wrong Dax was for me, the last part made me giggle. Dax hated when people said his work wasn't purely original. "Why didn't you tell me you didn't like him?"

"Would you have listened?" she asked.

I thought about it for a moment. "Probably not. But next time I date someone, will you let me know if you don't like him?"

She held out her pinky. "I promise."

With a smile, I linked my pinky with hers. And I made myself a promise that next time, I would listen.

27

COHEN

Even though I knew I'd see her tomorrow, I couldn't stop thinking about Birdie. With the bar taken care of and Ollie at his mother's and the house hunt on pause, there weren't a lot of things to keep me busy. It wasn't even late enough to go to bed.

A small thought popped into my head as I filled the watering can to take care of Ollie's plants.

Could she be thinking of me too?

Just the hope from that thought made me get out my phone and send her a text.

It was simple, just a hello, but if she was up to talk, I could be too.

Birdie: Hey. How are you?

Setting down the can, I went to the couch and sat down, thinking of that first night she'd been at my house.

And hoping, someday, she could spend the night again. This time, in my arms.

Cohen: Good. I'm looking forward to seeing you tomorrow.

I tried not to overthink what I would say, but I still read the message twice before hitting send. Birdie wasn't only kind and interesting. She was smart. I wanted to make sure my words were spelled correctly and the right punctuation was in place.

Birdie: Still no word on what we're doing?

Cohen: You'll see. :) How was your night?

Birdie: I helped my SIL paint her nursery.

Not knowing what SIL meant made me feel old as hell. I googled it real quick before replying.

Cohen: When is she having her baby?

Birdie: She's due in ten weeks. And of course she couldn't wait for my brother to take care of it.

Cohen: Those nesting hormones are intense. I remember staying up until two in the morning one night because Ollie's bed HAD to be put together. Never mind that she wasn't even in the third trimester.

Birdie: That's so sweet.

Cohen: You should have heard me complaining. You'd change your mind.

Birdie: Haha. Maybe.

She hadn't asked a question and I found myself more nervous than before. What did I say to her? How could I keep things interesting?

Birdie: Hey, I'm driving if you want to call.

My lips split into a grin. Of course I wanted to call. I got off the couch, pacing for a moment before dialing her number. I didn't want to seem to eager. Even though I definitely was.

After a couple of rings, she answered. She must have been connected to her car's Bluetooth because I could hear the rumbling of wind in the background.

"Hey," she said. "Thanks for calling. I couldn't sit in my brother's driveway texting for too long without raising suspicion."

I chuckled. "It's nice to hear your voice."

She seemed shy as she replied, "It's good to hear yours too."

Damn if I didn't smile. "How was work this week?"

"It was good. I had a few really good meetings with students, and Pam Alexander hasn't threatened to have me fired, so I consider that a win."

A protective instinct rose within me. "Pam wants to have you fired?"

"It's a long story." A heavy sigh came through the phone. "You know how some people are."

Oh, I knew. I definitely knew.

"What about you?" she asked. "How was your week?"

I frowned. It hadn't been completely terrible. But I was still down about the home inspection. "The house I was going to buy fell through. It looks like I won't be closing on anything until the summer, if then."

"If it makes you feel any better, I'm still on the apartment hunt."

I chuckled. "Not really. But I have a great realtor if you want help. I'm not sure if she does apartment searches though."

"The internet's been really handy," she said. "It's just a matter of finding something that's available. For the amount of people leaving California, it feels like there's still no housing."

"I hear you," I said.

"This is depressing," she said with a tinkling laugh. "Let's talk about something happy."

"I could mention your smile," I said. It was the first thing that came to mind.

"You're sweet," she said quietly.

I could hear the smile in her voice, and I wished I could see it too.

"You know," she said. "You have a nice smile too."

"I do?" I asked. My teeth had been messed up as a kid because dentistry was even lower than me on my mother's priority list. I'd since gotten braces and had my teeth whitened a couple times, but that old insecurity stuck around.

"Mhmm. It's...wholesome."

I had to chuckle now. "Wholesome?" I'd never been called that before in my life.

"Yeah, like you don't look like you have a mouth full of Chiclets. And when you smile big, your eyes crinkle around the corners and you look so happy. And then there's your smirk, which is really—"

The line went silent, and I almost worried we'd lost connection.

"Are you still there?" I asked.

A silent pause.

"Birdie?"

"Yes?" she said shyly.

My grin spread. "What were you about to say about my smirk?"

"That I'll see it, and you, tomorrow."

28

BIRDIE

Confession: I don't really like my clothes.

Frowning, Mara stood in front of my closet (well, technically her closet) and flipped through the neutral-toned dresses.

"What?" I said, already defensive.

"I didn't know this many shades of black existed," she said. "Does that school have something against color?"

Rubbing my arm, I sat on the bed. "You know what it's like to try to dress up as a big girl. Straight sizes are too small and plus sizes are too big. It's harder to shop for professional looks that aren't too revealing or skirts that are long enough to go over my ass or prints that aren't too loud."

"Okay, I will admit shopping a size eighteen sucks—which is why I wear leggings all the time—but there has to be more than this."

I shrugged. "I've sworn off buying jeans, so it's athleisure or dress clothes."

Mara's frown grew deeper—how that was even possible, I had no idea.

"Okay, now I'm feeling hopeless."

"No, it's not that. I'm sure he'd adore you in all of this." She gestured at my closet. "I'm just wondering how I've never noticed it..."

Her gaze on me saw way too much. "What?"

"Your clothes are a reflection of you," Mara said.

"So you're stretchy?" I asked with a wry smile.

She snorted. "Comfortable, relaxed. And you're..." She gestured. "You're in mourning!"

"What would I be mourning?" I asked.

"That's for you to find out." She shut the closet door. "In the meantime, I got the cutest dress last weekend. You should wear it."

I tried arguing with her at first. The tag wasn't even off the flirty floral dress yet, but she insisted, and I had to admit, I looked pretty cute. The colors even brought out the natural flush in my cheeks and the blue in my eyes.

We decided on stylish sneakers to match, then I'd worked one of Mara's bandanas through my curly hair as a headband. I'd never worn anything like this, but I realized I'd never felt more like myself. It made me want to go back to the store and find more dresses like the one Cohen had bought me.

It was silly, really. I should have been wearing a T-shirt and sweatpants to quell this sexual tension that lingered between Cohen and me. But just like that first night, I imagined his fingers playing with the hem of my dress, his knee parting my legs, his... I shivered. "Are you sure about this outfit?" I asked Mara.

"It's perfect. Not too casual, but also not too dressy," Mara said. "If he's not going to tell you where you're going, you have to be ready for anything. Speaking of, did you wear cute underwear?"

I turned to her and raised my eyebrows. "Absolutely not. Wearing cute panties would be like begging him to lift my skirt up and take me in the bathroom." Which gave me new ideas all together.

She bit her lip. "Now there's a date worth going on."

We were so on the same page it was scary, but we both needed to remember what could never be. "Mara, for the millionth time, I can't date him. The school—"

"—code of conduct expressly forbids it," she finished for me, mimicking my voice. "But do they say anything about one-night stands and banging it out with the hot barkeep?"

I shook my head, laughing, and walked toward the living room. Cohen could be here any moment, and I wanted to spare him a suggestive conversation with my overzealous best friend. I picked up my purse. "I'm going to wait for him outside."

"Uh huh. Don't do anything I wouldn't do."

"What's that?" I teased. "Anal?"

She cackled as I walked outside and shut the door.

Maybe Mara was right about 'banging one out.' I did want to fulfil my fantasy from that first night. If I wasn't such a chicken, we could have already had sex, and Cohen Bardot would be out of my system. But instead, I'd backed out and now here I was in not-dating purgatory with the hottest guy I'd ever met.

His car pulled into the driveway, and I could practically feel Mara's eyeballs on me as I walked to meet him.

He got out of the car, wearing fitted jeans and an olive-toned T-shirt that showed off his arms. I wondered when he worked out—if he got up early to do it or made time in the evening. But then I realized he was looking at me, and oh god, had he already said hello and I'd missed it?

"Hi," I said with an embarrassed smile. I still couldn't believe I'd almost called him sexy the night before when I was still trying to be his friend.

There was a twinkle in his eyes as he came and gave me a kiss on the cheek.

My skin felt hot where his lips had been, and I wished he could have kissed me longer. Could have moved his mouth just inches over so we could have that kiss I'd longed for the week before.

"Ready for your surprise?" he asked, as though completely unfazed by the contact.

"As long as it involves waffles," I teased.

"But of course."

I got into his car, and once we had closed the doors behind us, he lifted a hand and waved toward the house.

I distinctly saw a curtain whoosh shut.

"A friend of yours?" he asked, clearly amused.

"She was." I laughed awkwardly. "Actually, she's kind of my hero—letting me stay with her until I find a place and preparing me for not-dates." I gave him a look. "I had no idea what to wear."

"I'm sure she knows you look beautiful no matter what you're wearing."

Good thing I was sitting down, because his grin paired with those words made my knees weak. The back of my neck was hot already, so I reached up and brushed some curls away from my neck and looked out the window.

"So I know we're trying to stay out of Emerson," he said. "Have you ever heard of this place called Seaton Bakery?"

I lifted my eyebrows. "I didn't even know there were restaurants in Seaton. I thought it was just shut down factories and some housing."

He shook his head. "Spoken like a true rich kid."

"You're not wrong." I'd grown up exactly the way my parents had intended me to—going to Brentwood Academy, becoming skilled in an instrument I no longer played, learning languages I'd never use, and above all else, knowing how to groom myself for the public eye.

"No, there's a fishing pier there that's pretty fun on the weekends—they bring out food carts and kids fly kites and old guys cast reels off the dock. And then, of course, Seaton has a few shops and my very favorite place to get breakfast on the weekends."

"Yeah?"

"You're going to love it. And the owners—Chris and Gayle—they've become sort of like my business mentors at the bar, even though they're only ten years older than me."

"That good?" I asked.

He nodded emphatically. "Everyone who works there stays there forever because they're so great to work with, and their customer loyalty is through the roof. Of course, that might have something to do with their clean bathrooms." He winked at me.

My cheeks heated, but I smiled and said, "Possibly."

Soon, we reached a simple brick building painted white with discounts and specials written on the windows. It was unassuming, blending into the other places around it and the asphalt parking lot so broken up it may as well have been gravel.

"This is it?" I asked. The way he'd praised it, I'd expected...more.

He nodded and turned off the car. "Just wait 'til you get inside."

Skeptical, I got out of the car and walked alongside him, thankful at least for the fact that no one from the Academy would be caught dead here. It would be too much damage to their personal "brand" to be seen in a place that didn't use cloth napkins.

That made me like Cohen just a little bit more. He may have had money, but he also knew how to spot the diamonds in the rough.

A bell hanging on the door clanged as we walked inside. Despite its humble exterior, the inside of the shop exuded warmth. Couples and families and friends sat around mismatched tables and booths, and a display right up front showed off brightly colored cupcakes that made my mouth water.

The woman behind the counter smiled at us and said, "Cohen! This must be the girl."

My cheeks heated as I smiled at her, walking closer. "Hi, I'm Birdie." I extended my hand, and she shook it with both of hers.

"I'm Gayle. It's so nice to meet you." She had light blond hair and a smile that made her eyes crinkle. I immediately liked her.

The swinging kitchen doors opened, and a tall, thin man with a round belly and a head of gray hair walked through, rubbing his hands on his apron. "Is this her?"

I glanced at Cohen, and I swore I saw a blush on his cheeks. "Chris," he said, "this is Birdie."

Chris rubbed his hands yet again on his apron before

shaking my hand. "It's nice to meet you, Birdie." Just like his wife, his smile made me like him right away.

"Cohen's told me wonderful things about the two of you," I said.

Gayle grinned at him. Despite the lines forming around her eyes, she looked so young, so full of life. I could tell why Cohen was fond them. "Is that so?" she said.

Cohen shrugged. "Only how you two taught me everything I know.".

Chris batted his hand at Cohen. "He's been a smart one ever since he started working here at sixteen. That was just a couple years after we opened."

I raised my eyebrows. Cohen hadn't told me he used to work here. Did that mean he used to live in Seaton?

Cohen seemed shy—*shy*—and said, "Well, I thought I'd show Birdie the best of Seaton." He got out his wallet. "Can you send out some of your specialties?"

"Only if you put that thing away," Gayle said, nodding at his wallet. "You know your money's no good here."

Cohen shook his head and, tucking his wallet in his back pocket, said, "Stubborn as always."

Turning back toward the kitchen, Chris said, "You have no idea."

Cohen took my hand and led me to an open table near the corner of the bakery. I drank in everything—the old men playing chess, the young couple sitting on the same side of the booth, a family with kids running circles around the tables. There weren't any pretenses here. No, everyone was being exactly who they were. It took special people to make everyone feel so at home. People like my Grandpa Chester.

As we sat down, Cohen said, "What do you think?"

I smiled at him and said, "It feels like home."

He grinned back as if it were the best answer I could have given. "It does, doesn't it?"

"I didn't realize you used to work here."

"I had to," he said simply. "When your mom's an addict and your dad's nowhere to be found, someone has to put food on the table."

My heart wrenched, no matter how matter of factly he said the words. "Cohen, I—"

He shook his head. "Don't be sorry. I learned a lot from my mom."

I waited for him to elaborate.

"I learned quick ways to see who would be kind enough to share a meal. I found out how to live frugally, how to make myself scarce when another boyfriend came around, how to find a vein, you know..." He chuckled softly, but his eyes showed a vulnerability his casual words belied.

"That's awful," I breathed. Cohen and I had lived completely different lives, and although I disagreed with plenty my parents did, at least I never had to wonder where my next meals were coming from.

"It was. Gayle and Chris are more than my mentors. They were newly married, had just opened the bakery, and they were still the parents I always wished I could have."

I glanced over my shoulder at Gayle interacting with another customer. "They're lovely."

He reached across the table and took my hand. "And so are you."

29

COHEN

There was that blush again. It was so damn adorable. Even better was the fact that I'd put it there. Seeing how easily she clicked with Chris and Gayle was just the cherry on top of it all.

When Audrey and I had decided to divorce, I really thought I'd be a bachelor for life—dating around but mostly being on my own. Birdie made me wonder how I'd ever thought that would be enough.

Gayle came with a tray of food—she'd really outdone herself too. From sandwiches to their signature cupcakes, Birdie would get the best of the bakery. That was especially true when Chris came behind holding a few different cups.

"This one's a mocha, here's a latte, plain black coffee, hot chocolate, and of course, our signature lemonade."

Birdie's eyes lit up at the assortment. "It all looks so good."

Chris patted my shoulder. "She's a keeper, Co."

Now I was the one blushing while Birdie giggled.

"Do you make all this here?" she asked.

Gayle nodded proudly. "Chris is a genius in the kitchen. I don't know how he does it. Every time I try to make bread, it falls flat."

"It's the pH of your hands," Chris explained. "Some people just don't have the touch."

Gayle swatted his shoulder. "Okay, cool your jets or your head won't fit in here anymore."

Chris pretended to whoosh the air out of his head and said, "Enjoy, you two." He gave a pointed look at Gayle. "We'll give you your space."

She gave him an annoyed look before waving at us and walking back behind the counter.

Birdie smiled after them. "They're so cute together. They remind me of my grandparents."

"Yeah?" I said, opting for the plain coffee so Birdie could try all the special options.

She nodded, sampling the mocha. "They were high school sweethearts. Met when he was sixteen and she was fourteen. They dated and got married as soon as she graduated high school. It'll be sixty years this May."

I shook my head in awe. "That's incredible." Being divorced myself and knowing first-hand how difficult marriage could be, it was hard to believe anyone made a marriage last that long, much less had a happy one.

"I agree." She took another sip of the mocha. "It's nice though, knowing it's possible."

"It is." I glanced toward the register while Gayle worked with customers. I used to be jealous of what she and Chris had, wondering if I'd ever find it for myself. Now... I couldn't let myself think that far ahead. Instead, I asked, "What do you think of the mocha?"

"It's amazing," she said.

I nodded. "If I lived closer, I'd come here every day. You should try the latte too. And the hot cocoa. It's perfect for wintertime."

She sampled both and let out an adorable little moan at the hot chocolate. "Can they start serving this at the concession stands? Every time I go to a game now, I won't be able to drink what they serve!"

I chuckled. "Maybe you could put in a good word."

"You can bet I will." She gazed at the plate. "I want to try the cupcake, but I haven't had breakfast yet."

"So?" I said. "The only reason I ever made Ollie eat healthy food first was because it was the only way I could get him to eat the green beans." We both chuckled. "But you're not five, and Gayle didn't bring any green beans, so..."

She grinned at me. "So." She picked up the cupcake and tried a bite, her teeth sliding through the dessert and frosting landing on her nose. With the bite in her mouth, she closed her eyes, chewing. "Oh my god, it's so good."

"Right?" I said, my eyes following her lips. I wanted to lick the crumbs from them and taste the frosting on her tongue.

Noticing my gaze, she smiled shyly. "What?"

"You have some..." I reached out and swiped the frosting off her nose with my thumb. And then I put it in my mouth, tasting the sweetness.

Her cheeks heated more, and she crossed her legs. "Thank you."

I took my thumb out of my mouth and smirked at her. "You're welcome."

30

BIRDIE

Confession: I'm a beak geek.

I ate way too much at Seaton Bakery, but the best part? Cohen never shamed me for how much I sampled. Never suggested I opt for a water or black coffee instead of the mocha I ordered. Dax would have done all of those things and then suggested a walk after.

Cohen? He led me to his car and started driving. His hands stayed on the wheel, and I couldn't help but take him in while his eyes were focused on the road. The ridges of his nose made me think it had been broken, and after hearing how he'd grown up, I couldn't help but wonder how he'd gotten it.

My eyes traveled from his face to his hands to the

speedometer. His car was so fancy that it felt like riding in a cloud despite going eighty miles an hour. I checked. He only drove five miles over the speed limit at any given time. I liked it—like a small form of rebellion but also a sense of safety.

But what surprised and delighted me more was our final destination. He stopped in the parking lot of a new rainforest aviary outside of LA.

My mouth fell open as I looked from him to the sign. "I didn't even know this was open yet!"

"It isn't." He parked and pulled the keys.

"But how?" I asked, following him out of the car.

His grin was tantalizing. "I know a guy who likes to stay a little late at my bar sometimes."

I shook my head at him in awe, then went back to staring at the building. All of the cranes and cones and big chain link fences were gone, but the parking lot was still nearly empty. I'd been waiting to attend the opening all summer and fall. They hadn't announced a date yet, but it was set to launch sometime in December.

"I take it you're excited?" he asked, smiling.

"You have no idea. You know I'm a Friend of the Aviary? I donate a hundred dollars every year on Ralphie's birthday."

His smile didn't look as horrified as I might have guessed. Instead, it was encouraging.

"That's awesome," he said.

I nodded. "They spent a million dollars on the

windows alone—special glass so the birds won't ever try to fly into the windows from the inside or outside. There's a special etching process that hides their reflection while still letting in plenty of light."

Cohen pressed his lips together. "I'm assuming my friend won't be of much use as a tour guide then."

My cheeks warmed. "I'd love a tour."

"Great." He put his arm easily around my waist, and I tried not to act too excited about our contact. Something about the gesture was calming and thrilling at the same time. Eyeing me from the side, he said, "Go on. What else do you know?"

Grinning, I clapped my hands together. "Okay, did you know they built a fifteen-foot waterfall inside so the birds can perch and bathe?"

"Yeah?"

I nodded. "And they flew in plants from all over the world—they had to get special security clearance and the heads from both the Department of Agriculture and the Department of Homeland Security flew in to make sure everything was done safely."

His eyes were alight with wonder, and—was I too bold to hope?—admiration. "How did you learn all this?"

"I subscribe to their newsletter... and I may or may not have set up a Google alert."

He chuckled. "I like that about you—you don't do anything halfway."

I smiled at the compliment. "Why bother if you're not going to give it your all, right?"

"Exactly." The way he said the word made me think he was talking about more than just aviary research. But I didn't have time to think on it.

As we neared the front entrance, a guy in a tan suit stepped out and reached for Cohen's hand. "How are you, friend?"

"Great," Cohen said. "George, this is Birdie."

"Our aviary enthusiast," he said with the slightest Australian accent. "Are you in for a treat."

"I can't tell you how excited I am," I said.

Cohen chuckled. "She basically recited the pamphlet to me on our way here. I told you she's amazing."

My cheeks heated, but I couldn't help my smile.

"So," George said, leading us past the reception area. "She told you about the special glass? They use a special—"

"—etching process?" Cohen finished with a smirk. "Heard all about it."

George laughed. "She's a keeper, Cohen."

Cohen glanced at me, a heat in his eyes I felt to my core. "Agreed." His grip firmed around my waist, making my stomach swoop.

Together, the three of us crossed through a door and entered another world. The humidity was the first thing I noticed, along with the rush of water and rustle of wings and the botanical heat on my skin. I glanced around, catching sight of an employee walking toward us with a brightly colored macaw on her arm.

My eyes widened, and I stepped forward to meet them. "He's beautiful!"

"He sure is," the woman said. "This is Leroy."

"Hi, Leroy," I cooed, leaning forward slightly to take in his beautiful plume.

From behind me, Cohen muttered, "I think she forgot about me."

"With Leroy here?" I said. "Of course I did. No contest."

The guys chuckled behind me, and the employee—her name tag said Barbara—asked if I wanted to see some of the other animals.

"Of course," I said happily.

She led me down the first trail, pointing out all kinds of birds I knew and several I'd never heard of. They were all different sizes, different colors, and my eyes were wide as I took in all of them. "I feel like I'm cheating on Ralphie," I breathed.

Barbara said, "Your boyfriend back there?"

I chuckled. "My bird. I have a white dove at home."

Home. The school, actually, I thought with a sinking feeling. I wondered if I would ever find a place that felt like home.

"Doves are lovely. They have an incredible lifespan," she said.

I nodded, walking alongside her. "He's a little over nine now. He's practically my best friend."

"Sometimes birds can be easier to love than people... claws, beaks, and all."

I tended to agree.

We made the loop around the building, Barbara telling us all about the plants and the birds that had already made the space their new home. I could have listened to her speak for hours about their care routine and the plans for opening. But eventually, we found our way back to the main entrance.

George reached into his pocket. "I actually have a little gift for you, Birdie."

My eyebrows rose, and I looked from him to Cohen. "Really, I feel like I've gotten the best gift already. This place is amazing."

George and Barbara chuckled, and George said, "One more small present, for flattery if nothing else."

I took the envelope and opened it, finding an annual pass to the aviary and an invitation to opening day in December. "Really? This is so much."

George grinned. "With your enthusiasm, you'll make us look even better when the exhibit opens."

Enthusiastic was the perfect word to describe me. "This has been incredible. Thank you." I turned from George to Cohen, gripping his forearm. "Thank you."

Cohen smiled, putting his arm around me. "I'm glad

you liked it." He lifted a hand in a wave to George. "I'll see you around. Thanks for everything, Barbara!"

We all said our goodbyes, and once we got out of the building, Cohen asked, "What did you really think? It was good, right?"

My mouth opened and closed. "I don't even have the words to tell you how absolutely perfect it was. I think this has been one of the best days in—I don't know how long." Cohen had made today more special than Dax had made my last two birthdays. Accepted me in ways I'd never been accepted by a man before.

The wind blew a curl across my face, and he brushed it back, sending chills down my spine. "That's what friends are for, right?"

Friends. The word rubbed me so wrong.

Whatever Cohen and I had, it wasn't friendship, not even close.

31

BIRDIE

Confession: I used to be the mean girl.

The closer we got to Mara's house, the less I wanted to arrive. Cohen had this light around him that made me want to get his special version of sun kissed. And I knew the second he left to go home, all that brightness would be gone.

But where could he and I go that was private but wouldn't lead to more? His place? I wouldn't be able to control myself. And then I had an idea. The craziest, stupidest, most brilliant of ideas.

When it was time to make the turn back to Mara's place, I said, "Do you want to help me feed Ralphie?"

He seemed surprised. "Sure, if it's okay that we go to the school together. Aren't there cameras?"

"Yeah, but Headmaster Bradford says they're just for show. No one actually monitors them."

"I'm down. Anything to spend a little more time with you."

The butterflies in my stomach fluttered just like the birds in the aviary had. "Sounds great."

He knew the way to the school and easily navigated there while we talked about the birds and the best bird-watching places around Emerson. The more I spoke to him, the less I thought about Dax. The realization brought an even bigger smile to my face.

"Here we are," Cohen said, parking in the empty lot. There was no one on the premises, aside from us, which put me more at ease. I still had a rush of adrenaline at doing something so off limits. What was scarier? How much I liked it.

"Okay," I said, getting out of the car. "Our alibi is that Ollie left some of his homework in his locker and you called me to let you into the building to get it. Of course I obliged because he's struggling in school, and Emerson Academy will do anything to keep our parents happy, right?"

He bit his lip. "Anything?"

My mouth went dry, and I looked down to my purse, suddenly anxious to find my key ring.

He chuckled. "I was just joking. That sounds like a good plan."

"Right," I said, slightly disappointed for reasons I couldn't understand. Why was I such a mess? Hadn't I been telling Cohen all along we were just friends? We walked up the front steps, and I put my key in the hole, jiggling it. When we got to my office, I would let him know how much I enjoyed spending time with him, but that this had to be our last date. The last time we met outside of school.

Finally, the lock gave, and I pushed the door open. The halls were empty and dark sans emergency lighting casting a dim glow over the tiles.

He shuddered. "High schools make me uncomfortable. Especially when they're empty."

"Same," I said. "But I kind of think that's a good thing."

"Explain," he said.

I brushed my fingers over the row of lockers, feeling the cold metal against my skin. "No one grows or learns in their comfort zone. You always have to be a little uncomfortable if you truly want to get somewhere better than you were before."

With a smile, he shook his head. "You're romanticizing high school for me. I thought you said you had a hard time in school?"

A small sigh passed through my lips. If I wasn't going to see him again, I could be honest, right? It wouldn't matter after today. "I was the mean girl, Cohen."

He raised his eyebrows in disbelief. "What?"

"I was so mean." Tears pricked my eyes as I remembered the ways I used to torture those around me. "Now I know it was because of how controlled I felt at home—I was trying to get any amount of power where I could find it, and I was so miserable. I reached out to the people I hurt and apologized, but I still regret it." I looked down, not wanting to face him.

He linked his fingers through mine. "Everyone makes mistakes. It's what they do afterward that matters." He gestured around the hallway. "I'd say you more than made up for it."

"I try." I squeezed his hand, remembering the feeling of his rough palms against mine. The gentle scratch of the hair on his hands. But soon we reached my office and I had to let go. Unlocking the door took two hands and some jiggling of the knob.

As soon as the door opened, Ralphie fluttered his wings loudly inside the cage.

I grinned at my companion. "Hi, Ralphie. Do you remember Cohen?"

"Hi, Ralphie," Cohen cooed.

My bird seemed to settle, taking him in.

Cohen extended his finger, and Ralphie gently nipped it.

I smiled between the two of them, then realized I

should have been getting the food. Should have been looking anywhere other than at the man who was becoming more attractive by the second.

I reached into the filing cabinet to get his food and busied myself taking care of my bird. As I poured his food and water, Cohen leaned back on the table where I usually met with parents or larger groups, watching.

I felt his eyes on me with every move, and I wondered what he was thinking. Was he thinking about my size? My curly hair? The pattern on my dress?

Was he thinking about kissing me as much as I was thinking about kissing him?

I cleared my thoughts. This was dangerous—now that we were in the school together, alone, I couldn't believe I'd been so risky. All it would take was one teacher showing up to grade or pick up a forgotten item, and we'd be busted. I was the worst liar, alibi or not.

I spent a little longer fussing over Ralphie's dishes than I normally would, then put the food containers and water bottle away and rubbed sanitizer over my hands.

Cohen was still quiet, but when I drew the courage to meet his stare, he was looking right at me.

My breath caught in my chest as I took him in, the firmness of his jaw, the sharp swell of his cheekbones, the fullness of his lips. He was like a flame, and my moth's wings drew me ever closer. I needed to say it. That we couldn't be more than friends. That we couldn't be alone again. "Thank you," I breathed, "for today."

Only a couple of feet of space separated us, but he took my fingers, drawing me closer until I stood between his legs, my hips brushing either side of his denim-clad knees. "Seeing you smile was worth every second."

My heartbeat sped, and my brain begged me to do it. To stop this before I reached the edge where I knew I couldn't return. But instead, I stood frozen, only inches between us. I could see the folds of fabric on his shirt where it bunched around his shoulders. Watch the rise and fall of his chest. See his tongue wet his lips.

For a moment we stood, not parting, not drawing closer, our breaths mingling in the small space that separated us.

Then his eyes moved to my mouth, and I couldn't wait, couldn't stop, couldn't pull away. Not with my body calling for his.

As if on cue, his hand reached for the back of my neck, and he drew me to him until our lips met in beautiful, merciful, passion-filled lust.

My body responded to his in a way it never had to any other man's. My nipples hardened against his chest, my breathing grew ragged, and all I wanted was more. More of Cohen's mouth against mine. More of him against me.

I linked my arms around his shoulders as he moved his mouth from my lips to my cheek, his teeth grazing my earlobe, down my tender throat, and a moan of longing escaped my mouth. His hands slid slowly down my back to my ass and pulled me tighter against him.

How could I say no when my body was screaming, crying, yes? I wanted Cohen. Here and now. And by the hardness pressing into my hip through his jeans, he felt the same.

"I've wanted to touch you all day," he said, his voice husky in my ear.

The cool tickle of his breath combined with his words was dizzying. Intoxicating. "I've wanted you too," I admitted, placing a kiss along the rough stubble of his chin.

His fingers toyed with the bottom edge of my dress, setting the skin of my thighs alight with sensation. The reasonable voice in my mind saying this was a bad idea had been silenced by everything in me screaming to put an end to this need. To take him in my office like the bad girl I never thought I could be.

But then my eyes landed on my degree hanging on the wall. The one I'd worked so hard for and was still paying student loans for.

This career meant more to me than a moment of passion. And I'd deal with the fallout of that later, but right now, I stepped back and whispered, "Cohen?"

His green eyes searched mine, and he nodded. "Let's get you home."

32

COHEN

Birdie tried to apologize, but I wouldn't have it.

She set a boundary, and I needed to respect it. I did respect it. So I would walk away from this without any regrets.

That didn't mean it wouldn't suck. I still wished like hell the school's rules were different, but they weren't.

It sucked. There wasn't another word for it.

I kept my hands against my sides as I walked with her to the car. Knowing what her body felt like against mine, knowing how skillfully her lips worked and her hands fisted through my hair, made me want her that much more.

But I couldn't.

We rode in silence to her friend Mara's house, and I

fully expected her to walk inside the second I parked. But instead, she turned toward me.

"Cohen, I'm sorry." She bit her lip, her eyes shining. "I wish it were different."

A curl had fallen from behind her headband, and I wanted more than anything to reach up and tuck it behind her ear. Comfort her from the pain that was clear in her expression.

"Don't be sorry," I said for the second time that day. "Thank you for today. I had a great time."

"I should be saying that to you," she said, sniffling.

"It's okay." I smiled, because I couldn't show her how much this fucking hurt. How disappointed I was that the second I found something amazing, it slipped through my fingers, just like that goddamned house. "Maybe I'll see you around the Academy."

She nodded, but her lips tugged down like that idea hurt even more. "Thanks for everything, Cohen." Unbuckling her seatbelt, she got out of the car and walked down the sidewalk.

I didn't wait to see her go inside and officially shut the door on the possibility of us.

No, I drove straight to the bar. I needed a drink.

It wasn't even suppertime yet, but there were still people sitting around and drinking, eating food from the limited menu.

When Steve saw me approaching the bar, he grinned

and said, "How did it go?" But his smile quickly fell when he saw my face. He turned over his shoulders and called to one of his bartenders, "A bucket of beer, wings, and nachos."

The bartender got to work and Steve stepped around the bar, walking with me to one of the tables farther away from the servers. "What happened?"

I slid into the seat, sighing and scrubbing my hand over my face. "I wasn't worth the risk."

Instead of being a forty-year-old man, I was seventeen again, walking in after a shift at work and seeing my mom on the couch. Overdosed and cold to the touch. A sob rose in my throat, but I stifled it, swallowed it down.

I wasn't that boy anymore. I was a dad. I had a son. And I had a life.

Steve rubbed my shoulder briefly. "You tried your best." A server set a bucket of beers on the table and Steve cracked one, handing it to me.

I took a long drink, letting the bitter liquid fall down my throat and heat my insides. "I felt it," I admitted.

Steve nodded, letting me talk.

"She was something special, and I fucking lost it."

He frowned toward the table. "She said she didn't want you?"

"She kissed me," I said. "It was the best kiss of my life. Better than sex ever was with anyone else. And then she said she *couldn't*."

"That's not the same as saying she's out," Steve said.

I raised my eyebrows, frustrated. "Really? Because I'm at the fucking bar drinking and she's not here."

Steve threw a verbal punch right back. "So you're telling me some chick walks into your life and dating her would literally cost you the bar, everything you've ever worked for, you wouldn't have any second thoughts."

I thought about it, really thought about it. "Of course I would."

"Then why would you expect that of her? Why would you be upset because she can't?"

God, I was an asshole. "So that's it. I'm out an amazing woman because of a stupid fucking rule."

Steve set his beer on the table. "If it's that stupid of a rule, shouldn't be that hard to get it changed."

I looked down at my beer. Was that something I could even do?

"I've got to get to work. My boss is a hard-ass." He stood up. "Finish that food. If she's as special as you say she is, you better get your ass to work too."

33

BIRDIE

Confession: I don't follow all the rules.

Monday morning, I walked into my office and dropped my keys on my desk. The chairs around the table were shoved to the side, and I put them back, my heart skittering and my stomach aching. Kissing Cohen had been even better than I'd imagined, which was somehow worse than if I'd never kissed him at all.

Now I really knew what I had to sacrifice in order to keep my career.

Cohen had been a perfect gentleman afterward, adjusting himself and walking with me to the parking lot. He even smiled at me as he said goodbye, dropping me off outside of Mara's house. He didn't walk me to the door, which all things considered, was probably a good idea.

I still felt guilty. Sad. So many things. Because I knew what I wanted, and I also knew there was no way it could happen.

Maybe in a couple years, when Ollie graduated, Cohen and I could reconnect. If he was even available then.

The thought of him with someone else, of me missing my chance, made my throat constrict, and I began pulling the tray of wood shavings from the bottom of Ralphie's cage.

Ralphie tilted his head as if questioning me.

"I don't even want to think about it." I let out a sigh and emptied the shavings into my wastebasket, then used unscented baby wipes to wash the tray. "We can't be together. He's a parent. That's all there is to it."

Ralphie cooed sadly.

"I know." I blinked back tears. "But on the bright side, I got a promising lead on an apartment yesterday. The manager said they own another building closer to Emerson and they might have a vacancy if the tenant doesn't continue their lease next month. That means you can finally come home with me at night."

He chirped.

"And I didn't even tell you about the aviary..." That was a subject I could get lost in for hours, no matter how closely it was intertwined with Cohen. I told Ralphie about going to the aviary and all the amazing things I'd seen there as I got my schedule ready for the day.

During first hour, I had a couple of college planning appointments. One with a girl I'd seen with deep circles under her eyes lately. She needed my support, and I needed to be at my best for her.

Coffee was definitely called for.

I walked down the fairly empty hall, waving to my co-workers on the way, and went into the teachers' lounge. I used the sink to wash my hands, and as I reached for a paper towel, someone cleared their throat behind me.

I covered my heart with my hand and turned to see Headmaster Bradford shutting the door. "Oh, you scared me," I said nervously. Although, to be fair, I'd probably be a little scared even if I'd seen him coming.

Not only was Headmaster Bradford my boss, he also came from old money, old academia. He could just as easily recite Shakespeare as end my career at Emerson Academy.

He didn't chuckle at my fright or apologize. Instead, his lips pressed into a line, and his chest rose with a deep breath. "Ms. Melrose, I've gotten several calls from Mrs. Alexander the last few weeks."

I closed my eyes, thinking of Pam and her threats. I'd hoped they were empty, but judging by the look on the headmaster's face, I wasn't so sure. "And?"

"You're aware she and her husband are our largest donors, aside from the Rush family?"

I nodded, wishing I was brave enough to just ask him where he was going with this. Wishing the mere mention of Pam's name didn't make my blood run cold. I needed this job, though. Not only because I loved working with the students, but because any apartment complex would require income to pay my rent.

"It means we're dedicated to keeping our families happy," he said. "And lately, she's been quite unhappy with you."

"Because of Ryde?" I asked. "I only did the mandated college planning session with him and—"

"We're going to waive future meetings," he said.

I raised my eyebrows. "Every student has the meetings. It's a requirement for graduation." In fact, Emerson Academy's excellent record of Ivy League college placement was one of the things that made us a top high school in the country. "Won't it be holding him back to not know what his options really are? The long-term success of child actors—"

"If you're unwilling to fulfill the duties of your role as instructed," Headmaster Bradford said, "we can revisit your contract at the end of the year and see if Emerson Academy is a place you'd like to continue working."

I lowered my gaze and nodded. "Yes, sir."

"Great." He opened the door and walked toward the hallway, leaving me alone in the lounge. Except my stomach didn't much feel like coffee anymore.

Slowly, the door to the bathroom in the teachers' lounge opened, and Mr. Davis stepped out.

My cheeks instantly reddened with shame. "Did you hear that?"

"What?" he said, but his eyes told me he knew it all. "But if I did hear anything, just know that I've got your back."

He left the teachers' lounge then too, and I was alone with my empty cup. I filled it, if only out of habit, and walked back to my office. Leaving the door open, I sat behind my desk, waiting for Sierra Cook to come for her appointment, feeling worse than I had before.

Maybe I didn't want to work at this school. Surely Mara wouldn't mind me staying until I could find another job. Or...I could stay with my parents until I built up an employment record at another place. Maybe even a private business until I could find a position at one of the local public schools.

Except then I would have way more students to work with. Which meant I'd have less time with each of them to make any real difference. But I would be away from the school where I'd begun my career, getting a fresh start. And I would be able to pursue a relationship with Cohen...

I shook my head to snap myself out of that line of thought. What was I thinking? I hardly knew Cohen, and I was ready to throw away my career for a chance at what? Happily ever after?

As far as I knew, the possibility of that happening with

him or anyone else for that matter was slim to none. No, I needed to focus on my job, on my students, on finding a home for Ralphie and me.

I sighed. I hated that people could throw around their money and toy with someone's life. I'd seen my parents do it before, and now that I was on the receiving end, it made me sick.

The first bell rang, and soon after, the tread of Sierra's loafers signaled her presence.

I set aside my upset from this morning and gave her a smile. "Hi, Sierra, how is your morning?"

She dropped into a chair, sitting back and folding her arms across her chest. "Okay." Although, her face told me she was anything but. There was far too much shadow under her eyes for any girl her age, and her lips pinched down at the corners. Even her hair seemed askew, as though she'd attempted a braid without a mirror.

"Are you okay?" I asked.

Her eyes darted toward the door she'd left open, then she looked down as she nodded.

Gentle. "Let's talk about colleges. You're interested in studying art, right?" I reached into my filing cabinet for the information packets I'd gotten from schools with some of the best art programs. "UCLA, of course, has a good program if you'd like to stay closer to home."

She shook her head.

I put that packet aside, then held up the other two. "Yale has a strong reputation for their program. I've also seen excellent artists come from the Art Institute of Chicago. Do either of those locations appeal to you?"

Looking withdrawn, she folded her arms across her chest. "Can I be honest with you, Ms. Melrose?"

"Birdie," I said. "And of course."

"I don't think I want to go to college."

My stomach bottomed out, and I rose to shut the door. If a teacher heard her say that, she would never hear the end of it. Especially since she didn't come from big money or have acting plans after graduation.

"Is that so?" I said, clicking the door shut. "Now that we have some privacy...what are you thinking?"

She let out a sigh. "That I need to get as far away from here as I can."

"Yale is in Connecticut," I answered, taking my seat again.

With so much sadness in her eyes, she said, "Not far enough."

"Honey..." I paused. "Is everything okay at home?"

Her mouth opened as if she wanted to speak, but she didn't, her eyes shining. She couldn't answer me, and a pit grew in my stomach.

"Are you in danger?" I asked, keeping my voice gentle but firm. I needed to know how I could help.

"I'm not," she said simply, but didn't divulge any more.

"Do I need to call the cops? Is there any way I can help?"

She pressed her lips together, taking the packets for Yale and the Art Institute of Chicago from my desk. "I'll apply for these schools."

I reached out, taking the packets. "I'm your guidance counselor. And I'm supposed to help you reach your goals in life. Off the record, is this really what you want to do?"

Slowly, she seemed to relax back into her chair, and she shook her head. "I want to see the world. Outside of my father's control. And I want to see real art. Not just pictures in textbooks. And maybe, someday, I can make art like that too."

My mind worked the pieces together. The dark circles under her eyes. The fact that I'd only ever seen her mother at school functions. "You know… Plenty of students take gap years in Europe. But it would require some money for plane tickets, hostels, food."

"I have it," she said, a desperate excitement coloring her words. For the first time since coming in here, there was a light in her eyes. Hope. "I've saved everything. Birthday money from my grandparents. Everything from my jobs."

She needed this.

And me? I was here to help.

34

OLLIE

I shut my locker and did a double-take. Was that my dad, walking into the building? Why was he here?

With my brows drawn together, I walked toward him, looking around. "Dad, what are you doing here?" I asked when I reached him. I'd caught up on all those bullshit assignments. He couldn't be here to talk to Ms. Melrose.

A frown crossed his face for a fraction of a second before he replaced it with a smile. "Just here to ask some questions about the handbook."

Okay, this was weird. "The *handbook?*"

"Yeah," he said, scratching his chin. "I, uh, you're always complaining about how you can't wear shorts with your uniform, you know, how it gets too hot. Thought maybe I could have that changed for you."

People were beginning to look at us, and dear god, the

girls were checking out my dad. I just threw up in my mouth a little bit. I had to get him *out* of here.

"You don't have to do that," I said, walking toward the exit.

He followed me slowly. "It's not a big deal, really. And your mother said I should get more involved."

"Since when do you listen to what Mom wants you to do?" I retorted. He'd turned down at least a million requests from her to use a personal stylist and update his wardrobe. (Not that I could blame him. My stepdad had used Mom's stylist, and now he looked like he was trying to be fifteen instead of fifty.)

Dad frowned, tilting his head. "Honey."

"Don't call me that at school," I whispered, looking around to make sure no one had heard. I didn't need to look any lamer than I already did with my braces and acne. One overheard pet name, and I'd be honey for a year.

His shoulders sagged, and I felt like an asshole. "I'll see you later, Dad?"

"Yeah," he said. "I'm just going to grab an events calendar while I'm here."

"Sure," I replied with a shrug and walked down the hall.

"Wait," Dad called.

I turned, trying not to be a dick. My therapist, Cecilia, said I needed to be easier on my dad. That I was misplacing my frustration. "Yeah?"

"Are you going to botany club tonight?"

I nodded.

"Pick you up at five."

With a wave, I turned to head toward the bathrooms.

Okay, so it might have been nice to wear shorts when it got hot as Hades in this freaking school, but I didn't need Dad poking his nose around. I already felt like I was living in a fishbowl with Ms. Melrose telling him about therapists.

The warning bell rang, and I looked toward the ceiling, frustrated I hadn't had a chance to piss before going to videography class with Mr. Davis. That was the one class I didn't want to miss any part of.

I hitched my backpack over my shoulders and walked through the crowd of students toward the videography classroom. One of the girls in the botany club waved at me on my way there.

"Hey," she said, "are you coming tonight?"

"I have to miss it," I said.

35

BIRDIE

Confession: I got my nose from my father, and my mother got hers from the plastic surgeon.

I used my best handwriting to write a note in the card for Anthea's baby shower.

Mara stood beside me in a pretty russet dress and shifted in her heels. She looked so pretty with her brunette hair in loose waves and bright red lipstick painting her lips. "I'm glad you could help her," Mara said. "I wish I would have had someone like you when I was in high school. When I dropped out, my principal told me I'd be a single mom working at the diner by the time I was twenty."

I shook my head. "I can't believe the way some people treat children."

"Me neither." She shifted the rings on her hand, clearly uncomfortable.

I tucked the card in the envelope. "She's going to make something of her life, you know. Go somewhere else. Experience things I've never even dreamed of."

"Don't do that," Mara said. "Don't undermine what you've done."

"What's that?" I asked, my eyes feeling hot. I hadn't heard from Cohen all week. I'd been threatened to be fired. I was living in my friend's guest bedroom. This was not the life I'd ever imagined for myself.

"You've *lived*, Birdie," she said, her hands on my shoulders. "You went to college, had a serious relationship, lived somewhere other than your parents' mansion. Why would you feel any less than the amazing woman you are?"

I shook my head as I taped the card to the wrapped gift. "It's not just that. Headmaster Bradford practically threatened to fire me if I *deigned* to discuss colleges with this one student."

Only Mara could look that disgusted and beautiful at the same time. "They're threatening to fire you when you're changing lives? And you're sure you want to work there?"

I picked up the present and began walking toward her front door. "The apartment manager said they don't have an opening at that other building for a month. So unless I want to lie and tell them I have a job that I don't anymore, losing this job is out of the question."

"You know you can stay with me as long as you want," she said, letting us out the front door and locking it behind us.

"I know, and I'm grateful—you know I am—but I'm embarrassed, Mara." I held the present against the car with my hip so I could unlock the door. "Look at me. The only thing I own is this car, and it's already well over a hundred thousand miles. I'm in student loan debt up to my eyeballs because I didn't qualify for financial aid, *and* I don't have a boyfriend."

"Cohen could be your boyfriend," she pointed out as she sat next to me in the car.

"Allegedly." I buckled my seatbelt and turned my key in the ignition. It fired up, and I pulled out of her driveway. "After what happened, he's probably not interested. No, I just need to help Cohen find out what's going on with Ollie and then get him out of my head."

"Are you sure?" Mara asked. "I don't want you to do something you can't undo."

I nodded. "It's probably better this way. I haven't been apart from Dax for too long, and I probably need time just to focus on myself."

Mara waggled her eyebrows. "I actually have something that might help with that."

"Ew, Mara."

"It's not used!" she argued, laughing. "This company sent me a few toys to review and share on social media if I like them."

I chuckled, shaking my head. "How is what you do a real job?"

"Some of us just like getting lucky."

My cheeks flushed as I giggled. "Okay, but no sex talk at the party. My parents might pop a blood vessel if they hear any mention of masturbation."

"Ugh, I still don't get why they're such prudes. Everyone there knows how you get to have a baby shower anyway, right?"

"You would think," I murmured.

The closer I got to my parents' house, the more uncomfortable I felt. I didn't want to be like them, but right now, having true financial security sounded like the biggest blessing in the world. If only I could grab a drink from the gas station without worrying about how it would affect my bottom line or my ability to afford a down payment for a place of my own.

"What work has your mom had done lately?" Mara asked. "I always like seeing her latest upgrade."

I rolled my eyes. "I have no idea. Anthea hasn't mentioned anything, but she's pretty preoccupied with the baby."

My parents' house came into view, and I pulled into the driveway, where a valet was waiting to take my car. The kid took my keys and handed me a slip of paper I tucked away in my purse.

Mara shook her head. "I want to have fuck-you money someday."

I raised my eyebrows. "F-you money?"

She nodded, stepping toward the front door surrounded by a cascade of pink balloons. "You know, like if someone makes you mad, you can just give them the big middle finger. Like you could pay your school off to date that hot bartender. Or if someone insulted my car, I could get a Porsche the next day, just for fun."

I laughed, realizing that's what my parents had. Plenty of fuck-you money. "I only have I'm-fucked money."

Mara cackled and pushed open the front door. People milled about my parents' sitting room, but the main event was happening out by the pool.

"So," Mara said, leaning closer to whisper, "you have to tell me who all the eligible bachelors are. You know, in case writing falls through on the fuck-you money front."

I rolled my eyes. "If there are any eligible guys here, my parents have them lined up to marry me."

"No fair, why do you get the reverse harem?"

I gave her a look. "I can't even handle one guy, obviously. I have one kiss, and I'm all flustered. I can't stop thinking about his hands on me." I closed my eyes, stifling those feelings before one of these rich partygoers caught my flushed cheeks or the crossing of my legs.

"Call him!" she said. "Plan to meet up with him later! This holding back stuff is literal insanity."

I opened my mouth to argue, but my mom assaulted us instead. "Hello, darling. Greetings, Mara."

Mara took my mother's extended hand and shook it. "Is that a new nose, Mrs. M? Amazing."

Mom made the shame symbol. "You are too sly. You know, if you like the work, I can refer you to my surgeon. He has a wonderful friends and family discount."

"You're the best, Mrs. M," Mara said. "Can you refer me to some cute man candy?"

I rolled my eyes behind my friend's back. My mom didn't see either—she was way too interested in scanning the crowd for single men with all the predatory instincts of a hawk.

I looked around on my own, seeing who I recognized. All these people were a part of my old life, going to bar mitzvahs and weddings and baby showers and whatever other excuse there was to drink and show off the latest designer purchase.

Now these people were nothing more than strangers. How had my life drifted so far from where I began? I always thought people on the outside looked so happy and free, but now that *I* was out of the loop, I wasn't so sure.

I had to worry about things my parents never worried about. Hoping my car wouldn't break down so I could get to work and pay my bills. Waiting until Friday to eat out so I'd have plenty on my card. Getting gifts on a store credit card so I could pay a little at a time.

But as I caught sight of Pam Alexander and her husband, I thought my parents and I did have some similarities after all. I still had to impress the right people to succeed in my career. I had to play the game.

I gave Pam a wave, and she lifted her chin, her lips lifted but her eyes cold.

While Mom introduced Mara to one of her approved suitors, I found Anthea talking to Great Aunt Mildred. "Hi, Auntie M!" I said, stopping her short in her infamous story about her pet Dalmatians. Her eyesight was so bad that for a week, she mistook her feather dusters for the dogs. Luckily, the maid was feeding the actual dogs while Aunt Mildred petted cleaning supplies and bragged about how well-behaved they were.

"I'm sorry," I said, "but I have to steal Anthea. Baby shower business."

Mildred pointed a crooked finger at me. "You take care of her, alright? Precious cargo!" She patted Anthea's belly.

I could practically feel Anthea's spine stiffen. As we walked away, she muttered, "I'm not a damn airplane. Or a Buddha statue. Rubbing my belly is *not* good luck."

"I know, I know," I soothed.

"Thank you for getting me out of there. If I hear about her damn dogs one more time, I'll shove her in the pool."

"I'd like to see that," I said with a giggle, leading her past the pool and toward the mound of presents under the cabana. The water was no longer pink, but sparkling clear once more. "How's everything going? How are you feeling?"

"Huge. Like a cargo plane."

I leaned my head against her shoulder, giggling, and she managed a laugh as well.

Anthea's smile fell though, and she stopped walking. "Oh no."

"What?" I asked, following her gaze.

Mom was coming our way with none other than Walter on her arm, the boring, straight-laced businessman she'd tried and failed to set me up with at the last shindig. Of course, Mara was nowhere to be found.

"Get me out of here," I said to Anthea.

"If I have to get called a cargo carrier, you can talk to the boring man."

I glared at her, then turned a smile on Mom and Walter. They would be getting here in three, two... "Hi there," I said with a smile that was far too forced.

"Hello," Walter said with all the personality of a saltine cracker.

Why did the sight of bland smiles and polished dress shoes make me want to run? Why did I have to be attracted to the artists of the world? To off-limits guys with rough edges and even rougher hands?

Walter wasn't ugly. No, he had straight teeth, probably from braces he had at twelve. He probably went to summer camps as a kid and church on Sundays with his parents now and probably did great work on the job too.

He was exactly the kind of guy who would give me a life of ease. The kind of guy my parents would approve of.

Mom put her hands on both of us, as if she could somehow transfer by osmosis her desire for us to be together. "Beatrice, I made a huge mistake." She frowned deeply between Walter and me. "I made reservations for your father and me at La Belle for after the party, but I accidentally set it two hours early. Of course, I've been trying to get in good with the maître d there for years, and backing out last minute would really hurt that relationship." Then her surgically altered face lit up. "Hey! Why don't you two take it? You would be doing me a *huge* favor. Charge it to our account, please, as a thank you."

Walter shrugged. "I suppose I could enjoy a free meal at LaBelle."

I shook my head with a frustrated, albeit admiring, smile. My mom was good. She was. But even she couldn't ask me to make such a huge transgression. "Are you sure I should leave my sister-in-law's baby shower?"

Mom pointed over my shoulder where Anthea had gotten sucked back into a conversation with Aunt Mildred. "Anthea should mingle with guests she doesn't get to see on a regular basis." She whipped out her cell phone. "I'll have the driver bring up a car."

36

BIRDIE

Confession: I can be a bit of a hot head.

This was the most awkward car ride of my life, and we hadn't even left my parents' property yet. Walter insisted he hold the door open for me, instead of the driver, so the two of them danced around until I'd finally opened the door myself and got in the car.

As Walter walked around, I sent a quick text to Mara.

Birdie: Mom wrangled me into dinner with a guy. Sorry. :/ Feel free to duck out any time. I'll have the driver take me home.

The other door opened, and instead of looking at my date, I moved to buckle myself in.

Walter helped me clip my seatbelt. I wasn't even struggling. He just put his sweaty hands atop mine like I was a child and pushed in the belt until it clicked. Then he'd turned those round eyes on me like he thought we were sharing a moment.

It was a little sexual—now that I think about it—and in a gross way. Like a teenage boy who obsesses about sex but never has it.

I quickly moved my hand out from under his and folded it in my lap. Thankfully, there was plenty of room between us in the back of the car.

I couldn't believe I'd gotten sucked into this. What was I? A powerless child? No! I was a grown woman with my own car, my own phone, my own job, my own schedule. I could have said no to my mother.

But I hadn't.

Maybe a part of me *wanted* to be here with Walter? Wanted to close the door on something with Cohen. Walter would be a safe choice, not only for my career but for my future. Walter was stable. Unmarried. Had a good job with my dad's company. A relationship with me would, of course, disqualify him from ever getting fired.

Maybe my life wasn't supposed to be about falling in love. Or not in the sense of relationships. The love of my life was my career. My students. My friendships. No one got their happily ever after in *everything*, right? That only happened in Mara's romance novels.

"So," I said, anxious to cut the awkward silence. "How

is work?" If my father was any indication, work was always a safe topic.

"We're working on a big merger now. Lots of meetings and late hours and golf matches on Saturdays."

I nodded. "Some of Dad's best negotiations happen on the greens."

He chuckled. "Your father is the master, although I have to admit your mother runs a mean game of her own."

Despite the heaviness in my heart, I laughed. He had a good point. "Imagine, making this reservation seem so accidental. We both know my mother never makes a mistake."

"Of course not. Behind every great man is an even greater woman."

"No great man keeps a woman behind him," I countered.

Walter didn't know what to do with that.

The car slowed and stopped, then the driver held the door open for me. Thankfully, I'd dressed nicely for the baby shower, because La Belle was one of the fanciest restaurants in the city. Of course, my mom thought that would be the place for Walter and me to spend time together.

A host led us to a table, and Walter kept his hand lightly on my midback. Very respectable.

Very boring.

We sat at a table, across from each other. He took the cloth napkin and folded it over his lap.

A second of silence fell over us, so heavy I knew we both had no idea what to talk about. We had nothing in common, except for my parents, which may just have been the biggest connection killer there was.

"So you're a teacher?" Walter asked.

"Guidance counselor." He'd asked that last time and hadn't remembered my answer. Mentally, I was even more checked out than I'd been before.

"Ah. The one who pushes college on students."

"And condoms," I quipped, not in the mood to argue.

He shook his head. "Isn't it crazy how schools push such a sexual agenda on their students these days?"

My eyebrows raised. "Excuse me?"

"You know, when I was a kid, the topic of intercourse was left at home where it belonged. Kids learned these things from their parents instead of being indoctrinated with 'sex ed' at liberal schools by liberal teachers."

My lips parted. "I'm—I'm not sure I heard you correctly. Sex ed indoctrination?"

"Of course. They want to make sure every *child* has access to *adult* contraception. It's entirely inappropriate." He extended a placating hand my way. "Of course I'm not blaming you for the work you do. You're just doing your job."

"Wh-what? Hold on." I sat in my chair, reeling from what he'd said. "What?"

"I mean, you understand." The waitress came by, and he tapped the empty wine glass sitting in front of him on the table. Even the gesture, his lack of words for her, was so pretentious. He took a sip, slurping slightly, and said, "Besides, why should schools be shelling out birth control anyway? With taxpayer money?"

Okay, maybe I *was* in the mood to argue. I stood up, because sitting would have been too much for this conversation. "So taxpayers' dollars can't provide contraception, but they can pay for housing for single teen moms when their parents kick them out? Or free school lunches for kids when their teen parents can't get an education and a good job because they're busy raising children they weren't prepared for in the first place? Oh, but you're probably against that too."

"Well, I, uh, you're, uh—" he stammered, half standing, half sitting.

"Well, I, uh, you're—" I mocked. I threw my napkin on the table. "Bye, Walter. Enjoy your free lunch."

I yanked my purse over my shoulder, storming away from the restaurant. Surely the car was still there, but I was gone. I was done playing by the rules of people who had no idea what the real world looked like. I was done thinking I was less than because I had less than others.

I didn't know how but I was going to make it work on my terms.

37

COHEN

I'd been working on this paper so long, my eyes were starting to cross. But I had to get it perfect before sending it on to Jonas to read so I could get his feedback.

Marjorie, the secretary at Emerson Academy, had seemed so confused at my question on how to get a handbook item changed, she sent me back to Headmaster Bradford. I'd hardly had any interaction with him other than watching him introducing the band at showcases.

He was a little shorter than me, but broad, with hawk-like eyes that made me understand why Birdie was so reticent to break any sort of rules at the school.

"To what do I owe the pleasure, Mr. Bardot?" he'd asked. So proper.

When I asked him how to have a line item in the handbook changed, he'd told me it practically required an

Act of Congress. I needed to get a hundred signatures on a petition from students, staff, or parents to even have the rule change *considered* by the board of trustees. Then, I needed to give a presentation in front of the entire board, showing that a new rule really was merited. The next meeting was a couple months away, so I had time, but that was the worst part.

I had time.

Time away from Birdie. Time to wait for her to get snatched up by some guy, because she would. She was beautiful and funny and sexy as hell. A man would have to be blind not to notice, but even a blind man could hear the clear chime of her voice and be smitten as well.

I had to stifle that feeling of hopelessness as I worked on the speech. On the email I would send to everyone in the directory if I had to.

Birdie had told me she didn't want to break the rule, which I'd respect. And if by some miracle I got the rule changed and she didn't want to see me, well I'd cross that bridge when I got there.

The thought of her dating someone else, the thought of her turning me away, it was too much to handle.

I finished the closing paragraph, knowing I would need to rewrite it a million times before it would be good enough for stuffy people like Headmaster Bradford. After saving, I sent it to the printer in the apartment complex's business office and took the elevator down to get it.

With the few crisp sheets in my hands, I took the

elevator back up and went to my room. I'd play some TV in the background while I worked over the writing again and eventually sent it to Jonas.

But as soon as I sat down, my phone started ringing.

I blinked at the name on the screen.

Birdie.

She couldn't be calling.

But I blinked again, and there she was, like a fucking star in the blackest of night skies. I hurriedly swiped to answer, trying and failing not to get too excited.

"Hello?" I said.

Her voice was a balm. "Come pick me up."

"Absofuckinlutely."

She giggled and said, "I'll send you a map pin."

"I'll be there."

I didn't think about what this meant, and I definitely didn't ask her as I said goodbye. This was the most hopeful I'd felt all week, and I was going to feel it for as long as I could. If I got shattered, well, there were more buckets of beer and wings to be had at the bar.

The pin came through my phone, and I looked at the address. She was near a fancy restaurant at Emerson Shoppes. Audrey liked shopping those boutiques, even though you could get the same thing for half the price at a department store.

I wondered why Birdie was there. Wondered what had made her think of me.

Grabbing my keys, I flew down the stairs and went to find out as fast as I possibly could.

38

BIRDIE

Confession: So maybe I talk like a porn star sometimes.

I waited inside a nearby shop, checking out the trinkets and jewelry that were far too expensive for me to buy, when my phone started ringing. Had Cohen made it here that quickly?

I held it to my ear and said, "That was fast."

"What was?" Mara asked. "Where are you?"

Surprised to hear Mara's voice, I said, "Sorry, Mom sent me on a date with a guy who was so wrong for me."

"I could have told you that," she said. "He was wearing a sweater vest underneath his blazer, Birdie. A *sweater vest*. At least the guy your mom introduced me to had a decent sense of style."

"Well, apparently some of us don't learn as quickly as you." I twisted the price tag on a necklace and immediately let it swing back. Way too much.

"So what's the news? Do you need me to come get you? Because this guy and I actually hit it off, and he asked me to go out with him."

"Actually..." I bit my lip. "I kind of called Cohen."

Mara squealed. "You're so bad!"

I couldn't help but smile. "I'm not bad. I'm just fed up with doing what everyone else wants me to do."

"Okay, if that's the case, I *don't* want you to have hot sex with Cohen and tell me all the sordid details."

I turned toward the back corner, hoping the shopkeeper at the register wouldn't hear me. "You know Cohen has to agree with the hot sex part before we can have it, right?"

"Oh, he'll agree."

"How do you know?" I asked.

From behind me, a low voice said, "Because I'm standing right here?"

My lips parted, and I turned, seeing Cohen standing in his full, handsome glory. "Mara...I gotta go."

She might have said something, but I couldn't hear it. Not over the rushing in my ears as I lowered my phone and held it limply at my side. "Cohen..."

His grin was just as disarming as his voice. "What's this about hot sex?"

A nervous giggle erupted from my chest. "Let's talk about the getaway ride first."

"I'm happy to oblige."

We left the store without purchasing anything. Outside the door, his hand rested on my lower back as he led me to his car, where he opened the door for me. As soon as I got in, I felt better knowing I was at least partially hidden by the tinted glass. Just because I was willing to play with fire didn't mean I wanted to get burned.

When he got to his side, he asked, "So what's with the getaway ride?"

Ignoring the guilty feeling in my chest, I fastened my seatbelt. "My mother set me up on a date, and I realized I'd rather be with you."

His lips curved into an almost imperceptible smile, but he didn't meet my eyes, instead looking over his shoulder to back out. "I'm guessing it didn't end well?"

"End well? How about start well. My mother basically conned me into leaving my sister-in-law's *baby shower* with a man who doesn't believe in sex education." I eyed him suspiciously. "What do *you* think about sex ed?"

He lifted his hands from the wheel for a brief moment. "Don't shoot."

"No promises."

"Well, obviously, I believe in teaching abstinence only." He cleared his throat. "No child, ever, should know about contraceptive options, sexually transmitted diseases, or any other dirty sex act that could or could not have anything to do with bananas." His face was straight and his voice level. It was like a literal nightmare. "In fact, I feel like they should learn everything on the internet or from their friends, just like I did when I was a teenager. Reducing teen pregnancy rates and teaching consent be damned." He turned to me, smiling now. "Does that answer your question?"

I fought a growing smile of my own. "I think it does."

We fell silent for a moment, but it wasn't the same kind of quiet I'd experienced with Walter. With Cohen, it always felt like something amazing was right around the corner, like at any moment he could say or do anything that would send the butterflies in my stomach soaring.

"You've been quiet this week," he said softly. "I wasn't sure I'd hear from you again."

I shook my head and looked over at him. "Maybe I'm tired of playing by the rules."

His lips lifted at the corners. "Where should we start breaking them?"

"Your place?" I asked.

"Perfect."

The drive to his apartment, and even the walk up the stairs, felt illicit. My skin tingled with that special brand of excitement you get when doing something even just a little wrong. But why was being with Cohen wrong? My boss didn't deserve to know what I did in my bedroom. Or Cohen's, for that matter.

And judging by the look in Cohen's eyes as he locked

the front door behind us and turned toward me, that's where we were going—if we even made it that far.

My heart sped as he crossed the living room toward me. It beat even faster as he took the strap of my purse and slid it down my shoulder, let it drop on the floor. My breath caught, but he caught my lips just as quickly with his own.

Words didn't matter now, not with our bodies so insistent on doing the talking. Falling into his kiss was as easy as breathing had been moments ago. I tilted my head, deepening the kiss, feeling the sweet taste of his tongue as it parted my lips and tangled with mine.

His hands adored my body, gripping my hips, my back, my ass, pulling me closer and closer to him and his hardening cock.

I nipped on his bottom lip, and he responded with a moan that only emboldened me more.

Why had I been holding back all this time? This felt amazing, and we'd barely rounded first.

I reached my hand down to rub the hard spot underneath his jeans, and he growled, a sound so sexy my stomach clenched in response.

"This is for you," he said against my mouth and picked me up, carrying me to the counter. *Carried* me. As though I were the lightest weight he'd ever lifted. God, it was hot.

He spread my knees and stood between them, kissing me harder, faster, and I wrapped my legs around his waist, wondering why on earth I hadn't taken him up on that offer the very first night.

His lips moved from my mouth to my chin, my neck, the cleavage peeking through the sweetheart neckline of my dress, and I shuddered with need.

He easily slid down the back zipper of my dress, revealing my strapless bra, which he shoved down, freeing my breasts. Catching one nipple in his mouth, he rubbed the pad of his thumb over the other. The sensation was dizzying. Intoxicating.

Why had I ever thought I could settle for a lifetime with Dax or Walter when Cohen could make me feel like *this*?

He moved his mouth to my other hardened nipple, sucking, playing, dancing his tongue over sensitive flesh.

"God," I moaned, dropping my neck back. "That's incredible." I wanted him inside me; I wanted him to fill me so I forgot where I ended and he began.

But instead, he lowered his mouth and pushed the skirt of my dress up, baring the lace underwear beneath. His fingers pressed into the flesh of my thighs, shoving them apart, then he slowly ran one finger along the part of my lips.

He followed with his tongue.

I fisted my fingers in his hair and moaned.

His tongue slowly circled my clit, sending shocks of pleasure through me. "You're so wet for me," he hummed against my sex.

"I want you," I breathed. "I've wanted you since I saw you at the bar."

"Then you can wait a little longer," he said and traced another circle around my clit, sucking this time and then blowing gently.

I shuddered against his mouth.

"That's it," he said, continuing to work tantalizing patterns against me with his tongue. "I've been thinking of you, fisting my cock just from our kiss." Then he slipped a finger inside me, then two, working every part of me with his mouth and his fingers until I had to grip the countertop with all I had just to stay upright.

"I'm going to make you come," he said, looking me in the eyes. "And when you do, remember, it's going to be even better when I'm inside of you."

Just his words, his cool breath on my skin, made me shiver.

And then he was back at it, pushing me higher and higher until I fell apart around his fingers, yelling out with the force of it all, of the way he made me feel. This was nirvana.

No, this was *Cohen*.

And I would never get enough.

39

COHEN

She clenched around my fingers, and I gently fucked her until the waves stopped coming. Everything inside me, including my dick, wanted to be inside her, sliding through her wetness that slicked my fingers. But I didn't want to race through my time with Birdie.

Her eyes were wide, her cheeks flushed as she looked at me in awe. "That was... incredible," she said, her voice breathy.

Knowing I made her feel that way gave me a heady rush. Wanting to watch her shudder, see the lust fill her eyes, I brought my two fingers to my mouth and sucked off her moisture.

She tasted so fucking good, and she gave me just the reaction I was looking for. Her lids dropped, heavy with heat, and her teeth caught her bottom lip, red and swollen.

My dick strained harder against my pants, and she knew it. Those soft hands of hers kneaded at the hard spot in my jeans, and I groaned. She reached for my zipper as I reached for her tits. I wanted to taste them and feel her nipples stiffen against my tongue.

Just as I sucked on her tit, she freed my dick and brought her hand to my shaft, pumping once and butting up against the sensitive tip.

Bringing my lips to her ear, I said, "I have a confession to make."

"Yeah?" she asked, pumping harder.

I moaned, my breath coming faster. "The first night you stayed, I had to take a cold shower you turned me on so damn much."

"Is that so?" Her beautiful lips quirked into a smile as she slid her hand farther down my length and cupped my balls. God, it felt good.

I kissed her mouth, hot, heavy, and she kissed me back, her hands working me so well I could feel my dick hardening even more.

"The shower didn't work," I admitted, and this time she moaned.

"Tell me about it," she said, her breasts hitching, pressing to my chest.

I reached her other tit, freeing it and working my thumb over her nipple. "My dick was so hard just thinking about you. I did it in the shower, thinking about eating you out from behind."

She moaned again, and I pinched her nipple, tugging and working it between my thumb and forefinger.

"I thought about thrusting my cock through those tits of yours and watching them bounce against my balls."

"Oh fuck," she said, and that dirty word coming from her sweet mouth turned me on more. She slid her dress down her hips, kicking it off, and slid off the counter. "Do it."

Between her hand off my cock and her tits on full display, my dick hurt. I needed her. Needed to release the well building in me. She knelt in front of me, maneuvering her tits so they surrounded my cock, and god, it felt good.

I thrusted, sliding against her soft skin, and I moaned.

"That's so hot," she whispered.

I agreed.

I thrusted against her again and again until I couldn't fucking hold it in anymore.

"I'm going to come," I moaned. But she didn't let go. Didn't let me have space.

Instead, she looked me straight in the eyes and said, "Come on my tits."

I'd never wanted anything more. I pumped against her chest, and when I couldn't hold it in anymore, cum spurted from my dick, wanting her tight hole but landing on her chest. Seeing my cum glistening on her tits was the biggest fucking turn-on of my life, and if I hadn't just come, I'd have her now—against the counter, on the couch, in my bed until she was screaming my name again.

Instead, I took her hand and said, "Let me show you the shower."

40

BIRDIE

Confession: Getting older is weird.

"You dirty little slut!" Mara said, walking alongside me down the empty halls of Emerson Academy. I had to feed and check in on Ralphie, and she wanted more details than I divulged over our morning cups of coffee.

I gave her a look. "I never understood why women call each other that."

"It's taking back the term," she said with a shrug. "If we call each other sluts as a compliment, body-shaming misogynists can't use it to hurt us."

"So it's a compliment?"

"Definitely." She waggled her eyebrows. "And what he did to you? Major compliment. I can't believe you didn't stay the night and see what he had planned for round two."

"I had to get my car," I said.

She raised her eyebrows. "Really? You had to get your car?"

"If I didn't want to explain to my parents how truly terrible Walter was and risk World War III."

"Why do you let them push you around like that?"

We reached my office, and I turned to put the key in the lock. "It's all a chess game with my family. If I let them feel like they have control, they don't work so hard to exert it over me... and maybe I'm still so used to being bossed around I don't know how to say no."

"It's exhausting," she said, following me inside.

Ralphie chirped happily to see Mara and me.

"You know," Mara said, "you could bring Ralphie home if you wanted."

As I began preparing his food, I thought it over. "I don't know if I want to move him until I have his forever home, you know? He'd probably be alone more there than he is here. And the students like him. I think he likes seeing them too."

Mara passed me, going to sit on my desk. "Anyone get pregnant lately?"

I snorted. "Hardly. Although, I am worried about a student..."

"What do you mean?"

If I didn't give her identifying details, I could talk to

her about Ollie... and maybe she'd have some advice. "There's this student, and he stopped turning in homework out of nowhere. He's sad, withdrawn. He's gay, but not out to the other students. His parents are divorced, but they have been for almost two years, so it's all out of nowhere."

"Is he being bullied?"

"Not that I can tell."

"Broken heart," she said easily, examining her nails.

I finished pouring water in Ralphie's dish. "You think?"

"Come on, you were in high school once. Everything feels like it's the end of the world, whether it's a bad grade or a fight with a friend or losing a boyfriend."

I thought it over as I put away the food and water containers. Could Ollie just be upset about a relationship ending? I didn't know of any other gay students, but that didn't mean they didn't exist—or that he didn't have a boyfriend outside of school. Maybe I'd ask Cohen about it next time I saw him.

I pulled a chair next to Ralphie's cage and sat. "How soon is too soon to text Cohen?"

"Depends. Which century do you prefer to abide in?"

I snorted. "Preferably the present. I know I'm all about girl power, but clearly I did something wrong with Dax."

Mara gave me a look. "In my opinion, whatever you did, you did it right. You got him out of here so you could get with the hot bartender who goes down on you!"

"But texting?" I said. "I have no idea how to date. It's been so long!"

"My advice? If you want a relationship without games, you have to start it without games."

She had a point. So I got out my phone and sent Cohen a text.

Birdie: Hey.

I let out a groan. "But what do I say?" I made my voice all breathy. "'Last night was amazing. Let's do it again?' It sounds so needy."

"He's the one who ate you out. I say a little clinginess is a natural consequence."

"Stop making me laugh," I said, staring at my phone.

Mara made her voice breathy too. "Dear Cohen, please let me come sit on your face."

I snorted with laughter. Then my phone dinged. Thankfully, Cohen had just messaged back.

Cohen: Hey, I keep thinking about yesterday.

I showed Mara the phone, and she giddily slapped my shoulder.

Birdie: Me too.

Cohen: Can I see you again? Saturday maybe?

"Yes!" Mara cried. "Tell him yes!"

I shook my head. "As if that answer were ever in question."

Birdie: I'll see you then. :)

I put my phone back in my purse and asked Mara, "Want to head to the beach?"

"Thought you'd never ask."

We drove back to her house, grabbed some beach towels, snacks, and our Kindles, and got in the car. The second my feet hit the sand, I felt better. Freer.

"How's your editor liking the book?" I asked Mara. "You haven't said much about it."

"She *says* she likes it." She fanned out her towel and sat on it, then retrieved her sunblock. "You know how it is. I always worry each book I write will be the last and everyone will figure out I'm a hack who doesn't even have a high school diploma."

I frowned. "But what does a diploma have to do with what you do now? Do all of those reviewers who say they love your books care about that?"

"I know they don't." She paused to lather sunscreen over her face. "But maybe I do."

"Have you ever thought about getting your GED?"

She was quiet for a moment. "I have. But I don't know if I want to. Getting my GED will be like proving all those people right who said I'd never amount to anything without it."

I smiled at my friend. I loved her spunk, right along with her spite. I felt a hundred percent confident that was what helped her get so far in life. "Well, my master's-degree-having ass is thankful for the house you got without graduating."

She gave me a smile. "For that, I'm sending you the book."

My mouth fell open. "Before your editor gets it back to you?" Mara *never* allowed me to read rough drafts, no matter how much I begged.

"It's about a formerly rich girl who falls in love, so I may need your advice."

"Well then, I'm your girl."

"Now, put on your sunscreen, or you'll be my girl with melanoma."

Laughing, I took the bottle from her. "Getting older is weird."

"Ain't that the truth."

We spent the rest of the afternoon on the beach, reading, relaxing, and enjoying each other. Because these really were the days. Someday, maybe, we'd have partners, children, and we'd long for these days spent just us girls. I was going to savor every moment.

41

COHEN

Ollie and I sat across from each other at the dinner table. Our plates were full of spicy chicken and rice. It was one of my favorite things to make, and thankfully he liked it too. He also seemed in a better mood today than he had last week.

Things were looking up. Finally. Therapy must be helping, and Saturday with Birdie... I couldn't think about things like that at the dinner table. Not when I still had until Saturday to see her—and it was only Monday.

"Did you have a good botany club meeting?" I asked Ollie.

He nodded, looking down at his plate full of food.

"No-word answers? That's a new one," I said with a teasing tone.

He rolled his eyes. "How much is there to say about it?"

"Apparently not much." I took another bite. "And what about your weekend? Mom doing well?"

"Yeah. She is."

"Good," I said. And I meant it. No one deserved to be alone. And even though divorce had felt like admitting failure, no one deserved to be in a loveless relationship.

I wondered what might have happened if Audrey and I had tried to stick it out—lived alongside each other like roommates in a house big enough to hold all of our possessions but none of our baggage.

I might never have met Birdie. Might not be seeing her Saturday.

"Dad?" Ollie said.

I nearly dropped my fork. It was the first time he'd initiated conversation with me in quite a while. "Yeah, son?"

"What happened to the house?"

I shook my head. "The deal fell through. We can look for something together this summer."

Ollie smiled softly, then frowned. "I'm sorry. I know you liked the house."

I raised my eyebrows. "What am I paying Cecilia? Whatever it is clearly isn't enough."

With an eyeroll, Ollie said, "Sorry, lapse in judgement."

I chuckled and took another spicy bite, following it with a drink of lemonade.

"Dad?"

Again? At this rate, I'd have to erect a trophy in Cecilia's honor. "What's up?"

"Have you ever thought about dating?" he asked.

My hand stalled on the fork. In fact, I'd thought about dating a lot lately, and more, even though it was way too soon. "Sometimes," I admitted.

He nodded, pushing rice around on his plate.

"Why do you ask?"

His shoulders lifted in half a shrug. "Mom just got married so soon, and I... I don't know. I haven't really seen you with anyone."

"I never wanted to introduce you to anyone unless it was serious, you know?" I wished I could tell Ollie about Birdie. How much I liked spending time with her. How lucky he was to have someone like her working at his school. But I needed to respect her privacy too, especially before we made anything official.

Ollie lifted a corner of his mouth. "Because of your mom?"

I nodded. "And because of you. You deserve the best, kid."

"You know, Dad?" he said. "So do you."

♥•♥•♥•♥

That conversation with Ollie left me feeling as high as the moon. Even while he went to his room to finish up on homework and go to bed. Even while I scrubbed the dishes and the table and the sink.

Even when the house was quiet and I went to bed. I couldn't wait to tell Birdie about our breakthrough, about our first full conversation in weeks that didn't involve an argument.

Then I realized I didn't have to wait.

Cohen: You're not going to believe this. Ollie actually talked to me tonight at dinner. We had a really good conversation.

I settled into my pillows, wishing she was beside me.

Birdie: !!!

Birdie: Cohen, that's amazing! I'm so happy for you two!

Cohen: I'm happy too. Happier than I've been in a long time.

Birdie: :) what do you think made the difference?

Cohen: I'm not sure. Maybe a combination of things. Whatever it is, I hope it stays this way.

Birdie: Me too. You both deserve it.

Deserve. That word made me smile. When Ollie had said I deserved the best, he didn't realize she was coming over Saturday.

Cohen: Is it bad if I say I've been thinking about you all day?

Birdie: Not at all. I've been thinking about you too.

I wondered if she'd been having the same thoughts as me. Ones that left me wanting her even more.

There was only one way to find out.

Cohen: What have you been thinking?

It took a long while for Birdie's reply to come, but when it did, my mouth fell open.

Birdie: I've been thinking about you in my office and what I wished we could have done.

My free hand trailed down my abs to the waistband of my pants.

Cohen: What do you wish we could have done, baby?

I held my breath, mentally begging for her reply. That we could ride out this fantasy together on the phone even if we couldn't do it in person.

Yet.

Birdie: I would have let you bend me over the desk.

Cohen: I would have fucking loved that.

I ran my fist down my length, already turned on. The thought of Birdie thinking of me in her office, touching herself to us—god, it made me hard.

Cohen: Baby, are you touching yourself?

Birdie: I am now.

Cohen: Good.

Cohen: Imagine I bend you over your desk and tear down your panties. I pull up your dress. I drop to my knees and eat your pussy from behind, making you so damn wet you're dripping in my mouth.

Birdie: I'm moaning. It feels so fucking good.

Cohen: I want to make you feel good. I get my fingers inside you, licking your clit and all along your folds. You're getting closer, so I stop.

Birdie: I want to see you, so I turn around and unzip your pants, taking that cock of yours in my hands. It's wet at the tip. I lick it off.

I shuddered, pumping my fist faster over my cock. Fuck, even on the phone Birdie was sexy as hell.

Cohen: That's hot, baby.

Birdie: I'm so wet for you, Cohen. I want to feel you inside me.

I didn't know if she was talking about reality or the fantasy that was pushing me closer to the edge, but it didn't matter.

Cohen: I want to be inside you. I spread your knees and press the tip of my dick against your slit, teasing you.

Birdie: You're cruel.

Cohen: I push inside your tight hole, inch by fucking inch until my balls hit your perfect ass.

Birdie: Fuck me.

Cohen: I pull back, slowly, watching my dick slide out of you, seeing how wet it is from your pussy. And then I slam inside, grabbing your thighs to keep you exactly where I want you.

Birdie: I'm grabbing your arms, digging my nails in your skin. It feels so fucking good, Cohen.

Cohen: I pump inside you, rubbing your clit with my thumb.

Birdie: I'm moaning. Getting so fucking close.

Cohen: Come with me, baby. I want to feel you milk my cock.

Birdie: Almost.

I pumped faster, working myself harder and harder, silently begging Birdie to come so I can imagine her around me, the moisture of our orgasms slicking my dick.

Birdie: I'm coming. Cohen, I'm coming.

Fuck. I ripped off my shirt and pushed myself over the edge, coming into the cotton, wishing it was Birdie instead.

Cohen: That was... amazing.

Cohen: You're amazing.

Birdie: I can't wait to do it in person.

Cohen: I promise, baby, I'm going to make you feel so good.

Birdie: I'm counting on it. Goodnight.

Cohen: Goodnight.

42

BIRDIE

Confession: Being bad feels good.

When I reached Cohen's apartment building, a cool shiver went through my stomach at what he'd promised me the day before. That when he was inside me, I would feel better than I ever had before.

I completely believed him. The way he'd made me come was next level—I'd never experienced an orgasm that intense with Dax. Not even close.

I bit my lip, trying to stifle the thoughts running through my mind. I didn't want Cohen to think he was a booty call, because I liked so many other things about him too. I mean, the guy took me to an aviary, he liked my bird, he was easy to talk to and really thoughtful.

But the way he touched me...

I lifted my hand and rang his doorbell. As I waited for him, I could hear music playing. Something soft and soulful. And then there was a hint of spice coming from inside. Was he cooking?

The door opened, and I could tell he was making supper.

"Hi." He grinned and kissed my cheek. "I hope you're hungry."

"Always," I said honestly and followed him inside. There was a pot of bubbling liquid on the stove along with a boiling pot of noodles, and the oven light was on. "Are you making Italian food?"

"Absolutely. Gayle would be disappointed in me if I tried anything else."

"Yeah? I would have thought she'd expect sweets from you."

He nodded, reaching for a bottle of wine from the fridge. "That's why Chris is the one who handles most of the baking. Gayle's grandma was Sicilian, and she taught Gayle everything she knew. And then Gayle taught me."

I smiled. "I love it. My grandpa owns a diner, but my mother's just as embarrassed of him as she is of me."

"Which diner?" he asked.

"Waldo's Diner. It's on the east side of Emerson."

"I know the place." He uncorked the bottle of wine and began pouring it in my glass. "So your grandpa is the famous Waldo?"

I chuckled. "Actually, his name is Chester. He bought it from Waldo, but he doesn't really tell anyone he owns it. He likes to keep a low profile."

"We'll have to go there sometime," he said. "I used to take Ollie there for milkshakes all the time."

The idea of Cohen taking a small, curly-haired Ollie for milkshakes warmed my heart from the inside out. "I'd love that."

"Me too. And it would be nice to talk to another restaurant owner. I bet he'd have some good advice for me."

I imagined Cohen sitting across from my grandpa, and my heart felt full enough to burst. "I think he'd like that." Grandpa had never liked Dax, but I already knew he would fall for down-to-earth Cohen just as quickly as I had.

"Well, now that I know I have some competition, I'm a little more nervous to serve you dinner," he said with an adorable grin.

I giggled and took a sip of my wine. "I'm sure it will be amazing."

He drank from his own wine glass. "Here's to hoping. How was your day?"

Sitting at the counter, sipping on wine while he cooked, I told him about my week, and it all felt so *right*. I could imagine us doing this every night. Which was maybe why Cohen was so dangerous. Why he never would or could be just a rebound for me.

The timer on his stove went off, and he retrieved a pan of garlic bread that made my mouth water just from the smell.

Once it was on pads on the counter, he began dishing plates with pasta, sauce, and salad, then carried both of them to the table. "Want to get the drinks?" he asked.

"Of course," I said, topping off our glasses before following him. "It looks amazing, Cohen."

He grinned. "I hope it's Birdie-approved."

The first bite told me it was more than approved. We sat at the table and ate together, just enjoying one another's company. I couldn't believe I'd ever thought of following the school's rule and passing on a chance with Cohen Bardot. We could figure out the details, but not a missed opportunity.

His smile alone was enough to make the risk worth it.

But then he ran his fingers over the bare skin of my thigh, and I knew without a doubt how worth it this was.

I glanced into his eyes, cautious, curious, and found heat within the green depths.

His gaze flicked from my eyes to my lips, and my breath caught. He wanted to kiss me; I wanted that and more.

Slowly, I leaned in, and his fingers lifted my chin, bringing my lips to meet his.

I melted into him, letting the heat of his breath and my attraction to him wash over me.

As we kissed, his fingers trailed down my chin, down

my neck, to my cleavage. My nipples peaked, familiar with his touch, begging to feel it again.

"Come to my room," he breathed against my lips, his voice husky. "I want to be able to fuck you the right way."

My chest heaved at his words, and I stood, all parts of my body forgotten except for the heat between my thighs and the tenderness of my breasts.

He walked behind me toward his bedroom, pulling down on my dress sleeve to nip at the bare skin of my shoulder.

I shivered as I reached his room and turned to flick the lights off.

He stopped, breaking from me, and flicked them back on. "I want to see you, Birdie Melrose. Every single inch."

Even in my dress, I felt more exposed than ever before. Did he really want to see *everything* in the light?

Before I could disagree, his fingers were toying with the hem of my dress, lifting it, pulling until I stood before him in a skimpy bra and thong.

But he didn't shy away at the cellulite on my thighs or the expanse of my stomach that hung lower than I'd like.

No, he looked at me in awe. "You are the sexiest woman I've ever seen." His words, the rawness behind them, made tears prick my eyes, because I could tell how much he meant them.

And because it made me feel beautiful. Accepted in a way no one else had ever accepted me before.

He took me in a kiss, his hands exploring the bare skin

of my back, cupping my breasts through the lace, rubbing at the sensitive part of my sex and soaking my panties through.

I wanted to feel him closer, not the fabric of his shirt, and I worked the buttons loose, kissing him all the while. When the shirt was finally free, he ripped it away from his arms, and now we were closer than before.

The smooth, rippled skin of his stomach, the crisp feel of his chest hair, and the firmness of his erection pressed against me, hard and soft meeting in the sexiest of ways.

"You turn me on, Cohen Bardot." I reached for his pants, unbuttoning them and releasing his erection. It tugged against his underwear, a dark spot already forming.

I had to see him. Had to feel him.

I reached for his dick, pulling back at his waistband, but he gripped my wrists, taking my arms over my head and walking me backwards before flattening me on the bed.

My lips parted to argue, but he captured my mouth with his own, kissing me breathless, then moving down to bite back the sheer fabric of my bra and take my nipples in his mouth, one at a time, licking and nipping and tugging until need rose within me so strong I was ready to beg if I had to.

Holding my wrists above my head with one hand of his own, he reached down and tugged the fabric of my panties aside, running his fingers along my crease, looping a slow circle around my clit and sliding a long middle finger into my sex.

He pulled it out, glistening wet, and slipped it into his mouth, sucking my wetness off of him, and moaned. "God, you taste good, Birdie."

I moaned in return underneath him. "Cohen, please."

"Once we do this," he said, his eyes searching mine, "there's no going back."

But I didn't want to go back. Not now and not ever. I moaned, writhing underneath his straddle on me. "Cohen, please. I want you."

43

COHEN

Her words were music to my ears and fucking magic to my cock. I smirked at her. "That's better. Now take off your bra."

I let go of her hands, and she pushed herself up to reach for her bra, but stopped. "You first."

My smirk grew into a grin. "Excuse me?"

"You first," she repeated, glancing at my dick where it pressed against my underwear. "I want to see it."

My girl was a fucking goddess. I pushed myself off the bed, taking my jeans off the rest of the way first, and turned to the side, showing my cock tented against my underwear. "You do this to me, Birdie."

She wet her lips, moving toward me. Close enough now, she reached for my underwear and pulled, freeing my cock, and god, was it begging to be freed. Her eyes stayed on my veiny length for a long moment, and I saw her throat move with her swallow.

It was so fucking hot.

She put her hands on my hips and brought her lips to the pink tip, kissing it, and slowly bringing me into her mouth. Velvety smooth, wet, and tight.

I groaned, fisting my hand in her hair, careful not to pull her deeper than she wanted to go.

Her tongue flicked my tip, and I doubled over with a grunt, trying to control myself. "You are so hot, Birdie."

She rewarded me by taking me deeper, letting my shaft fill her mouth, my tip press against the back of her throat. I dropped my head back, gazing toward the ceiling but seeing stars instead. If she kept this up, I'd come before I ever had a chance to feel her hole.

I pulled my hips away, taking my dick away from her mouth, and pushed her down onto my bed, covering her body with hot kisses. Birdie was insecure about her body, trying to cover up her stomach, the folds of flesh at her hips, but I wanted it all. She was pillowy soft and buttery smooth, and her body was everything I needed and wanted.

Unable to stop myself, I hooked a finger through her panties and tugged until the seams ripped and the fabric fell away, leaving nothing between her and me. If she wanted new panties, I'd buy them, just to fucking see her like this.

"Are you on the pill?" I huffed in her ear. "I want to fuck you like I want."

"Yes," she said, begged. "Fuck me." She spread her legs, and my tip pressed against her slick entrance.

Her hold was so fucking tight, so fucking perfect, it had to stretch around my girth. Just like in our dirty texts, I slowly pressed into her, letting her feel every single inch. And once I was all the way inside, I flexed.

Birdie cried out in pleasure. "Cohen!"

"This is just the start," I promised, whispering into her ear. I wanted her to feel good. So fucking good she would never look at another man, because Birdie was mine. And fuck, I was hers.

She tightened around my cock, and I rolled my hips slowly, rhythmically, pushing deeper inside until we couldn't get any closer. Until she tightened on my cock and I pulled back, giving her a moment of reprieve before doing it all over again.

Her nails dug into my shoulders, sliced into my back, giving me the best pain. Her body was beautiful underneath mine. *She* was beautiful. I looked in her eyes, those pretty blues. "I love your body," I said. "So soft." I dipped my head down and kissed her neck. "So sexy." I moved my mouth, biting and sucking and teasing until she writhed underneath me, moaning.

"I'm going to come," she gasped.

"Not yet," I ordered, pulling out.

She bit her lip, eyes shining. "Cohen, please."

"Together," I said. We'd started this together, and I wanted us to see how high we could go, together.

My brave, sexy girl nodded, and I leaned forward, placing my hands on either side of her head. Her wild blond curls tickled my wrists, and her breath puffed against my chest before I pushed inside her again, filling her to the brim.

"On the count of five," I said. "And don't you dare come before."

She bit her bottom lip, quivering around me.

"Five," I said, pumping slowly.

She turned and bit my forearm, barely holding on. That made two of us.

"Four," I commanded, moving faster, slamming into her.

Her legs shook around me.

"Three."

She let out a scream.

"Two, damn it. Not yet," I said to both of us, slamming into her again.

Then I lowered my mouth to hers, covered it with my own. "One."

She screamed into my kiss, falling apart around my cock, milking my come as we shuddered with wave after wave, her vagina pulling me deeper and deeper inside, milking me for everything I had and more.

I pumped until the waves of our orgasms faded to aftershocks. And once I was sure my girl was finished, I slowly rolled aside, holding her tight. Birdie was everything, everything and more. I kissed her perfect lips, and she kissed me back, her soft fingers grazing the back of my neck and into my hair.

I wasn't sure how long we lay there—minutes, hours maybe with her twisting her fingers through my hair and me holding her body against mine.

It was heaven, pure fucking bliss.

Until I heard the sound of a key in a deadbolt.

44

BIRDIE

Confession: I like pink.

Cohen jumped out of bed, faster than I'd ever seen another human move.

"Who is it?" I hissed.

"Ollie!"

My eyes widened, and I got out of bed, hurrying to throw on my dress and what was left of my underwear. Ollie seeing us together would be the end of everything, especially my job.

"Get in the closet," Cohen whispered. "I'll tell you when you can go."

I grabbed my sandals and my purse and ran to the closet, trying to stifle my breathing and stay as quiet as possible.

I couldn't believe this was how today was ending. That I was hiding in a closet like the other woman. But then again, wasn't this what we'd signed up for? Wasn't this all supposed to stay a secret?

Through the door, I could hear dishes quickly being put away. Soft voices. Footsteps in the hallway, a bathroom door opening.

I closed my eyes, shaking my head. This was so humiliating. I wanted to get out of here as soon as possible and then find my own place even sooner than that. Then Cohen could come over and we wouldn't have to worry about interruptions or anyone catching us. I could still feel his cum sliding out of me, for Christ's sake.

There were voices, laughs, and then I heard the front door open again. Soon after, the closet door opened, and Cohen took me into his arms.

"I'm so sorry about that," he said, kissing the top of my head.

For some reason, I felt like crying, but I blinked and shook my head. "We lost track of time. It's no big deal."

"You know I had an amazing time." He stepped back, his hands on my shoulders. He was dressed in sweats and a T-shirt now and sitting in a bed I'd only slept in once before. "I wish you could stay."

I managed a smile. "The closet probably wouldn't be comfortable overnight."

He chuckled and ran the pad of his thumb over my

cheek. "He just came home early this weekend. He'll be here until Friday. Can you come over after work?"

I smiled and nodded, trying to ignore how long just six days away from Cohen felt. "I need to be at the football game that night to take tickets, but I can come after." I bent and slipped on my sandals, then stood to face him. We both knew it was time for me to go. Accepting that fact—that was another story. "Am I safe to leave?"

"Ollie went to get us a snack from the drive-through." Standing again, he slipped an arm around my waist, pulling me closer until he could place a soft kiss on my lips. "Someday I'll be able to take you out. And you'll be able to stay the night. And I'll parade you around like the queen you are."

Smiling, I kissed him back. "I'll look forward to that." I hoped that day would come, but I knew better than planning on happily ever after. All I had with Cohen was the best night of my life and a dream.

As I pulled out of the apartment's parking garage, I realized I didn't feel like going home right away. So instead, I went to the store Cohen had taken me to the first night we met. The thought of going back to work in boring black was impossible when Cohen had shown me every color of the rainbow.

I walked down the aisles of clothing, casually combing through the larger straight sizes and smaller plus sizes until I found a couple of brightly colored dresses and even a hot-pink pencil skirt.

None of the teachers at the Academy dressed so colorfully, but maybe it was time I started. Something Cohen had said that first night stood out to me. He'd said that by dressing how I chose I would wordlessly give students permission to be themselves.

But maybe I needed to give myself that permission as well.

45

BIRDIE

Confession: I fall...fast.

Walking into school on Monday in my new clothes, I felt like a new woman. I could still feel the effects of Cohen on my body. The tender spots on my hips where he'd grabbed me tight. The way any little thing could send my mind back to thinking of him.

For the first time in a long time, I felt giddy, infatuated, whatever this was, and I couldn't get enough.

On my way to get coffee, one of the popular girls, Olivia Nelson, greeted me. "Nice skirt, Ms. M. I need some sunglasses with you around."

I knew she was making fun of me, and my first instinct was to shy away. To make some self-deprecating joke. But then I noticed Sierra Cook a few lockers down and thought of her being brave enough to make her own choices after high school. I could wear a skirt.

"Thanks, Liv!" I said cheerily, doing a half turn. "Isn't it so cute? And stretchy too."

She blinked, shocked at my response no doubt, and I continued walking to the teachers' lounge, running right into Headmaster Bradford.

His eyes traveled my outfit, and he swallowed. "Ms. Melrose, may I speak with you?"

"Of course." I lifted my chin, refusing to look away, even though I could feel the eyes of other teachers in the room on me.

I followed the headmaster to his office—one with heavy wooden furniture, stacks of gilded tomes, and even a taxidermized bear.

The bell rang as he shut the door behind us. Ignoring it, he said, "Do you have a copy of the Emerson Academy handbook?"

My eyebrows drew together. "Yes."

"And have you referred to the dress code section recently?"

"Not recently, no, but my skirt is below my knees. And my top covers my shoulders and isn't made of cotton material."

He pressed his lips together, making his short mustache flatten. Then he licked the tip of his finger and flipped to a page in the handbook. "All staff are required to dress business professional. For men, slacks, dress shirts, and ties, jacket optional. For women, close-toed loafers or heels, dresses or skirts knee length or longer, or full-length pants, as well as professional tops."

"Yes," I said. "I'm not sure how I'm violating the dress code?"

He looked pointedly at my skirt. "Professionalism not only includes pieces, but prints and colors as well."

I raised my eyebrows, already feeling hot behind my ears. "Viewing pink as unprofessional comes across as misogynistic, Headmaster. I'm sure that isn't the impression you'd like to make with your staff, students, or parents."

For the first time ever, Headmaster Bradford looked surprised, but he quickly gathered himself. "Please, keep professionalism in mind when building your wardrobe. That is all."

I walked out of his office, knowing, at least for now, I had won. The high carried me through the week, that and the texts Cohen sent me. On Monday, he showed me a picture of a cardinal that had landed in a tree outside the bar. On Tuesday, he sent money to my Venmo and told me to get a coffee on him. Wednesday, he asked for a selfie because he missed my smile, and by Thursday, my thoughts were consumed with how much I longed to see him again.

So much so that I got distracted meandering the halls between classes and was now late getting back to my office. I needed to make a call to a parent, and then I had some paperwork to complete after that.

I picked up the pace, my kitten heels clicking softly on the tile as I walked toward my office through the empty halls.

One student stepped out of a classroom, and I said, "Do you have your hall pass, sweetie?"

She smiled and held up a hall pass of the teacher's making.

"Great." I wished her a good day and turned a corner to take a shortcut through my office. I had to walk through the gym and past some sporting goods storage closets, but the gym teacher wasn't around to yell at me for taking my heels on the hardwood.

Something to my left rattled inside a closet, and I nearly jumped out of my skin. I took a few steps away from the doors, wondering if something had shifted inside, and then I heard another rattle.

Someone, or something, was inside there.

I had my keys, but just in case it was Coach looking for some gear, I knocked on the door. "Anyone in there?"

No voices came.

I worried an animal had somehow gotten into the building. I almost chickened out and left to fetch the custodian, but decided I was a strong, independent woman. Besides, if there was a racoon in there, it would probably run away, not jump for my face like in a slapstick comedy movie.

Taking a deep breath, I put my key in the knob, twisted, and stepped back, wincing in case there was, in fact, a raccoon inside.

Instead, I found something much more surprising.

Ollie Bardot and Ryde Alexander.

Their faces were red, their lips pink, and Ollie's curly hair was wilder than usual.

As they stammered out excuses, what had really been happening became quite clear.

I cleared my throat, trying to catch my own bearings. "Do either of you have a hall pass?"

They looked at each other and then shook their heads.

"Come with me," I said.

The walk to my office felt longer than ever. And they weren't in trouble. Plenty of kids skipped class, but both of them had fairly good attendance records. No, I needed to talk to them about safety—with their bodies and their hearts.

We reached my office, and I turned to the boys. "Ryde, will you wait in the hallway, please?"

Silently, he sat on the bench while Ollie followed me inside.

His eyes were on Ralphie, and Ralphie seemed to peer back at him with his big black eyes.

"Ollie," I said softly, "does this have anything to do with why your grades have been suffering?"

Ollie didn't quite meet my eyes. But he nodded enough to know the answer. "Are you going to tell my parents?" he asked. "Or Ryde's? His family doesn't know..."

"Oh, Ollie." I covered my chest with my hand, shaking my head slightly. I took a deep breath and spoke softly. "As it's a first-time offense, I'll let you both off with a warning." He turned toward the door, but I said, "Wait. I know how difficult this must be for you."

"Do you?" He turned on me, his eyes red-rimmed. "Do you know how hard it is to be gay in a small school where the majority of the student population is Christian? Do you know how hard it is for your sexual orientation to be an insult or the butt of a joke?"

His words had a bite behind them, but I knew the sting wasn't for me. "I don't," I said gently. "But I know how hard it is not to be free to date who you want to date." I pressed my lips together, shaking my head. "I wouldn't wish that on anyone."

"Me neither," he said.

My lips tugged into a shadow of a smile. "Why don't you get back to class? I'm assuming fourth-hour wasn't scheduled to take place in a utility closet."

He nodded and walked out the door.

Gathering myself, I took a breath and went to the hall to get Ryde to come into my office. But when I looked at the bench, he was gone.

46

OLLIE

Where the hell was Ryde?

When I walked out of Ms. M's office, he was nowhere to be found, and honestly, it kind of pissed me off. So I was supposed to take whatever consequences we had while he ran off and hid behind his parents' money?

To be fair, it hadn't been that bad. Ms. Melrose had been surprisingly cool about it. And even though I was terrified my parents would find out I'd been caught skipping class and making out in closets, they wouldn't be mad I'd been with a guy.

Ryde's parents would never be okay with his orientation. It would cost them too much money from Ryde's paycheck. He was going to be an actor—a famous one—and girls would go crazy over him. If they knew he was gay, he'd lose the fans who wanted to be with him.

I tried to point out to him that there were plenty of queer people who would love him, but gay guys weren't half the population like women were.

So we'd been sneaking around. Making out in closets and staying after school on Monday afternoons when my dad thought I was at botany club.

That was, until today.

On the way to class, I made sure no one was around and got out my phone to send him a text.

Ollie: Are you okay?

I looked at the screen for a moment...no response. Maybe he was already back in class.

Tucking my phone back in my bag, I went back to the English room. We were reading *To Kill a Mockingbird* out loud for the hour.

Making out in a closet had seemed like a much better use of my time. You know, until we got caught.

When I slipped back into English class, I made an excuse about needing to see the nurse and got back into my seat. For the rest of the hour and every hour until the final bell, I was on edge, waiting to see what Ryde would say.

As usual, I waited in the bathroom until most of the students cleared out, either going to a sports practice, meeting for a club, or heading home. After about fifteen minutes of scrolling social media and wondering why Ryde hadn't texted me, I left the bathroom and went to the A/V room.

It was technically Mr. Davis's office, but he was always gone by this time. The room made a perfect place to pass the time, crouched amongst the stacks of VHS tapes and recording equipment.

But today when I walked into the room, Ryde wasn't there.

I'd had a feeling he wouldn't show, but having my fears confirmed was the worst.

I looked around, wondering what to do. My dad wouldn't be here to pick me up for another two hours. I could call him and say botany club let out early...

But the thought of doing that just pissed me off more. Ryde was being a coward. He hadn't even asked how I was after being caught. This on and off was driving me insane, and we needed to figure it out.

I got my phone out of my pocket and dialed his number. It rang so long I thought he was going to screen my call. But then his voice came on the phone, and I swore my heart relaxed just at the sound.

"Ollie, I'm not going to make it today," he said with a sigh. Like he was already tired of talking to me and entertaining my emotions.

Half fueled by rage and half by desperation, I said, "Like hell you aren't."

"Excuse me?"

"Where are you?"

"I'm in my car. I thought about coming in, but I just... I just can't."

"Then I'll come to you. The least you could do is give me a ride home." My words came out a lot more confident than I felt. I just hoped like hell he'd wait long enough for me to get there and convince him this was worth it. That we were worth it.

I gripped my phone tightly in my hand as I left the A/V room. There was hardly anyone in the hallway as I walked outside, and eventually, I walked down the school's front steps, craning my neck to check the parking lot.

At the sight of Ryde's car, my shoulders relaxed, but that movement was too much, and I toppled down the last several steps, banging my elbow and then my shoulder hard on the concrete.

"Shit," I muttered, rolling on my back and holding my elbow in my hand. I could feel where the fabric of my blazer had ripped. But my pride hurt even more. Had anyone seen me?

A car door slamming shut and feet pounding on the sidewalk confirmed they had.

Before I could sit up all the way, Ryde was at my side, helping me to a seated position.

"Shit, Ollie," he said, taking my elbow in his hands. "Are you okay?" His hazel eyes intensified at the sight of my arm. "You're already bleeding."

"I was bleeding before I fell," I muttered.

Letting go of my arm, he said, "What does that mean?"

"It means you're hurting me," I said, tears stinging my

eyes. Maybe from the pain of falling down the stairs. Maybe from the pain of falling for Ryde. "One second you're happy to have me and the next you're nowhere to be seen, and I swear I have fucking whiplash from it all!" I hissed.

Ryde still looked around, making sure no one could hear us. I was so sick of the secrets. Tired of the lies.

He gently tipped up my chin with his bent fingers. "I'm not as brave as you are, Ollie."

I blinked, sending a tear falling over my cheek. "I'm not that brave. I just love you."

Ryde's lips parted at what I'd told him. It was the first time saying the words out loud, but I meant them. I knew they were the truth. When he'd broken things off between us last time, I'd fallen apart. Why wasn't I good enough for him to love me out loud? Why wasn't I worth the risk?

"Ollie..."

I braced myself for the worst. That he didn't love me back. Or that he did, and it still wasn't enough, just like it hadn't been enough for my parents.

Ryde sat beside me, a regretful look on his handsome face. I'd never seen someone who looked like him—with shaggy blonde hair that got lighter at the tips. Or golden skin so perfectly tan. And his eyes. They held me, just like they always did. "I do love you."

The words were exactly what I'd wanted to hear, so why was I crying harder now? "Why do you look so upset about it?"

"I didn't want to love you," he said. "But I do. And you know why I can't be open about it. But when it's just the two of us...it's perfect."

I looked away from him. I was tired of the secrets. But was I willing to give him up?

"Come on," Ryde said. "Let's get out of here."

He helped me up and walked with me to his car. I got in, resting my arm on the center console. As he drove away from the school, our pinkies touched. It wasn't much—no one could see—but it was enough. For now.

47

BIRDIE

Confession: I'm keeping a secret from Cohen.

I thought all day about how to tell Cohen what I'd discovered without betraying Ollie and Ryde's privacy.

I decided to let it rest until Friday. Cohen had asked that I come over after the game, no matter how late it was. A tingle of excitement worked its way through me at the thought of spending an entire weekend with Cohen, knowing we'd likely be in his apartment the whole time as to protect our privacy.

After I finished selling tickets at the game, I got in my car and drove to his apartment. There was an overnight bag in my car, but I left it there so I wouldn't seem too presumptuous. I'd be just as happy to have an hour with Cohen as I would to have a weekend.

When I reached his door, I heard the now familiar sound of indie music and smiled to myself. So much had changed since I first saw his apartment. I liked it as much as I had then, but I liked the man who lived here so much more.

Seconds after I rang the doorbell, he appeared at the door holding a bottle of wine and two glasses. "Have you ever had Cupcake wine?" he asked as I stepped inside.

I grinned. This had to be fate. "Mara and I drink it all the time."

"I should have known." He chuckled, setting the glasses on his island countertop. "It's not very expensive, but it's so good. One of my bartenders turned me on to it."

"Sounds like they need a raise," I said, taking the glass from him

"Right?" he said. "I'm kind of embarrassed to admit I drink it."

"Look at that. Misogyny working against men?"

With a laugh, he said, "True. I should be drinking whiskey neat, right?"

"Exactly." I took another sip.

He reached out a fingertip and adjusted a curl on my shoulder. "If you haven't noticed, I like sweet things."

My cheeks warmed, and I smiled up at him. "Thank you."

"Of course." He stepped back and began walking to his fridge. "Are you hungry? I have some leftovers from supper, but I could order in too."

"Can you stop being so nice?"

He chuckled. "I think it's a habit from being a parent. Like even if you can't fix a broken heart, at least you can make sure they have good food."

My heart warmed. "Speaking of Ollie..." I glanced to his couch. "Can we sit down?"

A look of concern crossed his features. "Sure. What's going on?"

I went to the couch with my wine glass and sat with my legs tucked under me. "I figured out why Ollie has been upset."

Cohen's eyes widened, and he leaned forward as if to hear me better. "What is it?"

"He's been seeing a boy at school who, I think, is even more private about his sexuality than Ollie is."

"Wow." Cohen let out a breath and rubbed his chin. "Who is it?"

I frowned. "I can't say. Ollie also asked me to keep his identity private."

"I guess it doesn't matter who so much as the fact that Ollie's been heartbroken all this time and hasn't felt like he could tell us." Cohen shook his head, blinking quickly. "Poor Ollie."

The guilt Cohen so clearly felt made my heart ache for him. I reached out and put a hand on his wrist. "I think

Ollie was more worried about protecting this other boy than protecting himself."

Cohen looked up at me, then stood, pacing back and forth in front of me.

Worry immediately flooded me. Was Cohen mad I hadn't revealed the other student's identity? "Cohen, I'm so sorry."

He paused, turning toward me, looking genuinely confused. "For what?"

"I just..." I stood, setting my glass on the coffee table. "I wanted to help, but I feel like this answer is so messy."

He cupped my cheek with his hand. "Birdie... If parenthood, marriage, divorce has taught me anything, it's that *life* is messy." He ran his thumb over my cheekbone. "I used to want to run away from it all, but now I know better."

I looked into his green eyes, searching for the answer in the depths. When I couldn't find it, I asked, "What do you want now?"

He smiled, then dropped a gentle kiss on my lips. "Someone to sit with me in the mess."

His answer caught me off guard, and I smiled. "No one's more acquainted with messiness than I am."

Taking me hand, he pulled me onto his lap on the couch. My back rested against his chest, and the rise and fall of his breaths calmed me in a way I hadn't felt for a very long time.

"What do you mean?" he asked, running his fingers lightly over my forearm.

I leaned back against his shoulder, looking at the ceiling. "I had to leave my place because my boyfriend left me, and I didn't have enough time to find another apartment. So I'm staying with my best friend, who doesn't even have a high school degree and makes more than I ever will. Oh, and did I mention my boyfriend was actually my fiancé?"

"Oof," he said. "That hurts."

"On a multitude of levels."

"Well, if it makes you feel any better, I was the one who blew my marriage."

I twisted to look at him. Cohen was so even-keeled and kind. Why wouldn't his wife want to stay with him? "What do you mean?"

"Our relationship was always...more effort because we got married out of obligation instead of love. Keeping things going was hard under the best of circumstances, but starting the bar made it even more challenging. I focused more on my business than I did on her because I didn't want her parents to keep funding our lifestyle."

I raised my eyebrows.

"They paid for Ollie to go to the Academy, they put the down payment on our house, her mom would take her shopping during the week. And there were always these comments, like I wasn't enough for their daughter." He shook his head. "So I tried to be enough in all the wrong ways. And then she found someone who actually was."

His hand had stalled on my arm, so I held it, lacing my fingers through his.

"Messy," I said.

He nodded. "But without it, I wouldn't get the beautiful moments either. Ollie. The bar." He squeezed my hand. "You."

My heart warmed, and I twisted, kissing him with everything I felt but couldn't find the words to say.

Our embrace deepened, his hands tangling in my curls and my fingers fisting in his shirt until there was too much between us to let it go any longer.

He peeled off my Emerson Academy shirt, baring my chest to him, and looked at me in awe, loving my body with his eyes. "I'm never going to get used to how beautiful you are," he said, almost to himself.

I would never get used to how beautiful he made me feel. I closed the gap between us, kissing his lips where sweet words always seemed to flow, and reached down to unbutton his jeans. All of these feelings, I wanted to pour them out, to show this man how much I absolutely adored him.

Once his jeans were off, I slid from his lap, kneeling before him on the floor and coming closer to his hard, veiny length.

"Birdie, you don't have to," he said.

"But I want to." Before he could argue, I took him in

my mouth, swirling my tongue around the tip, savoring each twitch of his hips and the deep moans emanating from him. Sucking gently, I pulled him deeper in my mouth, sliding my lips and tongue over the length of his cock.

It was too long to take all the way in, so I used my hands to cup his heavy sack, gently pulling and kneading until he moaned again.

"Fuck, Birdie."

It was all the encouragement I needed to take him that much deeper, all the way to the back of my throat until my lips rested near the base of his shaft, and I held still until he writhed against my touch.

"I'm going to fucking come," he gritted out.

All I could think was, good.

I worked my mouth back and forth, faster and faster, until he said, "Let me pull out."

I clamped my mouth around him, grabbing his hips, and sucked him until his dick throbbed and pulsed.

"Birdie," he moaned... and then he released.

I swallowed fast until every drop was gone, ready to collapse over his lap, but he took me in his arms instead, held me close, and kissed me over and over again.

48

COHEN

God, this woman was beautiful. Especially when she was sleeping with her curly hair messy around her face and her full lips parted.

Ever since she'd walked into my bar, I'd been captivated by her, but every second I spent with her made me like her more. I knew she was worried about her job, but I wished I could tell her I'd take care of her. That she didn't need to worry about a place to live or food to eat or anything at all. But it was too soon, and the last thing I wanted to do was scare her away.

Time would make all the difference, and as far as I was concerned, she could have all of mine.

I wanted to take her out and show her to the world, but I had a different idea instead. I kissed her awake, placing my lips on her shoulder, her chin, her cheek. "What do you think of birdwatching?" I asked her.

She curled closer into me, her body so so soft. "I love that idea," she said in that sweet voice of hers. "But are you worried someone will see us?"

"There's a trail at Emerson Trails that no one ever goes on. I honestly think they've forgotten to maintain it at this point."

Her blue eyes brightened. "Yeah?"

I nodded. "I even got a couple pairs of binoculars."

"You did that for me?" A smile formed on her lips.

Would it be bad to admit I'd bought binoculars on Amazon moments after she'd told me she liked birdwatching, just so I wouldn't forget? "Of course," I said instead.

"Let me get ready and then we can go," she replied. The moment her body left mine, I felt cold, but I knew it wouldn't be long before I was holding her hand again. Going a moment without touching her felt like too long.

I got dressed and did my hair, and then we went down to my car. As soon as I had the car out of the parking garage, I took her hand in mine. Her hands were so soft, aside from the silver ring she wore stamped with birds in flight. Sometimes she spun it around her finger, usually when she was nervous, sometimes when she was in thought.

We stopped at a drive-through for a quick breakfast and coffee and then continued toward our destination.

"How did you find out about this trail?" she asked.

"I run in the mornings, and one time I took a wrong turn." I shrugged. "Happy accident. But last time I was running, I noticed a few woodpeckers and even an owl. I'm not sure what kind it was, but I thought maybe you would know."

Her eyes lit up just like I'd hoped they would. "I'm your gal." She gestured her free thumb toward her chest, and damn, if I hadn't been driving, I would have let myself get way more distracted by her full tits and what I could do with them to make her scream my name.

I shifted, hoping to hide the way my body reacted so easily. I was like a fucking teenager, tenting my pants at even the hint of a breeze.

Luckily, the trails weren't too far from my apartment—one of the reasons I'd chosen the place—and I adjusted myself on my side of the car.

She got out and said, "You're right. I didn't even realize this was here. You can't see the turnoff through all the trees."

"Exactly," I said, walking her way. She easily walked along my side, and I slipped my arm around her waist, squeezing her lush hips toward me.

Just as easy as breathing, she tilted her beautiful face toward me, and I bent to kiss those luscious lips.

We walked onto the trail, barely wide enough for us to walk side by side, and the trees enveloped us in shade and silence. We couldn't even hear cars on the road once we got a little ways down the trail.

"What do you see?" I asked her.

"Birdwatching is a misnomer," she said. "In my opinion, it all starts with bird hearing." She paused, turning toward me and putting her arms around my waist.

I felt like fucking Superman with her holding onto me like that. I put my arms around her too, listening to the quiet of the trees around us. Soon, a small twitter came, and Birdie pointed in the direction the sound had come from. She lifted her binoculars and whispered, "Butterbutt."

I snorted. "What did you just call me?"

She rolled her eyes, laughing. "That's what the bird's called." She pointed to a spot midway up a tall sycamore.

I followed her finger with the binoculars and found a bird with a patch of yellow on its rump. Butterbutt. That name was adorable. I wanted to tell Ollie about it. "I see it," I said.

"Nice," she replied.

I glanced sideways to see her looking at it, a small smile on her pink lips. All her lipstick was long gone by now, but I loved the natural color of her mouth and the flush that so easily came to her cheeks.

The knobbly sound of a woodpecker came above the Butterbutt's song, and I turned my binoculars that direction. I spotted it with my eye first, then zeroed in on it, pointing for Birdie to follow.

"Do you ever wonder if they get headaches?" she said.

I laughed. "What?"

"I mean, banging their beaks against wood all day can't be comfortable."

"I never thought about it," I said, smiling and shaking my head. "But you're probably right. Think we should toss him some aspirin?"

She chuckled. "A little birdy aspirin for Mr. Woodpecker? I need to ask the vet at Ralphie's next checkup."

The thought of her taking her white dove to the vet like a doting parent made my heart want to burst out of my chest, and I looked away, searching for another bird. "Want to walk farther?"

"Sure," she said.

We walked, hand in hand, her walking ahead when the trail narrowed. We spotted a few birds she said were pretty common, like the California Towhee and the Oak Titmouse. My personal favorite was the California Scrub-Jay with its beautiful blue feathers.

"Stop!" Birdie cried, and I froze mid-step.

She rushed off the trail, kneeling before a small nest of twigs and leaves. I immediately saw what she had—a bald baby bird, its skin still pink, lying beside the nest.

My heart wrenched at it and then the dead sibling just a foot away. "Where's its mom?" I looked around, as if I could spot its parent. Obviously, its mother was nowhere to be seen.

Birdie shook her head. "I have no idea." She looked around, her eyes darting all over the ground.

"What do you need?" I asked.

"Something soft so I can carry it. Do you see anything?"

I undid my top button and slipped my shirt over my head, stripping down to my plain white undershirt. In the back of my mind, I was glad I had just bought a new pack, but the thought quickly went away as I saw how gently Birdie took the little fledgling into the shirt.

Her eyes were wide with worry as she stood, holding the bird in my shirt close to her chest.

"Let's go," I said, even though she was already walking toward the car. She was a woman on a mission, and I had to lengthen my stride just to keep up.

We made it to the small dirt parking lot in a fourth of the time it had taken us to walk on the trail, and I held the door open for her so she could carefully slide inside. I even reached across her, doing the belt so she didn't have to jostle the baby.

As soon as I got in, she said, "Head toward LA. There's a vet that specializes in birds between here and there."

I nodded, shifting the car into gear and taking off down the road. In Birdie's lap, the little bird cheeped softly, and she cooed to it, talking so gently as if even her words could cause it to break.

"Hey, little guy," she whispered. "I know it's so scary to fall out of your nest and be away from your mommy. Cohen and I are taking you to the best of the best. Dr.

Needermeier is going to take amazing care of you and get you back in the forest in no time. I promise."

This woman was amazing. I couldn't believe anyone had ever let her go. I promised myself I'd do my best to keep her as I quickly took the roads toward LA.

She told me which exit to take off the freeway, then guided me down city roads until we approached an animal hospital.

I wanted to help her out, but before I could even get to her side of the car, she was out and hustling toward the building.

The second we were inside, she greeted the receptionist by name and said, "We have a rescue."

Judging by the way everyone jumped to action, I realized this wasn't a new experience for any of them. My shoulders instantly relaxed as the veterinary technician promised Birdie they would care for it well and take it to the animal rescue as soon as its medical needs had been cared for.

Birdie transferred the bundle to the vet tech and looked at me. "Is it okay if they keep your shirt?"

All this worry for saving a bird and she was thinking of me? "Of course," I said.

The vet tech turned to walk away, and Birdie said, "Wait, can I say goodbye?"

Of course she wanted to say goodbye.

She leaned over the small bundle and whispered softly to the bird, her eyes shining with tears.

I was utterly convinced Birdie put every other human to shame. I wasn't sure what I would have done if I'd happened across the bird on my own, but I knew it wouldn't have been greeted with a tenth of the love Birdie had shown it in the limited time we had with it.

I leaned over Birdie's shoulder, looking at the pink bird, and rubbed her back. "You're going to do great, little guy," I promised. "Birdie found you for a reason." Just like me.

49

BIRDIE

Confession: All future boyfriends require Grandpa's approval.

Sunday morning, I woke up in bed next to him, fully naked and fully happy. His arm curled around my waist and his chin nuzzled into my shoulder blade, and I felt the steady rhythm of his breath play over my skin.

Yesterday had been a bigger day than either of us expected, but I'd loved the way he'd taken me seriously as we worked to save the bird. He could have easily dismissed it as a hopeless cause or gone along with it all just to appease me, but I'd seen it in his eyes. He'd truly cared, and that mattered to me more than he'd ever know.

My eyes caught paper on his nightstand, and I carefully leaned forward, curious what he'd been reading. I paged the top sheet over and began reading...

It was Emerson Academy's bylaws, but with revisions and a speech to present to the school board.

My lips parted. Cohen was trying to change the school's rules, just so he could be with me. It was possibly one of the sweetest things someone had ever done for me.

Slowly, I rolled over in his arms, kissing him awake.

He smiled into the kiss and in that delectably sexy morning voice said, "Morning, babe."

Babe. I could have melted right then. "Good morning," I sighed, the happiest I'd been since I couldn't remember when.

"How'd you sleep?" he asked, eyes still closed.

I took in the peacefulness of his expression, the dark fringe of eyelashes and the small specks of gray in his morning scruff. "Really well. For how long I did sleep."

He chuckled, blinking his eyes open. "It's hard to keep my hands off you." He squeezed one of my ass cheeks, and I giggled.

"I can tell."

Kissing me again, he said, "I wish I could take you out to breakfast."

I bit my lip. "Why not?"

His smile was brighter than the sunlight filtering into the room. "You tell me."

I turned in his arms, facing him and trailing my fingers up his muscular arm. "I thought maybe... you could meet my grandparents? There's a back room at Waldo's Diner."

"I'd love to." He kissed my hand, then nipped at my knuckle. His eyes were hot on mine, and I felt his erection growing harder by the second.

My stomach swooped, and I was seconds away from begging him to take me again. "What happened to breakfast?"

"Baby, you're better than any meal."

I smiled, then kissed him again. "You're more sugary than syrup, Cohen Bardot."

"I think that's you." His kissed my cheeks and then the tip of my nose.

I smiled, closing my eyes, then blinking them open again. "Is it okay if I shower before we go? Curly hair's a little crazy without some help."

He grinned. "Ollie's told me that a time or two. Can I get you anything while you shower?"

I bit my lip. "I brought a bag just in case I stayed. It's in my car."

"In case?"

I smiled. "I didn't want to be too clingy. Or eager."

"I'd say you were eager last night." He gave me a teasing wink.

My cheeks flushed, and I gently hit his shoulder. "If I remember right, you enjoyed it."

"Oh I did." He pulled me closer, nipping at my earlobe.

"Okay." I disengaged, standing and wrapping a sheet around myself before he could get any more ideas that would keep us in bed all day. "You grab my bag from my car, and I'll shower."

"Fine," he groaned.

With a smile, I shed the sheet, letting him see my curves in all their rolled and dimpled glory, then walked to his bathroom and shut the door, locking it behind me.

He tried to twist the knob, then laughed. "You're sneaky."

"Save it for later," I retorted and twisted the knob for the water. Since I had the water to cover the sound, I sat down and went to the bathroom. Everyone pooped, but that didn't mean he needed to know I was doing it in his toilet.

When I finished, I flushed and got into the shower. Thankfully, there was curl product in there for Ollie's hair. At least, I hoped it was Ollie's hair. I tried not to think about it too much as I put a bit on my hands and worked it through my curls.

The water felt amazing on my body, cleansing away sweat and more from the night before. Usually in the shower, I thought through the day before, the students I worried about, the things I could have done better in the staff meeting, but now I just thought about Cohen. About possibilities.

If his proposal went through the school board, which it might according to the paragraph he included about other top-tier high schools that allowed parental-teacher relationships, our lives could change. What would it feel like to go out with Cohen? To sit with him at a school play or ride home with him after school?

To live together someday?

I smiled at the thought. It was still too soon, but that didn't keep me from dreaming.

A few knocks sounded on the door, and Cohen called, "I'm holding this bag hostage until I can see that beautiful body of yours."

I giggled. "I'm almost done."

With the product washed out of my hair and steam filling the room, I turned off the water and stepped out of the shower, rubbing a thick towel over my face, then wrapping it around my body.

I walked to his room and found him rolling the sleeves of a shirt. Leaning against the door frame, I said, "You look handsome."

He grinned at me. "Thanks, babe."

I could get used to him calling me babe. "You didn't want to shower?"

Coming closer, he kissed me on the lips. "I'm not washing you off all day."

My cheeks heated, but I smiled and walked to my bag he'd set on my side of the bed.

My side.

I bit my lip to hide how happy that thought made me and pulled out a long-sleeved dress for the day. Now that we were getting later and later into fall, the air had a chill to it. Cohen's eyes were hot on me as I put on one of my lacy bras and underwear, then slipped the dress over my head.

When I met his eyes again, he was smiling at me. "I don't think I'm ever going to get used to how beautiful you are."

"You're sweet," I said.

His smile was genuine. "I try to be."

I used the towel to soak moisture from the ends of my hair and scrunched it with my fingers. The curls would air dry eventually and look pretty good when they did. "Ready to go?"

"That's it?" he said. "It's not going to take another two hours for makeup and wardrobe changes?"

"Ha ha," I said.

"You're amazing me more and more every day." He came to me and kissed me.

I smiled, wrapping my arms around his waist and looked up at him. "Ready?"

"I am now."

50

COHEN

As we drove to the restaurant, she kept one of her hands in mine and the other on her phone. I listened as she spoke to her grandpa. She clearly adored him. And judging by the way she smiled at me as she got off the phone, she adored me too.

"We're good to go," she said.

I grinned at her, happy she was happy. "Anything I should know before I meet him officially?"

She chuckled. "Well, he's very protective of me."

"Why am I more nervous to meet him than your dad?" I asked.

"Because he's the one you need to impress."

I lifted her hand, drawing her knuckles to my lips. "I'll be on my best behavior."

"Just be yourself. He's going to love you."

Did that mean she already did?

When we got to the diner, she showed me where to park around the back, where the servers and cooks always left their cars. She got out and looked around, making sure there wasn't anyone from the school there before hurrying me inside.

I didn't like being her secret. Keeping our love on the down-low, but I reminded myself it wouldn't be forever. I had to believe my case would be good enough to change the rules about staff dating parents. I wouldn't let myself worry otherwise.

Inside the building, I could hear the sounds of the kitchen, but she brought me to a small back room with a table inside. It wasn't the kind of dining tables from the main restaurant, more like those white plastic ones you saw at craft fairs and business meetings. Two of them were pressed together, forming the place I figured we would eat.

"Where are your grandparents?" I asked.

Just then, the door cracked open, and the old man who always sat three booths into the diner came in, holding his wife's hand. They were a cute couple—him with his plaid, pearl-snapped shirt, her with curled white hair and a string of pearls around her neck. When she smiled at me, I could see where Birdie got her grin.

"You must be Cohen," Chester said.

Birdie held on to my arm. "This is him." Her voice radiated pride, and I realized I wasn't her secret. Not where it really mattered.

I extended my hand and said, "It's nice to meet you, sir."

Chester shook my hand. "It's Chester to you." He turned toward his wife. "This is my bride, Karen." The love in his eyes was clear, just as clear as it was between Gayle and Chris.

I liked them both instantly. "It's nice to meet you, Karen," I said.

She took my hand in both of hers. "Don't let us scare you away," she whispered.

Chester batted his hand at her and said, "Let's sit. I'm having Betsy bring back burger baskets. I hope that's okay..." He raised his eyebrows. "Unless you're a vegetarian."

"No—Chester," I said, and at his smile, I had a feeling I'd passed some sort of test. That was good because I could tell this mattered to Birdie, which meant it *really* mattered to me.

"Good," he said. "And how are you around the house?"

"As in cleaning?" I asked.

"Among other things," he said, despite looks from his wife and granddaughter. "Can you fix a pipe? Replace a doorknob? Change the wax seal on a toilet?"

"I used to work in construction," I said simply. "If I don't know how to do something, I'm pretty good at figuring it out."

Even Chester looked impressed at that answer.

"Good," Karen said. "Now can the interrogation stop?"

Chester gave me a wicked grin. "It's only just begun."

Although Chester joked about an interrogation, the next hour was filled with laughter. We talked about business, and he gave me tips on the food service and employee retention side of my business. I referred him to Jonas since Chester's accountant was retiring.

Karen asked me about my son. She and Chester both remembered us coming into the restaurant for milkshakes.

"He was the most adorable boy," Karen said. "With those pretty brown curls and big brown eyes."

I grinned. "He was always the most beautiful thing I'd ever seen. I don't know how he came from me."

She chuckled, her eyes shining. "Our children have a way of surprising us, don't they?"

"Always," I agreed.

Under the table, Birdie gripped my hand, and I knew without a doubt everything was going just as it should.

51

BIRDIE

Confession: My hero writes romance.

Introducing Cohen to my grandparents couldn't have gone better. They adored him—Grandma even pulled me aside after to tell me to bring him by the house sometime. They'd never asked that of Dax, opting to meet at the restaurant instead, and we'd been together for two years.

To celebrate, Cohen and I decided to grab dessert from Seaton Bakery before going to Seaton Pier. Most people from Emerson preferred Brentwood's beaches, so the risk of being seen was pretty low.

He held my hand on the way to the bakery and told me about some of the music that came through the speakers as we drove. Most of the musicians on his playlist had played at his bar one night or another.

"I can introduce you to the bands when they come," he said. "They usually have awesome stories."

The hope in his voice hurt. "When we can be together in public."

He gave me a look. "Academy parents don't go to bars like mine."

I tried to imagine any of the parents I worked with at Collie's, either on the dance floor or drinking a five-dollar draft while eating peanuts. I couldn't. "Good point," I said.

He turned another corner and pulled into the parking lot. "And besides, I don't think we'll have to keep doing this in secret for long."

"Really?" I asked. "Why do you think that?"

Taking both of my hands in his, he looked me in the eyes. "I'm taking the issue to the school board and changing the rule. It's archaic. And frankly, a pain in the ass."

I giggled. "It is. And I saw your speech."

He tilted his head, confused.

"You left it on your bedside table."

"Well then... any notes?"

"It was perfect."

He leaned across the console and gave me a gentle kiss before unbuckling and getting out. Walking into Seaton Bakery this time already felt like home. Gayle greeted us with a smile, and despite the Saturday morning rush, Chris came out to personally say hello.

With our orders in, Cohen and I sat at a small table by the window. I watched people around us eating and enjoying each other.

"You're very observant," Cohen said.

"Says the person observing me," I teased.

"Fair."

I shook my head, smiling at him. "When I was growing up, I was only allowed to be around one kind of people. I was friends with the kids of my parents' friends, and my parents were friends with people who could get them further in life."

"I know the type," Cohen muttered, looking at his clasped hands on the table.

My eyes traced his fingers. There wasn't a hint of his ring anymore—no indentation or tan line. Just a tattoo of an ocean wave on his middle finger. "When did you get that?" I asked.

He glanced down to see what I was referencing, almost as if he had forgotten it. "Seventeen. My mom chased me out of the house with a frying pan, and I decided it was probably time for me to leave."

My heart broke. Cohen didn't open up much about his past, but every time he did, I found myself wanting to hug the sweet man in front of me and the hardened teen he must have been.

"You're sad."

I shook my head. "Only sorry."

"Sometimes it feels like all of that happened to an entirely different person."

"I feel the same way about myself in high school. If I saw myself back then, I wouldn't recognize her."

"Maybe that's a good thing. A snake doesn't look at the skin it shed and see a snake."

Gayle brought coffee and cupcakes to the table and gave Cohen a kiss on the head before walking away.

I smiled between the two of them. "So how did seventeen-year-old Cohen spend his time? You know, other than getting tattoos."

He chuckled. "I spent a lot of time at the beach. Knew a guy who ran the surf shop and he always let me borrow boards on slow days."

"Really?" I hardly pictured Cohen as a surfer boy, but I liked the idea.

"Oh yeah. And sometimes a guy at the pier would fish with me, and we'd take them back to his house. If I cleaned them up, I ate like a king with him and his wife."

I smiled. "I'd love to see it through your eyes."

His smile alone lit the room. "Are you sure? Sometimes Emerson people go to the pier."

"We're friends, right?" I teased.

"Friends," he said, reaching for my hand and running his thumb over my knuckles. "And more."

I reveled in the sensation of this closeness with him, then when I realized I looked as googly eyed as some of my students, I pulled my hand back and took a sip of my latte.

We nibbled at the sweet cupcakes and drank our coffee, then Cohen took me outside with the promise to see Seaton Pier through his eyes.

It wasn't a far drive, maybe ten minutes from the bakery, and we had parked. The beach wasn't as pretty here as it was farther down the coast, and the air had the distinct smell of rotting fish. But the people here seemed happy. Kids chased each other over the battered wooden planks, and a long pier extended over the ocean with fishing poles silhouetted against the bright sky like multiple antennae.

"This is it," Cohen said, shutting off his car.

I smiled. "I already like it."

"Wait until you meet Carl."

"Carl?"

"He runs the corn dog stand and he's been here for as long as I can remember, but no one knows how old he is. He never ages."

I laughed. "So this is what Seaton urban legends look like."

"Something like that." He got out and came to my side of the car, taking my hand in his for a few seconds. My heart fell the second his fingers slipped from mine, but I reminded myself why we couldn't hold hands in public.

The closer we got to the boardwalk, the more I could hear the sounds of the people around me. It blended with the crash of waves, and I felt pleasantly at ease. Maybe it was the ocean, but more likely it was the strong and steady man next to me.

He pointed ahead of us, and I followed his finger to an unassuming dingy white cart with a man in equally dingy white clothing behind it.

"That's Carl?" I asked.

He nodded. "And he serves the best corn dogs you'll ever eat."

"I mean, Mara's made me microwave corndogs before, so the bar's set pretty high."

He chuckled. "You talk about Mara like she's your hero."

"She kind of is," I admitted with a small laugh. "I think you'd like her."

"I'd love to meet her one of these days. Maybe you could meet some of my friends too."

It wasn't a big deal, meeting someone's friends, not really, but it felt big to me. Like our lives were becoming even more intertwined, and he wanted it that way.

As we approached the cart, Cohen lifted his hand in a wave. "Hi, Carl."

"Cohen! How you doin', pal?"

"Good." He gestured at me. "Carl, this is my friend Birdie."

Carl grinned a happy smile missing a few teeth. "Let me get you two a dog, on the cart."

"You don't need to do that," Cohen said.

"I don't need to do anything." He reached into the cart and pulled out two corn dogs wrapped in thin paper. "I want to."

"Thank you," Cohen said, shaking his head and taking the food from Carl, then handing one to me.

We both thanked him and took our corn dogs, walking toward the pier.

"What are you thinking?" Cohen asked.

"I'm trying to picture a seventeen-year-old you out here."

He chuckled. "I can scowl for you if it would help."

I shook my head. "You're funny, Cohen Bardot."

"And you're beautiful, Birdie Melrose."

I smiled and nibbled at the corn dog. "Oh my gosh," I moaned. "Okay, I'm going to tell Mara this kicked her corn dog's ass."

"Told you," Cohen said, chuckling.

He approached an open space on the railing between two fishermen and leaned against the rail overlooking the ocean. I followed his gaze, admiring the space where the sky met the sea. "I can't believe I've never been here before."

He smiled over at me, the wind ruffling his hair. "I'm just glad you're here now."

Maybe it was the rush or the ocean waves, or maybe it was the way he smiled at me, but I felt brave, bold, and completely in love.

I closed the distance between us and pressed my lips to his.

He curled his arms around me, holding me close and kissing me like it was the first and last time.

And then I heard a stunned voice say, "Dad? Ms. Melrose?"

52

COHEN

Birdie and I parted and turned to see Ollie and Ryde Alexander staring at us in shock.

Shit. Fuck. Shit.

Ollie looked betrayed, Ryde look like he'd just discovered gold, and Birdie stepped farther away from me, covering her mouth with her hands. This day had been incredible. Too good to be true. And now we were getting yanked right back to reality. The reality where it was very much against the rules for Birdie to be kissing me. And where the son of a woman who wanted her fired had just seen it. The reality where I'd told my son I wasn't dating anyone serious.

The two people who mattered so much to me stood on either side, but I had to choose.

"Ollie—" I began, stepping toward my son, but Ollie stepped backward.

"You said you weren't dating anyone serious," he accused, his brown eyes narrowed.

"Ollie," I warned.

"You didn't mention you were fucking my guidance counselor."

"Whoa." That was way over the line. Birdie didn't deserve to be talked about like that, especially by my son. "You have no room to talk." I gestured at him and the boy next to him. "Is this the boy you've been sneaking around with?".

Ollie stared between me and Birdie with hurt in his eyes, the mirror of my own. "You said you wouldn't tell!" he yelled at her.

Birdie stepped forward, her hands outstretched like she was trying to soothe him without touching him. "I didn't say who it was," she said gently. "But I did need to tell him what I saw. He's been so worried about you."

Ryde paled, but Ollie's cheeks reddened as he looked between Ryde and Birdie and me.

"Ollie," I said, putting an arm protectively around Birdie's shoulders. "I said I wasn't seeing anyone seriously because it's against the rules for me to be dating your guidance counselor. No one needs to know about Birdie and me, just like no one needs to know about you and Ryde."

Ryde straightened, a cool expression crossing his

features. "What is there to know about us? We're just friends."

Ollie stiffened at the words, nodding jerkily. "Exactly. I wanted to show him Carl's corn dog stand."

The hurt in my son's voice shot straight to my heart. Ollie wasn't as good of an actor as Ryde, and his pain was as clear as the expanse of ocean before us.

"Your father was showing me the same thing," Birdie said, breaking the silence.

Ryde snorted. "Thought he was showing you how far his tongue could reach down your throat."

"Watch it," I snapped. What was this little prick's problem? Birdie had clearly kept his secret for him, and now he was treating her like this? Treating my son like he was a dirty secret?

This was ridiculous. I was a damn adult, and Birdie wanted to be with me. That should have been the end of it.

"Listen, boys," I said, my voice low, commanding. "I'm an adult, and I'm allowed to see whoever I please, whenever I please, as long as she's agreeable. What your parents or the rest of the school thinks doesn't have a place in my bedroom."

"Your bedroom?" Ollie asked, aghast. Then a look of realization changed his features. "Was Ms. Melrose at our place last Friday? Is that why you had extra dishes out?"

I didn't respond. Not fast enough.

Ollie shook his head, turning to leave. "Come on, Ryde."

"Hey," I said, grabbing his arm. "You don't just get to walk away from this."

Ollie glared from my hand to my eyes. "You don't get to act like you haven't been lying to my face."

Ollie and Ryde walked away down the pier, and I ran my hands over my face, dragging them through my hair.

Birdie stepped beside me, giving me plenty of space.

"That was awful," I said.

Birdie blinked quickly, tears pooling in her eyes. "Can you take me home?"

I only nodded. I couldn't speak. Not with the overwhelming feeling of dread chilling my gut.

This was it. The other shoe that had been waiting to drop.

53

OLLIE

Ryde trailed beside me as I stormed away from my dad and our guidance counselor. "Holy shit," he said. "You didn't know your dad was boning Ms. M."

I shot him a look. I was so not in the mood for theatrics today.

That was until we reached the boardwalk and Ryde said, "My mom is going to have a field day with this."

As shocked as I'd been to see my dad with Ms. Melrose, I was more surprised to hear those words coming out of his mouth. "What did you say?" I turned to face him, nearly running into a little kid.

Ryde stepped off the boardwalk into the sand, shucking his leather sandals and holding them in his fingers. "Mom's been looking for a way to get rid of that hag all year."

I jerked my head back. "What? Why?"

Ryde looked at me like I was the crazy one. "Maybe because she's obsessed on wasting my time learning about college when everyone knows I'm going to get an acting deal. The only reason I don't have one now is because Dad wants me to graduate from the Academy." He rolled his eyes like his dad was the stupidest person alive, but I was beginning to think maybe *I* was.

"That's her literal job, Ryde," I said. Birdie had done so much for him, including keeping his secret. He owed her at least a little respect. "What else is she supposed to talk to you about in those meetings?"

"Maybe she could help me make connections with alumni. Or just skip them like my mom wants her to."

I narrowed my eyes at Ryde. "Aren't you the one who's frustrated your parents are controlling your life? Maybe Ms. M's just trying to give you a way out."

Ryde scowled, shaking his head. "She has no idea about my life."

I shook my head, stepping underneath the pier and walking toward the beach. I couldn't believe Ryde. I'd just found out my dad had been lying to me, and all we were talking about was Ms. Melrose and his acting career? Why wasn't he asking how I was feeling? Because right now, my stomach was just as wavy as the ocean.

"What?" Ryde said, walking behind me.

I stopped at the water's edge and turned back to him. "I'm fine, thanks for asking."

The slats of wood above cast long shadows over his body, just as perfect as ever. But I couldn't see that now. No, all I could see was the way one side of his mouth rested higher than the other. The way the tips of his ears protruded through his hair. He wasn't as beautiful as he'd been moments ago.

"Lee," he said, using his special name for me. "I'm sorry." He glanced around, and when he was sure no one was watching, he took my hand. "It's okay. If they didn't want to get caught, they wouldn't have been in public."

I pulled away from him, shocked, disgusted. "That's my dad, Ryde."

He nodded. "And you hate him."

My eyebrows drew together. "I was mad at him for being nosy. I was complaining about him. But he's still my dad."

Ryde stepped forward again, taking my shoulders in his hands. "Lee, I'm sorry. I know that must have been crazy to see your dad like that." His hazel eyes studied mine before coming closer for a kiss.

My brain short-circuited. Ryde was kissing me.

In public.

My heart beat faster as his fingers worked through my curls, and I took his face in my hands, kissing him back.

Asking Ryde to keep my father's secret could wait.

54

BIRDIE

Confession: I'm the ugliest crier.

We rode back to his house in silence, because what was there to say?

His son had seen us making out and been none too pleased about it. Ryde Alexander was there too, and if he had half the distaste for me that his mom did, Pam Anderson would have me and my bird on our asses in two seconds flat. I was so stupid. So stupid to have let my heart get in the way of my head. So stupid to ever have left that apartment with him in the first place. Stupid to think a rebound was what I needed to fix my broken heart.

It felt broken now, and I didn't even know if I'd lost

my job or not. Didn't even know if Cohen wanted to deal with all this drama.

I fought tears the last half of our drive, and when Cohen reached over to hold my hand, I let my fingers rest in his. He wanted to fix this—I could tell—but what could possibly be fixed?

He pulled his car into the apartment building's parking garage and turned it off with a sigh. "Let's go upstairs and order some food. Think this through. The next school board meeting isn't for another couple weeks, but maybe Headmaster Bradford will agree to a probation until then. If it's even a big deal. Just because it's a rule doesn't mean they'll enforce it."

I lifted Cohen's hand to my lips and kissed his knuckles to stop the nervous stream of words flowing from his mouth. "You don't need to do a thing."

His expression was guarded. "What do you mean?"

I shook my head, looking out the window at the dim lot and cars parked about. My car was only a few spots away. "I mean I think we've done enough damage for one day."

"Damage? Birdie, we were just kissing on the pier like adults."

"We were breaking the rules. Rules I told you about the second I found out you were Ollie's dad. You should have listened to me." Anger grew in my chest, because it was easier to blame him than it was to admit I wanted this too. More than I ever should have.

"What are you saying? You were the one who wanted to go out today! I was fine ordering in and spending time with you in private until we could change the rules."

My eyes stung with tears, and I blinked quickly. "If it wasn't today, it would have been another day, another place, another person to catch us. It would have only delayed the inevitable."

"And what's that?" His words were a challenge, and I lifted my chin to meet it.

"You told Ollie this wasn't serious. Did you think we were going to last forever?" I pushed open the door and got out of the car.

He didn't answer.

"Goodbye, Cohen." I turned and walked toward my car, toward my escape, toward heartbreak and the last chance I had at saving what was left of my job.

Cohen was still in the parking garage as I drove away. Standing by his car looking furious. Looking *hurt*.

I thought about driving home, but instead, I went somewhere else. I went to the school to see my best friend.

Tears streamed down my face as I reached my office and jiggled the key in the door. I burst inside as fast as I could, desperate to see the one creature who had always been there for me, who had never disappointed or hurt me.

I took him from his cage, and he curled his feet around my finger, holding on tight as if this was the best way he could hug me. I drew him closer to my chest, sobbing about everything I had hoped for and everything that would never come true.

55

COHEN

All I could see was Birdie asking me if I'd thought we were going to last forever.

I'd said nothing. Because the truth was, I had. Forever might have been a naïve thing to believe in, especially with my history, but Birdie made me believe in so many things I hadn't before. She'd made me believe that a person could be wholeheartedly good, like she was. She made me believe I could have a relationship, even with all the baggage I brought with me.

And now she made me believe my heart could break in half. The pain of it had brought me to my knees, made it nearly impossible to make it up to my apartment and drag myself to the couch.

I sat on the hard surface, replaying the day in my head. It had been so perfect. Waking up next to her, meeting her family, showing her Seaton and seeing it through her beautiful blue eyes.

Until Ollie and Ryde had seen us together. The look of betrayal on my son's face had cut me just like Birdie's exit.

I should have been honest with him, told him I was in love with a woman I shouldn't have been dating at all, and trusted him. He wasn't a child anymore. That much was clear.

My chest ached more as I realized I might not get another chance to speak with him. What if he decided he wanted to stay with his mom from here on out? Our custody agreement was fifty-fifty, but Ollie was sixteen. He had a say in what happened in his life, and I wouldn't force him to stay with me if he truly didn't want to.

At this point, I wouldn't blame him.

But I couldn't just give up. Not with him and not with Birdie.

I tried calling Ollie's number to explain, but it only rang once before going to voicemail. He had ignored my call. So I sent him a text and hoped like hell it got through to him.

Cohen: Ollie, I'm sorry about today. Can we please talk? On the phone or at the apartment or the bakery? Wherever is okay with me.

I let out a shaky breath, knowing I had another call to make, and scared as hell she would ignore me too. She and I didn't have a history like Ollie and I did. There was nothing stopping her from cutting me out of her life forever. The thought of never seeing her again was too much, so I pressed the call button and hoped like hell she'd answer.

But just like with Ollie, the call went to voicemail.

My fingers shook as I typed out a text message.

And then my shoulders shook with the force of my sobs when she didn't reply.

56

BIRDIE

Confession: I'm not above begging.

Mara and I stood in her bathroom, trying to make sure I looked as professional as possible today. I'd worn my plainest black dress that I hoped screamed "keep me on as your guidance counselor."

I worked a thin strip of black liner along my lashes.

"I still don't understand why you're trying to change yourself," Mara said. "You're great at what you do."

"I know, but I need them to know that too."

My phone vibrated on the countertop. A new text from Cohen.

I swiped away the notification and got back to work on my makeup.

"You can't ignore him forever," Mara said, sitting on the edge of the bathtub.

"What would I say to him? I let sex get in the way of my career?" I capped the eyeliner and reached for the mascara.

"It was more than sex, and you know it," she said.

"But who knows how long it was going to last anyway?" I asked. "Was the risk of my career really worth it?"

"Judging by how happy you were, I'd say yes. You hadn't acted like that in a long time, not even when you were dating Dax. It was like you were finally yourself."

I frowned. Because she was right, and I didn't want her to be. I uncapped the mascara and leaned close to the mirror to swipe some over my lashes. "Did you want me to clean the bathroom this week? You sitting on the tub reminded me."

She glared at me. "You're trying to divert the topic, and that's fine." I opened my mouth to argue, but she held up her hand and said, "I'm going to say one more thing and then let it drop."

"Fine."

"If you already think your career is over, what else is there to lose by going all in with Cohen?"

"If I'm going to have any chance at keeping my job, I need to prove it was a minor indiscretion that isn't happening anymore or ever again. I need to show I'm more committed to my job than to sexual pleasure."

"But why not both?" Mara asked. "Why can't you be good at your job and have good sex?"

"Because I don't make the rules." I turned back to the mirror to finish my makeup. I had no mental bandwidth to argue with Mara, not when she was right and my heart was breaking.

It wasn't fair, any of this, but life wasn't fair. My parents had more money than they knew what to do with, while people like Cohen's parents numbed their pain with drugs. There was no fairness in that. No fairness in finding someone you really liked, only to have the door slammed in your face.

The sooner I learned to accept it and move on, the sooner I could heal. And I wanted to heal. So badly. I wanted to forget how awfully Dax had treated me and what a knight in shining armor Cohen was in comparison.

Mara stood and waited for me to finish my makeup before giving me a hug. "You're going to get through today, Birdie. You're stronger than you think."

Tears pricked my eyes as I hugged her back and then stepped away. "If you keep being nice to me, I'm going to cry and ruin my makeup."

With half a smile, she reached out and cupped my cheek. "You're my best friend, and I'm a romance author. Either I have to be nice or we have to make out eventually."

I giggled. "Thank you." I hugged her again quickly and stepped back. "I better get to work."

She nodded. "You've got this."

With a small smile, I left the bathroom, picked up my purse, and went outside to my car.

Maybe someday I'd be able to find someone like Cohen. If he'd done anything, it was prove that men like him existed. That fact alone should have made me feel better, but it only saddened me more. Deep down, I knew Cohen was one in a million. But that didn't mean he would like me long enough to make a sacrifice like this worth it. Especially after how I left him yesterday.

My nerves felt like they had been lit on fire as I drove to Emerson Academy. The entire walk inside, my legs felt weak and my hands shook around the handles of my purse. This could be my last day walking into this building.

Just the thought of saying goodbye to this place, my students, nearly brought me to tears. This was my first real counseling job. In the last three years, I'd helped multiple students get into Ivy League colleges, gotten engaged, been broken up with, and worked with some incredible people along the way. How could it all be over so quickly?

I couldn't let it.

As I walked up the stairs, I made a promise to myself. I'd set my pride aside—I'd beg, I'd plead, I'd bargain—anything to keep this job I loved so much. And the second my job was secure, I'd find an apartment, any place that would take me so I could start living on my own and be the adult I should have been through all of this.

Inside the building, I marched past the main office as

if it were any other day. Because really, it was. My relationship with Cohen didn't have to interfere with my work. If anything, it made me a better guidance counselor. He and I had worked as a team to help solve Ollie's issue. With a little more parental involvement, it could be the same with the other students.

Why did we have to sit in our ivory tower at Emerson Academy like we somehow weren't on the same team with the parents and students?

I reached my door and jiggled the knob until it opened, saying hello to Ralphie as soon as I saw him. He cooed in response and tucked his beak under his wing a few times.

"I'm okay," I said, not convincing either of us. So I tried again. "We're going to be okay." It was more of a wish than the truth.

A few knocks sounded on my open door behind me. Marjorie stood in the doorway, looking me over with a disappointed expression. "Headmaster Bradford would like you to come to his office."

My heart stalled, and I felt dizzy for a moment. This was it. The moment of truth.

"I'll be there in a second," I said. I needed to gather myself, to make myself as confident as possible before setting foot in his intimidating office.

"Mhmm." She turned and left my office, as if even she knew I was a dead woman walking.

Taking deep breaths, I knelt before Ralphie's cage.

"That man who came in here mattered to me, but this school, this job, these students matter to me more. I'm going to tell headmaster that. And everyone makes mistakes—it's what you do after that matters."

Ralphie tilted his head, and I took that to mean he agreed with me.

I wiggled my finger through a slat in his cage, and he gently nipped at it with his beak.

"I'll be back," I promised.

He cooed.

With another deep breath, I stood, held my chin high, and walked toward the headmaster's office and whatever fate awaited me.

57

BIRDIE

Confession: Sometimes I want to punch my students in the face.

I'd expected the intimidating wooden furniture. Headmaster Bradford's hands folded on the desk. Even Marjorie's smug smile as she shut the door behind me.

What I hadn't expected to see was Ryde Alexander slouched in a chair next to his mother. Pam Alexander sat in a bright red dress and killer black pumps with the smile of a cat who'd just killed a poor, innocent canary.

"Sit," Headmaster Bradford said to me. His voice was formal, cold.

Trying not to show the wobble in my legs, I did as I was asked.

"Mrs. Alexander and her son came to me this morning with interesting news," Headmaster Bradford said. "Do you know what that might have been?"

I kept my gaze even. Because if I didn't, my eyes would have shot daggers at both of them. I didn't like the game, the way they were treating me like I'd committed an unforgiveable crime. "I'm curious," I finally said.

"Very well." He let out a sigh and shifted forward, steepling his fingers atop his desk. "It has been brought to my attention that you are having intimate relations with a parent."

I opened my mouth to speak, but he already had out the blue leather handbook with Ad Meliora embossed in gold.

"Article III, section 12b," he said. "'Teachers are strictly forbidden from having any relationship with an Emerson Academy parent, aside from that of a collaborator for the betterment of a student's education. Romantic involvement is prohibited except in the case of teachers who are also parents.'"

Every inch of me was screaming at myself to crawl into a hole and stay there until this was over. I knew the rule full well. I'd cited it to Cohen before we'd taken things further than we ever should have.

Headmaster Bradford continued reading. "The consequence for breaking these rules can be as minor as probation or as severe as dismissal." He glanced to Pam, who smiled even wider, and Ryde, then turned back to me.

"The bylaws state severity of the consequence is determined by past performance assessed by—"

"—an Emerson Academy parent and student," I finished. That was why Pam was here, along with her son. She wanted to weigh in on my behavior.

"So you are familiar with at least some of the bylaws," he snipped. Then he lifted a folder. "I've reviewed your achievements and reprimands during your time here. Mrs. Alexander and her son have shared their experiences working with you, and I've come to a decision. We're letting you go, Ms. Melrose, effective immediately. You may have the morning to clear your office."

He rose to stand, but my head was still spinning.

"W-wait," I said, blinking quickly. That wasn't how this meeting was supposed to go. I was supposed to be bold and in charge, state my case. I'd barely even had a chance to defend myself.

"Yes, Ms. Melrose?" Headmaster Bradford said.

"Can I not speak for myself?" I asked, firming my voice, my resolve.

"As you well know, sordid actions speak louder than words."

His words hit me like fists, but I pressed on. "My actions at this school have always been in the best interest of the students. I've worked late, made connections, helped countless students get into their goal colleges. How has my performance not been satisfactory?"

"If you must know," Headmaster Bradford said, "we

were on the fence about keeping you past this year. Especially as of late, you haven't been presenting the polished front we prefer for Emerson Academy."

"Are you talking about my new clothes?" I asked. "I don't wear these for me! I wear them for students like him." I gestured at Ryde. "I wear them for students who are so *afraid* of being who they truly are that they'll lash out on innocent people. I wear them so students can see it doesn't matter what anyone else thinks, only what you think of yourself."

Headmaster Bradford pressed his lips together. "Perhaps that ideology will be better received at a public school."

My lips parted. Everyone in the room knew that was an insult. But I wasn't ready for him to make me leave without a fight. "And you brought in Pam Alexander as your parent of choice? That's hardly an objective representative of my time here."

"I'm assuming you'd prefer to have Mr. Bardot brought in instead?" Headmaster Bradford asked, raising an eyebrow.

I sputtered, unable to argue through the red I was seeing in my eyes. Through the helplessness that permeated every inch of who I was. "This job is everything to me. *Everything.*"

Ignoring my plea, he stood and walked to his office door, holding it open. "I have a security company on standby. Please do not make this more difficult than it needs to be."

Every word hit me like knives to the back. In the last three years, I'd given everything to this school, to my students. And now they were casting me aside without a second thought.

Numbness settled over me, and it felt like I was walking in a trance on the way back to my office. All around me, students were flooding the halls, happy to see each other, getting ready for first hour. They had so many new beginnings every single day, but this was my end.

I choked on a sob and covered my face so no one would notice. But I could feel them staring just as surely as I felt the throbbing lump in my throat.

I ducked into my office and shut the door behind me. My hands shook as I took a canvas bag one of the college recruiters had left and started shoving items inside.

I tried to grip the handle of the bag, but my fingers shuddered, and I dropped it, collapsing beside it on the floor. I didn't even have it in me to tell Ralphie what had happened. That we were leaving this place he had called home for so long. That our new home would be with my best friend, who had already done far too much. That getting a new job and a new place to live were going to take that much longer.

That not only had I lost my job, I'd lost Cohen too. He would never forgive me. And even if he could, I'd never be able to look at him again without thinking of all I'd lost because I just couldn't say no.

58

OLLIE

As I walked into the building, I caught sight of Ms. Melrose slipping out of Headmaster Bradford's office. Her shoulders curled in on themselves, and her eyes stayed on the floor. Dread pooled in my gut as I looked from her to the office and saw Ryde and his mom walking out.

I glanced back down the hall and saw Ms. Melrose hurry into her office and close the door behind her.

What had Ryde done?

His mom kissed him on the cheek, to which he rolled his eyes, and she walked past me out of the building, not even giving me a second look. This was all a game to her, a power play to show who ruled the school. And Ryde? He was no different.

Why didn't he seem bothered as he sauntered toward

his locker? The confident walk that used to be so attractive to me now made my lip curl. What had happened in that office? How could he be so carefree?

Ryde preferred we communicate by text when we were at school to maintain his privacy, but to hell with that. He clearly hadn't kept Ms. Melrose's privacy or my dad's.

I walked straight up to him and tapped his shoulder, harder than I meant to. "Ryde, can I talk to you?"

The friends he was already flanked by laughed, joking about why a sophomore would be talking to a senior as popular as Ryde.

He played right into the act, shutting his locker and grinning at his friends like he couldn't believe it either.

Rolling my eyes, I walked away, going into the boys' bathroom. There was a person in the stall, but I banged on the door. "Out."

A freshman came out looking surprised and left without washing his hands. Gross.

Then Ryde came in, looking pissed, and said, "What the hell, Lee? I thought I said not at school!"

Well, I wasn't the only one who was ticked off. "What were you doing in the office with your mom and Ms. Melrose?"

His shoulders stiffened, confirming my fears. I felt cold, like icy acid was dripping over my skin, ruining everything exposed to Ryde.

"I thought I asked you not to tell your mom about my dad and Birdie!"

He raised his eyebrows. "Oh, so now she's Birdie? I thought you were pissed he kept it from you? Serves him right for keeping secrets."

My mouth fell open, and I wanted to scream. I didn't know who the hell this pompous ass was standing across from me, but it wasn't Ryde. It wasn't the guy I'd spent hours with locked in the A/V room, sharing secrets and kisses.

"It wasn't your secret to tell," I said.

Ryde shrugged. "It's done, Lee."

"That's it?" I stammered. "You destroy our guidance counselor's life and probably ruin my dad's chances with her and all you can say is 'it's done'?"

Ryde rolled his eyes and started to walk out of the bathroom. "I don't have time for this. I need to get to class."

I grabbed his shirt, not finished yet. "Birdie was the only one who advocated for your education and the one who cared enough to keep us a secret from your parents and mine." I studied his face, seeing the contempt there. The utter lack of guilt. "You don't care."

"I don't," he said. "I only care about you." He leaned closer, almost pressing his lips to mine, but I stepped back.

His eyebrows drew together. "What the fuck?"

"You can't just kiss me and fix this!" I hissed.

"What are you saying?" he demanded.

"You ruined lives, Ryde. And all you've been doing is

playing with mine." I lifted my middle finger and held it up. "Fuck you."

I walked out of the bathroom and left him in my past, exactly where he belonged.

59

BIRDIE

Confession: Potato chips are my comfort food.

I walked down the sidewalk to Mara's house, holding Ralphie's cage in my arms. Before I even reached the front door, I saw the curtains fall back and the door open. Mara came rushing out.

"They fired you?"

Tearfully, I nodded.

She took Ralphie's cage, setting it on the ground, then pulled me into a tight hug. "Let's put Ralphie inside, and then we're going out."

I stepped back, looking at her in shock. "Go out? All I feel like doing is lying in my bed and crying. And then maybe drawing some circles around want ads."

"There will be time for both of those things."

We carried Ralphie inside, then went outside to her pickup. My body was so numb I didn't have it in me to argue. It didn't matter whether I was in the guest bed at Mara's place or riding in her pickup—I'd still lost my job. Still lost the man I loved.

Holy shit. I loved him. I cradled my head in my hands. That made everything so much worse.

"Aren't you even curious where we're going?" she said.

I shrugged. "Where are we going?"

"The store—I thought we could get some snacks and then hang out on the beach."

That didn't sound terrible. "Maybe I can pick up a job application at the store."

She reached across the truck and hit my arm. "You're going to find an even better job where they'll let you date who you want to date."

"That's not even all of it," I said, tears stinging my eyes. "They said I 'didn't present the professional look expected at Emerson Academy.'"

Her mouth fell open. "That place is toxic, Birdie. You're good to get out of there."

"And what about you?" I asked. "I can't get an apartment if I don't have income."

"You'll find something. There are a million jobs out there."

"And only five local high schools."

"See?" she said. "That's five chances! And you don't

have to start as a counselor. I'm sure there are other jobs in a school you're qualified for."

I knew she was trying to cheer me up, but honestly, I felt as lost as a beach ball floating away in the ocean. Who was I without my job? Without my students?

A small part of me wished I still had Dax. That I could have gone home to him, fallen in his arms, and had him kiss the top of my head.

My eyes widened. How could I have forgotten? This was supposed to have been our wedding weekend. Instead, I was a homeless, jobless, single wreck.

Although I offered to wait in the truck, Mara insisted I come into the store with her. We went down the snack food aisles, grabbing chips and candy and frosting and pretty much anything that would help me feel even a little bit better.

Once we had three grocery bags full, we got back in her truck and stopped by her house to change. I talked to Ralphie, who was sitting in his cage on the dresser, as I put on my high-waisted bikini bottoms and full-coverage top.

"We're going to the beach. I don't see us being gone long though. Mara started a new project, and she's on a deadline. I'll be back, lying in here and watching TV with you before you know it—just like old times."

From across the hallway, Mara called, "If you're done talking to your bird, I'm ready to go now."

"His name is Ralphie," I called back, picking up my

sunhat, then I waved goodbye to Ralphie and followed her back out to the car.

We drove to the beach and laid out our towels in the usual spot. Even though it was fall, it was still warm in the sunlight. The water was getting colder, but that didn't matter. I didn't plan to swim.

In fact, I realized, I didn't have any plans at all. I closed my eyes, thinking of my next steps. I needed to apply for jobs, of course. I'd look at all the local high schools and see if I could slide into an open position there. If one existed. Then maybe I could try for administrative jobs at other places that served teens. I used to work as a barista in college—I could do that to get by until I had a new permanent role.

Or maybe I could move, I thought.

There had to be a rural town somewhere looking for a guidance counselor. I could get a fresh start, away from my family, away from this place that held so many memories for me.

But that would mean leaving my best friend too.

I opened my eyes and looked over at her. She lay on her stomach, reading a paperback.

My mouth fell open at what I saw past her on the beach. "Fuck," I hissed.

Mara's eyes widened as she looked at me. "I know you're upset, but—"

"No, no, look," I said, nodding toward the couple walking along the shore.

"Is that... Dax?" Mara asked.

"Yes!" I frantically rolled the chip bag shut and shoved it underneath my towel. Then I brushed off my chest, making sure there weren't any greasy crumbs there.

"You look great," she said. "You can hardly even tell that you've been crying."

"Great," I muttered. Of course I had to see Dax on the worst day of my life. But what I saw beside him was even worse.

The girl he'd left me for had a baby bump. It was obvious by the dress she wore. She had to be at least in her second trimester...

Dax and I had only broken up a couple months ago. She'd been wearing an oversized dress then...

"Is she..." Mara asked, not even finishing the sentence.

I nodded slowly, because they were close now, and Dax had seen us.

His smile didn't quite reach his eyes, but he said, "Hi, Beatrice, Mara."

"It's Birdie," I said, my words coming out like venom. He had never called me that before. It was like looking at a complete stranger.

His new girl looked from him to me. "How do you two know each other?" His new girl clearly didn't recognize me, and that hurt even more. I wasn't just disposable; I was forgettable.

My lips parted, but what was there to say?

Beside me, Mara said, "He fucked her over and hung

her out to dry." She got up and grabbed her towel and bag. "Come on, Birdie. We're getting out of here."

I stood, numbness threatening to slide over me and keep me from speaking, keep me from feeling, but I wasn't ready to leave yet. A look of recognition crossed her face, but Dax only seemed... uncomfortable.

I'd thought of what I'd say if I ever met him again, but frankly, all of it fell short in reality. All I really needed to say was, "Thank you."

Confusion overtook his features. "Thank you?"

I nodded. "Thank you for sparing me a lifetime of being disappointed by you."

With my head held high, I picked up my towel and followed Mara to the truck, where I promptly broke down and cried.

60

COHEN

Ollie's forehead creased and his lips were set in a hard line as he walked to my car. What had happened in school today? Worry flooded my mind, and I begged he wouldn't tell me Birdie had been fired. Or that today was his last day coming home with me.

I had my apology ready for the second he opened the door, but instead, he said, "Dad, we've got to do something."

"What do you mean?" I asked.

He shut the door behind him, turning toward me. "They fired Birdie today."

I felt like I was going to throw up and pass out at the same time. "They did what?"

"I saw it this morning—she came out of the office looking really sad, and then Ryde and his mom came out after. I asked him about it and..." He swallowed hard. "He did it. He was the one who did it, Dad, and I feel so guilty. He never would have seen you and Ms. Melrose if I hadn't brought him out there."

"Whoa, whoa, whoa," I said, my mind reeling in an attempt to pick up all the pieces. Birdie lost her job. Ryde told the secret. Ollie was sorry. "We're on the same team?"

The person behind us laid on their horn, and with a frustrating grunt, I whipped out of the spot and parked.

Ollie said, "I'm pissed at you for lying, but I'm on your team. This isn't right."

I shook my head, gripping the steering wheel so tightly my knuckles turned white. "What can we do? The next board of trustee meeting isn't for another month."

"We need to talk to Headmaster Bradford," Ollie said. "He's the one who fired her."

I nodded slowly.

Ollie opened the door.

I raised my eyebrows. "Now?"

Ollie nodded. "We've got to fix this, Dad."

I couldn't disagree. I followed my son out of the car, proud of him for standing up for what was right, but also mad as hell. The headmaster of my son's school had fired a woman who so clearly cared for her students just as much as herself. Getting rid of her was doing a disservice to every student in that damn school.

We walked up the stairs and went to the front desk where Marjorie was packing her things. She gave us wary looks, and Ollie said, "We need to speak to the headmaster."

"Keep it short," she said.

Oh, it would be short. As long as he made the right decision.

The door was cracked open, so Ollie pushed it the rest of the way and walked in. Headmaster Bradford turned away from the filing cabinet he had just shut and faced us. "Ah," he said, "I wasn't expecting this so soon."

I narrowed my eyes. I already wanted to punch him in the face.

Ollie said, "Headmaster, you need to give Birdie her job back."

His dismissive smile made me want to punch him that much more. "Ms. Melrose and your father broke rules very clearly written in the Emerson Academy bylaws."

"But I read them," Ollie said, "and it didn't say she had to be fired. Why not place her on probation? Because of what the Alexanders say? Ryde's going to be gone in a year, his sister will be a freshman, and then what? We have a new guidance counselor who doesn't care half as much about the students as Birdie does."

I watched in awe as my son stood up for me, for Birdie, and clearly spoke his case. He wasn't my little boy anymore. He was a man.

I put my hand on Ollie's shoulder and said, "When I first met Birdie, I didn't know she was employed at the school. I came in a week later to discuss concerns I had for

Ollie, and even though she told me we couldn't date, she worked tirelessly to make sure he was cared for academically, in his friend circles, and at home. I pressed her to date me because I was so amazed by her. If you're going to blame someone, blame me. I'll pay a fine; I'll speak to the board of trustees. I'll do whatever it takes."

"The time has passed," Headmaster Bradford said, nodding toward my son. "I want you to see this, Oliver. Actions have consequences. We must choose our actions carefully. The results, negative or positive, are up to you."

My hands clenched at my sides. How dare that prick talk to my son about me like he knew anything about me.

"That's bullshit!" Ollie said.

My thoughts exactly.

The headmaster let out a sigh. "Learning quickly, I see. That will be a week of out-of-school suspension."

My mouth fell open. Was that really what they were teaching here? Comply or die?

"You're going to regret this," Ollie said, his eyes shining with angry tears.

"Come on," I said, putting my arm around his shoulders and turning him away. As we walked out of the school, I made a promise as much to him as to Birdie. "We're going to figure this out. No one deserves to keep their love a secret."

61

BIRDIE

Confession: I'm a backslider.

A call coming in from an unknown number interrupted my television binge. I'd been holed up in my room for most of the last few days, passing the time talking to Ralphie and watching shows I'd already seen a hundred times.

The call went to voicemail, and I waited to see what they said. But instead of leaving a message, they called again.

Worried it could be news from the hospital, I picked up. Anthea was thirty-two weeks pregnant, so not full term. Would she be okay if she delivered early?

"Hello?" I said, trying to keep my voice steady.

"Hi, is this Birdie?"

"It is," I said. "Is everything okay?" If it was bad news, I wanted to hear it already instead of fearing the worst.

"Hi, um, it's me, um, Walter?"

Walter. His voice registered in my mind, and I almost hung up. Almost. "Yes?" I said, my voice cool.

"I, um, this is awkward, but I was wondering if you might go out with me again?"

"What?" I was shocked that he would even ask.

"I know I messed up last time, but you did give me a lot to think about. That's what I want in a woman, someone who will challenge me, even if they are misguided."

"Are you serious?" I asked, baffled.

"I know I might not be your dream guy, but I would be able to take care of you."

"Take care of me?"

"I'm blowing this, aren't I?"

The bit of vulnerability in his voice softened my heart, if only a bit. "Kind of."

He chuckled. "Do you think there's a possibility I could get a second chance? Do dinner the right way? I'll take you anywhere you want."

I glanced in the direction of the kitchen, which held all of my sandwich supplies. Until I found a job, I was on a barebones budget, which meant no coffee shops, no driving unless necessary, and definitely no eating out. Would it be bad to get a meal with him?

After all, he was right. He would take care of me, financially at least. A life with someone like Walter would be easy. No passion, but also no heartbreak. No head-clouding lust that would keep me from making the right decisions.

"I'll go to lunch with you," I said. "Let's go to Waldo's Diner. Say noon?"

I wanted to see my grandpa anyway. Also, if Walter could refrain from insulting the diner while he was there, he might stand a fighting chance at redemption.

"I'll be there," he promised.

As I got ready, I called Grandpa Chester. He answered on the third ring, and I could hear wind in the background. He always stepped outside to answer a call, saying it was rude to talk on the phone in a restaurant.

"Hi, Birdie," he said. "How's my favorite granddaughter?"

"I've been better," I said honestly. "But I wanted to let you know I'm coming by the restaurant today. And I'm bringing, a, um, friend."

"Cohen?" he asked, full of happiness. "I was hoping you'd bring him back around."

My chest ached, because I'd been hoping the same thing. "That didn't work out, Grandpa. It's someone else. Nothing serious. But I thought maybe I could get a coffee with you after?"

"Of course. When will you be here?" he asked.

"We're eating at noon."

"That works great. I need to take Grandma to the doctor at eleven, so we'll be by at one."

"Everything okay?" I asked.

"You know your grandma. Healthy as a horse."

I smiled. Just talking to him was like a balm to my soul. "Good. I'll see you then."

"Bye, sugar. Love you."

"Love you."

♥·♥·♥·♥

Sometime around eleven, I threw on the first clean dress I saw in the closet, put my curls into a bun, slipped on some sandals and walked out the door, not even bothering with makeup.

Losing my job, seeing Dax so happy, it had messed with me. What was wrong with me that I couldn't have that kind of happiness? That the universe conspired against me having both a job and love and now I had neither?

I couldn't even bring myself to call Cohen. It would be pathetic. And what would I say anyway? *Well, since you came in second to my job and I no longer have it, I guess we can see each other again?* It fell flat even to my own ears.

With a sigh, I grabbed my purse and went out to my car, making the drive to my grandpa's restaurant.

When I got there, it was immediately clear which car was Walter's. It had to cost at least twenty grand more than all the other cars in the lot, and it shined in the sun like it had been freshly detailed.

When I got out of the car, I saw his driver's side door open. "Hi, Birdie," he said with a smile.

I forced a small smile on my own lips and waved. "This is it."

He glanced back at the restaurant. "Looks like a good local haunt."

Well, that wasn't quite a compliment. But not an insult either. "I know the owner," I said. "And the food is great."

"Looking forward to it," he said, walking alongside me toward the door. "And honestly, I'm thankful for another chance with you." He crossed his fingers. "Here's to hoping I don't blow it."

It was kind of adorable, all the effort to make amends. Maybe I could set aside his opinions about high school sex ed. After all, he'd probably change his mind once he heard all the facts and figures about how important it was.

The diner was bustling with customers when we arrived, and we found a booth near the back. I smiled at the waitress, Betsy, as she walked by in a hurry and said, "I'll be with you shortly."

"They need more help," Walter mumbled. "Maybe you could make that suggestion to the owner?"

I gave a noncommittal shrug. Grandpa had the best help. He didn't let just anyone into the family if he didn't think they'd care about his customers as much as he did.

And besides, there were usually two waitresses during the lunch shift. Someone must have called in.

"So," I said. "What inspired you to want a second chance?"

"Well, first of all, you're beautiful."

I found that hard to believe in my undone state.

"And clearly opinionated." He chuckled. Like my opinions were *cute*. God, this guy was already rubbing me the wrong way.

"Mhmm."

"And you come from a great family," he continued.

"Spoken like a true Melrose Insurance employee."

"It's a great place to work," he said. And apparently that encouragement was all he needed to launch into a spiel about work and how it was going and how much he looked up to my father.

I was thankful when Betsy came and took our orders, just for the brief reprieve it gave me from hearing about my family.

They surrounded themselves with people who worshipped them—employees, friends, business partners. I wondered when the last time was anyone had disappointed my parents. Or if I was the only disappointment in their life.

"Tell me about your job," he said.

I took a deep drink of the soda in front of me. "I got fired."

"Oh, wow." He raised his eyebrows at the table and

tilted his head, as if he were mulling over the news. "But you know, that might not be the worst thing. Now you have an opportunity to be who you were meant to be."

That was surprisingly astute for Walter. "I guess it does give me the chance for a fresh start."

"Exactly. Now you can get more involved in the family business. That would make your parents awfully happy."

I looked toward the ceiling for a moment. I didn't even have it in me to argue. Because he was right. My family would take me back with open arms—probably even let me work as an assistant or something until they could get me married off to someone as vanilla bean as Walter. And they would pat themselves on the back thinking about how much they'd helped, not caring how miserable I was along the way.

For the rest of dinner, he asked me about my skills and what I'd learned in college. It was like the worst possible combination of a job interview and a date.

"You know," he said. "I'm actually looking at getting an assistant. Maybe I could put you in to your father?"

A weathered hand gripped my shoulder, and I looked up to see Grandpa Chester. He was like sunshine bursting through rain clouds. I stood and hugged him tight, already near tears. "Hi, Grandpa."

"Hi, sugar. How are you?"

"Great now." I grinned at him, then spotted Grandma Karen behind him.

I gave her a hug, and she kissed my cheek, surely

leaving a red lipstick stain that always drove my own mother insane. "It's so good to see you."

"You too," she said. "Why don't you introduce us to your friend?"

"This is Walter," I said, gesturing toward him.

He stood, wiping his hand on a paper napkin, then said, "I should probably get back to the office, but it was nice meeting you folks."

Grandpa Chester waved with an amused smile, but as soon as he walked away, his lips settled into a frown. "Beatrice Karen Melrose. What in the hell was that?"

62

BIRDIE

Confession: I want to make my grandparents proud.

Suddenly, I felt like I was five years old again, trying to let their pet finches out of the cage. "I-I-" I began, not sure how to finish.

"Let's sit down," Grandma said, settling into the booth where Walter and I had been. She carefully took the plates and stacked them near the edge of the table so Betsy could grab them on her way by.

Grandpa was still watching me, though, waiting for my answer.

"It's a long story," I said.

"We have time," he deadpanned.

I shook my head, not wanting to explain to my

grandpa, one of my all-time heroes, how acquainted I'd become with rock bottom.

Grandma reached across the table, covering my hand with her own. "We're here for you, sweetie."

My eyes stung at her kindness. I knew I'd gone far too long without telling them about my job and my failures with Cohen, so I opened up. "I was on a date with him."

"That suit?" Grandpa said, confused. "What did he say about you working at your father's office? What happened with Cohen? Why would you ever leave that school when we both know you're doing what you love?"

I shook my head, wiping at my eyes. "I got fired, Grandpa."

He and my grandma looked astonished.

"What?" Grandma said. "What happened? Was it that woman? I'll give her a piece of my mind, and she won't even know what hit her."

"No, no, no. Cohen was a dad at the school, and dating parents is against the rules. The headmaster found out."

The lines on Grandpa's forehead deepened. "That's a stupid fucking rule."

Grandma gave him a look, then said, "I agree. Without the cursing."

"And they let you go," Grandpa said. "Just like that? No warning or nothing? That's not how you run a business."

"It's how the Academy runs their business," I said with a sigh. "And I-I don't know what to do."

"Of course you do," Grandpa said sternly.

"What?" I leaned forward. "Didn't you hear? I got *fired*. Lost my job. Lost my boyfriend. Lost the roof I was keeping over Ralphie's head, and I'm living in my friend's spare room." Grandma opened her mouth to speak, but I shook my head. "And no, you can't talk me into living in the senior apartments with you. I'd stand out like a sore thumb, and you'd get in trouble."

"You're down," Grandpa said. "I get that. I've been kicked in the teeth a few times myself. Why do you think I have dentures? But you weren't raised to mope like this, to settle for suits like that jackass." He jerked his thumb over his shoulder toward the exit Walter had gone through. His voice was almost mad as he continued. "You're going to get your ass up, pick up the pieces, apply for jobs at other schools, and show your shit-for-brains boss at that stupid fancy school that they made a mistake in losing you. But under no condition, Birdie Karen Melrose, are you allowed to settle for anything less than you're worth."

I looked toward the table, my vision blurring. "I don't feel like I'm worth much at all."

When I looked back up, Grandpa's lips quirked. "Sugar, you're worth the sun, the moon, and all the stars."

My heart melted at the words and the sincerity behind them. But something held me back from accepting them as truth. "Then why do these things keep happening to me?" I asked. "Why do I keep losing all the things I want?"

Grandma and Grandpa exchanged a glance, then Grandma said, "You made a huge leap in going to college, and I wonder if you thought you were done with hard decisions after that? Life rarely happens to us, unless you let it."

Had I been letting life happen to me? I hadn't chosen for Dax to break up with me. Hadn't chosen for the school to fire me. The only thing I'd chosen lately was to take a risk with Cohen, and even though our relationship had been short, it had been amazing.

"Can I give you some advice?" Grandpa said.

I gave him a sardonic smile. "Now you're asking?"

He chuckled, then reached across the table, taking my hands in his. "One step at a time, Birdie. That's all anyone can do."

Grandpa was right. I couldn't fix all my problems. Couldn't change the fact that Dax had clearly cheated on me throughout our relationship. Couldn't change what I'd said to Cohen or that I'd been fired from my job. But I could direct my next step, and it was going to be one that made my grandparents proud.

63

COHEN

Ollie and I sat together at the table, both of us bent over our computers, hard at work. I'd called every single person on the board of trustees, only to get the same answer. Headmaster Bradford had the power to make the decision he had. I could attempt to change the rule at the next meeting, but it wouldn't cover the past.

So there was only one thing left to do to make sure our voices were heard.

64

BIRDIE

Confession: I want to live on my own.

I sat at the kitchen table, filling out a tenth job application. I knew because I was keeping track. I had a spreadsheet with the company website, application date, the best contact to follow up with, and the results of my efforts.

Most of these applications took for-freaking-ever. A resume wasn't enough. You had to enter all of your past experience in the stupid website and then add all the information from your past employers. My chest ached every time I had to advise the employer against contacting Emerson Academy. They had already done more harm to my career than good.

Mara came into the kitchen, heading straight to the coffee pot. Now that we were both home all day, we went through way more than I cared to admit.

"Any bites?" she asked.

I shook my head. "But I have it on my list to follow up with Seaton High today. I'm going to drive over there and drop off my resume."

"Nice," she said, taking a sip of her coffee. "I think I'm going to head to a coffee shop to write this afternoon. I need to get out of the house. Do you think your grandpa could give me a pep talk too?"

I laughed. "Head by the diner and ask. I bet he'd oblige."

"I might just do that."

"Have fun," I said, looking back to my computer. I wanted to fill out at least a couple more applications before going to the print shop to get a few resumes printed out.

She left with her cup of coffee, and I giggled, realizing she was taking a to-go cup of coffee on her way to get more coffee. Living with Mara as an adult was different than living with her when we were two twenty-year-olds treating LA like our personal playground. But some things never changed.

I spent the rest of the morning on the job hunt. I dressed nicely in one of my demurer dresses, printed resumes on the fancy paper, and dropped them by the office at Seaton High. The woman behind the desk said the principal was busy and they weren't looking for a counselor, but she would pass on my information.

"I'll do any role I'm qualified for," I said. "Even substitute teaching."

"Great," she said with a smile. "I'll pass it on."

Feeling a little dejected but trying to keep up hope, I left the school and began driving back to Mara's place. Like she'd said, there were a million jobs in the world. I just had to find one that would take me, even if it meant working my way up to a position I loved or waiting patiently for something to open up. Heck, maybe someone from another school would take my job, and I could fill their empty position.

Out of the corner of my eye, I saw a vacancy sign in front of an apartment building not too far from Mara's house. It wasn't in the best part of Emerson, and the paint was peeling, but it wasn't as scary as the place I'd toured in Seaton.

On a whim, I pulled into the parking lot and drove through the complex until I found a sign for the main office. Immediately, doubts started whipping through my brain. What if I couldn't afford it? What if I couldn't find a job? What if they wouldn't want me?

But I took a breath and listened to Grandpa's words in my ears. One step at a time.

When I walked into the main office area, a woman

behind the desk smiled at me warmly. "Hi there, how can I help you?"

"I was wondering if you had any one-bedrooms available?"

"A few, actually, would you like to see one?"

I hesitated, then stepped forward. "What are your screening criteria?"

"All we ask for is your last two pay stubs and a credit score."

That was it? I could show them my last two pay stubs. And I promised myself I would get whatever job I needed to pay the rent. Speaking of rent... "How much is it per month?"

Her answer took me aback. It was actually in budget, even if I found a job making less than I had at the Academy.

"Would you like to take a tour?" she asked.

I nodded. "Very much so."

She hung a sign at the desk and walked around the counter to me. "I'm Henrietta, by the way, but all my friends call me Hen."

"That has to be a sign," I said, absolutely giddy. "My name's Birdie."

"See?" She clapped her hands together happily. "Match made in heaven."

As we walked toward one of the open units, she showed me around. There was a small gym on-site with a few treadmills, laundry in the basement of every building, and even a small pool. I pictured all the hours I could spend with Mara, laid out on folding chairs, getting even better tans.

And best of all, it would be mine. Something I had gotten for myself, by myself, even in the darkest of times.

Hen led me into the building and walked me up to the third floor. I wasn't crazy about all the steps, but it would be good exercise, right?

She opened the door to the unit, saying, "This one's available at the end of the month. I never asked you when you were looking?"

"As soon as possible," I said honestly. Before my past could bite me in the butt again and keep me from a place like this.

It was simple, with carpeted floors, a small kitchen, and a decent-sized bedroom.

"There's no bathtub," she said, "But we do have excellent water pressure."

"That's fine." I wasn't particularly fond of baths anyway. Why would anyone like sitting in their own dirt water?

"Do you have any pets?" she asked.

I smiled. "A bird named Ralphie."

"Great. There are no rules against caged animals like birds or even spiders. We don't allow cats, but we do allow small dogs."

My eyes lit up. Everything about this place was perfect. "Can I fill out an application?"

She grinned. "Of course. The best unit comes open in a week. Come with me."

65

BIRDIE

Confession: Everything I know about childbirth comes from a college textbook and Gray's Anatomy.

"I leave for one day and you get an apartment?" Mara asked as we sat at her table, eating the spaghetti supper I made for us to celebrate.

I twirled spaghetti around my fork. "It would have been better if I'd gotten a job, but I'll take it."

She frowned. "You know I'm going to miss living with you. This was just like old times."

"Me too," I said with a small smile. "But you'll be thankful when you bring a guy over and you won't have to coordinate with me." I drew my eyebrows together. "Mara, it's been a while since you brought anyone over."

She finished chewing and swallowing her bite. "I just haven't met anyone worth messing with."

"What do you mean?"

With a shrug, she said, "I don't want to bring a guy over for the sake of bringing a guy over. I want it to actually be a good time, for both of us."

I raised my eyebrows. "Who are you, and what have you done with my best friend?"

She held up a meatball on a fork. "Don't worry, I still like meat."

"Good," I teased. "How else would you write romance?"

"I don't know. Sometimes I feel like a fraud, writing all these love stories when I've never experienced happily ever after."

"You can dream, right? How are you supposed to know what you want if you can't imagine it?"

"Oh my gosh," she said with a smile. "You and your grandpa have superpowers."

"Did you get to talk to him today?"

"Yes." She grinned. "We had two cups of coffee, and he told me all about how he and your grandma met. They're seriously the sweetest couple ever."

"I know," I said. "Whoever I end up with has big shoes to fill."

"Exactly. Don't ever settle for someone like Dax again. Or the 'suit,' as your grandpa calls him."

I chuckled and held out my pinkie. "And promise

you'll do the same?"

She hooked her finger through mine. "Promise."

We shook on it like we were young again, but my phone rang loudly from my purse, interrupting us.

"I better go get that," I said. "It might be a job."

"Go, go," she replied. "All this talking is distracting me from eating."

I chuckled, rising from the table and going to the living room, where my purse hung on a hook by the door.

When I looked at my phone, it was a call from Doug. As soon as I answered, he said, "Birdie, Anthea's in labor."

"Where?"

"RWE Memorial."

"I'll be there in fifteen minutes." I hung up and leapt to action, running to the kitchen. "Anthea's having the baby!" I cried.

Mara got up. "What can I do? How can I help?"

I shook my head. I realized I had no idea what to do at a time like this. Would I get there and see a precious baby, or would it be hours of waiting? Did I need a book? A computer?

"I've got it," I said, hurrying to grab my purse with my tablet and charger. That was close enough. "I'll call you when there's a baby!"

She clapped excitedly. "See you later, Auntie."

The word brought a smile to my face, and I wore it all the way to the hospital. I couldn't wait to see what my niece would look like. How Anthea and Doug would be as parents. I hoped my parents would be more affectionate and loving as grandparents than they had as parents. Baby-girl-to-be-named deserved it.

As soon as I got to the hospital, I parked and ran inside, looking for any sign of the maternity wing. A nurse pointed me to the third floor, and I rode the elevator up, eager to see what was happening.

When I reached the waiting room, I couldn't see my parents, so I went to the nurses' station and asked for Anthea Melrose.

"Three thirty," she said.

I thanked her and looked at the plaques on the walls, following the numbers to the right room. I couldn't hear screaming anywhere, like I'd expected in the maternity ward, but there were couples walking around, checking in, hushed noises behind closed doors.

The door to Anthea's room was cracked, but I knocked anyway.

Doug's face quickly appeared, and he pulled me into a hug.

"Hey," I said gently. "How's it going?"

He stepped aside, letting Anthea answer.

She had cords and monitors strapped all about her body, but despite the situation, she looked beautiful with curled hair and perfectly done makeup.

"My water broke at dinner with a client and her husband, so I'm absolutely mortified," Anthea said. "I'm five centimeters dilated, my back hurts, and they haven't given me an epidural yet. Does that answer your question?"

I chuckled softly, then covered my mouth. I didn't want her to think I was being insensitive. "What can I do? How can I help?" I asked, echoing Mara earlier.

"I can't eat," Anthea huffed. "So nothing. But when this is all done, I want the greasiest cheeseburger and fries you can find."

"You got it," I said, going to her and sitting by the bed. "Is your mom or sister coming?"

Anthea rolled her eyes. "My labor interrupted their nail appointments. They'll see me and the baby at the house when I'm ready."

I nodded, twisting toward Doug. "Mom and Dad?"

"On their way."

A funny thought crossed my mind. "Can you imagine them in the waiting room?"

Anthea snorted. "Your mom will have the décor updated and the coffee upgraded before the baby even gets here."

"True," I said, giving her a hug. "I know you're going to do amazing."

Doug said, "Do you mind if I duck out for a minute to use the bathroom?"

"There's one here," I pointed out.

He and Anthea exchanged a glance.

"Go ahead," Anthea said. "I'll call you if I'm crowning."

Doug rolled his eyes and left the room.

"What was that about?" I asked.

Her laugh was a little embarrassed. "I told him if he stinks up the room while I'm giving birth, I'll make him change every diaper from now until she's potty trained. The baby and I are the only ones allowed to shit in this room."

I laughed. "Fair enough."

She shifted, then adjusted her gown and reached for the remote. "Want to watch something?"

"Sure. Whatever you want."

She winced and began taking deep breaths. A line on one of the monitors spiked, and I leaned forward, worried. "Are you okay?"

"Contraction," she gritted out, squeezing the railings until her knuckles turned white. "If that damn anesthesiologist doesn't get here soon..."

"I can ask the nurses?" I offered.

She shook her head. "Doug's already asked three times. He's on his way—allegedly." Her body visibly relaxed, and the line on the monitor went down. "Maybe we can watch the news. Seeing someone else in a worse situation might make these contractions not as bad."

"Makes sense to me," I said, watching as she flipped the channels on the TV. When she landed on the news station, my mouth fell open.

"What?" she asked.

I pointed at the screen. "That's Emerson Academy."

66

BIRDIE

Confession: I always think I deserve less than I do.

The image on the screen depicted the Emerson Academy courtyard flooded with students and parents holding signs in protest.

"What's going on?" Anthea asked.

"Turn it up!" I said.

The screen cut to a newscaster holding a microphone in Ollie's face. Instead of his uniform, he wore a bright pink shirt with a bird on the front. Behind him, there were signs with words like.

BRING BACK BIRDIE
JUST SAY "YES" TO BIRDIE
TEACHERS DESERVE GOOD S3X TOO

My mouth fell open at the words, but nothing shocked me as much as the interview.

"I'm here with Ollie Bardot, Emerson Academy student and the organizer of this protest. More than a thousand people have gathered around the school, demanding a job for the guidance counselor who was fired for fraternizing with this student's father."

"No freaking way," Anthea whispered. "That's all for you?"

On the screen, Ollie said, "Emerson Academy has been around since the 1800s, and some of its rules are just as old."

The newscaster brought the microphone back to herself. "You're referring to a rule that forbids staff from dating parents."

"Exactly," Ollie said confidently. "We believe if it doesn't affect their ability to do a good job, then it shouldn't matter who they decide to love."

My heart melted at his words.

"And you believe she was doing a good job, despite breaking the rule?" the newscaster asked.

Ollie looked straight at the camera. "She did the *best* job. She cares about her students like no one else. She deserves to work at the school, and we students deserve to work with her."

They cut away from Ollie, showing helicopter footage of all the people in the courtyard. There must have been no one left inside the school.

"This brings an excellent question to the public eye," the reporter said. "Is our private life truly private? And should it matter if you do an excellent job? I think you can tell where the students stand on the matter."

My cheeks felt wet, and I realized I was crying.

Anthea rubbed my arm. "Birdie, you're amazing."

I sobbed, wiping at my eyes. "I'm not supposed to be the one crying today!"

"It's baby day," she said. "Everyone's supposed to cry."

I shook my head, turning back toward the screen. Now the news anchor stood with one of my co-workers, the videography teacher, Mr. Davis.

"How was it to work with Birdie Melrose?" she asked.

He smiled at the reporter. "She's a woman like no one else. Completely her own person. It's a true disservice to all the students and staff at this school to lose her."

"What would it take to change the headmaster's mind and bring her back?" the reporter asked.

"An act of God." Mr. Davis shrugged. "Or for the board of trustees to overturn the bylaws."

The reporter smiled into the camera, showing straight white teeth. "Trustees, if you're watching this, you have a lot of people to answer to about this bylaw!" She held her earpiece for a moment. "We'll be covering the protest and providing updates on the case throughout the week! If you'd like to chime in, you can use the hashtag #BringBackBirdie to let us know what you think."

The screen cut to commercial, and Anthea grinned at me. "You are *so* getting your job back!"

I was still stunned, numb, as Doug walked into the room.

"Why's she getting her job back?" he asked.

Anthea opened her mouth to explain but winced as another contraction spiked on the monitor. Doug immediately went to her side, holding her hand.

I felt like an intruder in that moment. Like this was an experience for Anthea and Doug to share together. As soon as the contraction passed, I excused myself and told them I'd be waiting in the lobby if they needed me for anything at all.

Then I gave Anthea as good of a hug as I could with all the wires. "I love you," I whispered in her ear. "You're going to do great."

She kissed my cheek, just like Grandma Karen would do, and I knew, without a doubt, that everything was going to be alright.

I went back to the lobby and pulled out my phone to call Mara and tell her what I'd seen. Immediately when she answered, she said, "Is there a baby there already?"

"No, Mara, you need to go look at the news! They're doing a protest at the school to try to bring me back. Cohen's son is spearheading the whole thing!"

"What!" she cried. I heard her moving throughout her house and things clattering around. "Do you think Cohen asked him to do it?"

"Cohen wasn't there," I said, trying to ignore how sad that fact made me feel. "I think if he would have been, they would have put him on screen."

"You never know," she said. She was quiet for a moment, then I heard the TV in the background, the newscasters covering more of the protest. I got my own tablet out so I wouldn't miss anything, even though notifications were dinging in my ear. Other people were trying to get a hold of me too, no doubt about the news.

"This is amazing," Mara said. "They have to hire you back now."

"You think?" I asked, doubt filling my mind. Headmaster Bradford was proud, and it was no secret that the Alexanders had a lot of pull at Emerson Academy. "It would mean admitting they were wrong."

"Honey, if they don't, it doesn't look like they'll have any students left to serve."

My heart warmed, and I whispered, "I can't believe they're doing this for me. I always knew how much I loved my students, but I didn't know they felt this way too."

"You're easy to love," Mara said. "Just ask Cohen."

I wiped at my eyes, my throat feeling tight. "I treated him horribly, all because I thought it would save my job. He'd never trust me again."

"Are you sure about that?" Mara asked. "Get on video chat with me."

I drew my eyebrows together in confusion as I accepted her video call. Her camera was pointed toward the television screen in her living room, and the most handsome man I'd ever laid eyes on was looking into the camera.

He looked just as good as always, in brown jeans and a button-down shirt. His eyes were full of emotion as he spoke to the reporter. "I understand having rules for good conduct, to teach our children what is right and wrong. But I never want my son to think loving another consenting adult is wrong, especially if it doesn't affect how you perform your job."

I covered my chest with my free hand. It was a love letter to his son, to his son's right to be who he was. And it made me fall for Cohen that much more.

A commotion sounded to my right, and I saw my parents barging into the lobby. "Sorry, Mara, I've got to go."

67

COHEN

A roar ripped through the crowd, and I leaned closer to Ollie, yelling to be heard. "What's going on?"

"They're having a board of trustees meeting tomorrow to talk about it!" he said, pumping his fist.

I hugged my son tight.

We had a chance.

Birdie and I had a chance.

68

BIRDIE

Confession: I care what my parents think.

"Mom, Dad," I said, walking toward them. The nurse they were accosting with questions looked relieved.

"They're in room three thirty, but only two people are allowed in at a time."

Dad quickly offered to get us both coffee.

"I'll go back," Mom said determinedly, carefully adjusting her hair with her hands covered in silk gloves. She was wearing exactly what you'd expect one to wear to a labor—a floor-length ball gown, diamond earrings, and curled hair with jewel-encrusted pins.

All I thought was poor Anthea.

She walked past the nurses, swinging her train as she went.

I shook my head behind her. My life was looking more and more like a cartoon every day.

I went back to the chair I'd been sitting in and waited for Dad to come back. He balanced three Styrofoam cups in his hands and set them carefully on the table in front of us. Once they were all down, he took one for himself and handed one to me.

"How are you?" he asked.

I raised my eyebrows. My dad hardly spoke to me, much less asked how I was doing.

"I'm alright," I said simply. "You?"

He shrugged and took a sip of coffee. "I spoke to Walter today."

My gut immediately sank as I waited for him to continue.

"Said he's looking for an assistant and wanted to hire you for the job."

Good thing I hadn't taken a sip yet, because I would have spat it out.

"I told him no," Dad finished.

My mouth fell open, and I set the cup down. That was the last thing I'd expected to hear.

"I don't want to hurt your feelings," he said, "but I don't think you'd do well in the company. And if my golf buddy on the Academy's board of trustees is right, you won't be able to take the job anyway."

My lips parted. "What are you saying, Dad?"

He turned to me, his eyes full of emotion I usually never saw. "Honey, I know your mom and I have been tough on you, but it's hard to be a parent and see your child reject everything you are... It makes you wonder if you focused on the right things after all."

Part of me wanted to argue with him, but he was right. I never wanted the kind of life he and Mom gave me. "I just wanted parents who loved me."

"And we do." He gave me a hug. It was awkward, like he'd never practiced how to give one before, but he'd made an effort, and that meant the world.

As he pulled back, I smiled and said, "Thanks, Dad. For the not-job offer."

He chuckled and took a sip of his coffee. "If history's told us anything, it's that you're not Melrose Insurance material. And Walter is not Birdie Material. Grandpa Chester made sure to tell me that."

I laughed out loud. Grandpa was always there looking out for me.

Mom swept back into the lobby with a weak smile. "They brought out the needles, and I had to leave."

My eyes widened. "You saw the needle?" No wonder she looked so pale. Mom wouldn't even go in with me to get my vaccines when I was a child. She'd had to bring the nanny along instead.

She nodded slowly. "Now, distract me. Tell me about the guy."

I grinned, glad for a chance to tell them about Cohen. I loved talking about him almost as much as I loved thinking about him, no matter how much it hurt. "He owns a popular bar in between Emerson and Brentwood."

"A business owner," Mom said, seeming impressed.

"And he's really kind. The first time I saw him, I had a drink spilled all over my dress, and he brought me to buy a new one, just like that."

Dad nodded approvingly. "Chivalrous. I like that."

"He is," I said, "and he's a great dad. He really cares about his son."

"Your student," Mom confirmed.

I nodded sadly. "But I don't think it's going to work out."

Dad frowned. "Why not?"

"Because I dumped him in an attempt to keep my job, and well, you both know how that turned out."

They were quiet for a moment, and I said, "It's not my day. It's Doug and Anthea's. Let's focus on that."

Begrudgingly, they agreed.

For the rest of the evening and well into the night, we sat in the waiting room, getting periodic updates from Doug on Anthea's dilation. I checked on the news, read texts from my co-workers and parents who were secretly rooting for me.

The entire day was so emotional, building and balling in my chest, so when Doug came out grinning and said, "It's a girl," I burst into tears.

I went back to the room with him first, my cheeks and even some of my dress completely soaked from all the happy tears. With his hand on my back, he led me inside, and I saw Anthea in the bed, a beautiful, pink-skinned baby swaddled and lying against her chest.

I covered my mouth, crying more, and sobbed, "She's so beautiful." I went to Anthea and gave her a sideways hug, admiring the baby she and my brother had made. "Have you decided on a name?"

"Amelia Birdie Melrose," Anthea said. "For her godmother."

My hands went to my heart, beating out of my chest at the honor. "Are you sure?"

Doug walked to the other side and nodded with his wife. "Would you like to hold her?"

I nodded quickly, wiping my tears away.

Doug gently lifted the little baby bundle from Anthea's arms and passed her to me.

Carefully taking her in my arms, I looked down at the little goddess, a perfect person in and of herself. "Hi, baby girl," I cooed, pulling back gently at the blanket by her fingers. "You are absolutely precious."

She blinked up at me, and her finger wrapped around mine, a direct connection to my heart.

"What can I tell you about life?" I asked softly, a tear slipping down my cheek. I ran my thumb over her tiny fingers. "It's messy. But it's awfully beautiful too."

69

COHEN

So many people wanted to attend the board of trustees meeting, they held it in the courtyard. The group of six old men and the headmaster sat along a table positioned at the top of the stairs like they wanted to physically remind us who was in charge.

But I think Ollie and I and the thousand people behind us had shown them differently. Even Audrey was here with her new husband, in support of the cause. This was bigger than Birdie and me. It was about love.

I kept that in mind as they finished opening the meeting and Mr. Davis handed me a microphone.

My breath sounded over the speakers, and I pulled the mic away to inhale deeply. I'd practiced what to say, but now it was time.

I held the mic closer to my mouth, and in the other hand, I held the sheet of paper that included my speech.

"Esteemed members of the board, I come to you today as a father. When my wife and I were considering where to send our child to school, we had a few requirements. The school needed a good student to teacher ratio. The academics had to give him any opportunity he desired. And he needed to be taught by those truly dedicated to bettering students' lives in every aspect.

"My son had one request. That the playground be epic."

A chuckle rang through the crowd, and I used the chance to take another steadying breath.

"Of course, we decided on Emerson Academy. I drove my son up to the building on his first day of school, walked him into the classroom, and he quickly felt at home. For the last ten years, he's learned more math than I could ever hope to know, has read more books than I've read my entire life, and dreamed bigger than I was ever told to dream.

"He's also grown as a man. He's gone from making friends on the playground to deciding which kind of person he'd like to date and which he doesn't. He's learned about self-respect and consent."

I paused, my hands shaking on the page.

"Lately, he's learned about rules, and specifically that not all rules are fairly created or applied." I looked toward the row of men sitting atop the stairs for a long moment.

They needed to understand they hadn't just affected mine and Birdie's lives, but they were showing thousands of people what they thought was right.

"In the Emerson Academy handbook, it says the first purpose of the school is to serve the students. Above your head, engraved in stone, it says 'Ad Meliora.' My son recently informed me that means 'toward better things.'

"I want you to think about what your actions and bylaws say to your students. That a woman cannot both love a man and care for a child and perform a job. That two consenting adults cannot have both a career and a relationship. That a person cannot decide who to love."

A cheer roared through the crowd.

When they quieted, I said, "Birdie Melrose loves her students and this school. And I hope you'll give her the opportunity to love me too."

70

BIRDIE

Confession: I want to wear more pink.

I made it back to Mara's place Friday around noon and collapsed into my bed, falling asleep instantly. The adrenaline and emotion of the day before had wiped me out, and I slept like a rock.

At first, I didn't know what the vibrating against my shoulder was. I blinked my eyes open groggily, seeing it was nearly dark outside. Then I realized it was my phone. And Headmaster Bradford's name was on the screen.

I grabbed it and scrambled to my feet, rubbing my eyes to try to wake up.

"Hello?" I said.

"Ms. Melrose, it's Headmaster Bradford."

I nodded, then realized he couldn't see me. "Yes?"

"The board of trustees has met and decided they would like to have you back."

My lips parted, my brain moving too slowly to process the words he was speaking. "You want to offer me my job?"

"That is the position of the board," he said.

I walked down the hallway, not seeing Mara in her room or the living room, and stepped outside, hoping the fresh air would clear my mind.

"And the rule about staff dating parents?" I asked.

"Updated in the bylaws. It is permitted as long as it doesn't interfere with your treatment of the students."

"Wow," I breathed, sitting back on the swing.

"So, can I inform the protesters that you're coming back? Because, to be quite frank, this has been extremely disruptive to our learning environment."

I almost said yes, but the tone in his voice held me back.

"Do you want me to take the position?" I asked him.

"I'm offering it to you."

"That's not the same thing," I said.

He was quiet for a moment.

"Respectfully, Headmaster Bradford, I would love to have my job back, I would love to work with the students, but I want to be on a team with my administrators. I don't want to walk on eggshells anymore while trying to do my job, especially not with what I wear or the information I offer students."

He cleared his throat. "We are trying to prepare children for the professional workplace."

"Right," I said. "And I'm trying to teach students to never let anyone dull their sparkle. Our students aren't graduating to be employees; they're training to become *world changers*. How can they do that if they're playing by all of the rules, some of which are illogical?"

Headmaster Bradford was silent for so long, I checked my phone to see if the call had ended.

He let out a heavy breath and said, "This week, I've learned many things. Particularly that a small, unique voice can speak louder and resonate more than a powerful, established one."

I waited for him to explain what that meant.

"I think it's time for me to start listening to that voice instead of trying to silence it."

My lips lifted into a smile.

"So please," he said, "do me the favor of working with me again. I can't promise I'll be perfect, but I can promise that in the spirit of Emerson Academy, I'm willing to learn."

I bit my lip, smiling. "I'd appreciate a raise, for the extra instruction."

There was a smile in his voice. "Done. I'll see you, and Ralphie, Monday."

71

BIRDIE

Confession: I have a soulmate.

Mara and I sat on the couch I'd found just as another couple was dragging it out to the curb. They were moving out of another unit in the building and were planning on buying a new one for the house they had just bought.

All of my boxes were spread about the apartment, some of them half-open—like the sheets for my bed that had been waiting for me in Mara's garage or the wine glasses I'd gotten out for the bottle of Cupcake wine we shared.

Ralphie's cage rested on a box by the couch, and I couldn't help but be proud of the home that I'd found for both of us. With my salary, this place was within my budget, and I could finally start building wealth for myself, feel more secure in a place that was all mine.

We'd spent all day Sunday moving my things up the three flights of stairs, and I was exhausted, but also incredibly happy.

"I have a feeling," Mara said, taking a sip of the rosé.

"What's that?"

She smiled against her glass. "I have a feeling that the best years of your life are only just beginning."

I grinned back at her. "I can feel it too." My chest was light for the first time in months, and I finally felt like I could walk into Emerson Academy on Monday as myself, without having to work to be someone I wasn't. The freedom was amazing.

"How are Doug and Anthea doing with baby Amelia?" Mara asked. "Have you heard from them today?"

"Anthea sent me a picture." I got out my phone, going to my text thread with her, and pulled up the picture of her, Doug, and Amelia in the nursery. "They just got home this morning."

Her lips formed a wistful smile as she looked at the picture. "They're a beautiful family."

I nodded, setting the phone on the arm of the couch. "It'll be our turn someday."

"Someday." She took another drink of her wine. "Well, I'm proud of you."

"Thank you. And actually..." I got up from the couch

and started walking toward the bedroom. "I have something for you."

Mara had done so much for me, especially after Dax had moved out, leaving me high and dry. I knew I'd never be able to repay her, but I hoped she knew how much it truly meant to me.

I found the gift bag in my room and carried it out to her. Her eyes lit up as she saw it, and she immediately pulled out the tissue paper, unearthing a small jewelry box.

She looked up at me, curious, then flipped it open. Inside, there was a ring with a pink stone surrounded by small diamonds.

"What is this?" she asked.

"The other day, you were talking about how you feel like an imposter for writing romance even though you don't have your own happily ever after. But you are the most loving person I know. If anyone knows about love, it's you. I got this ring to remind you."

Tears shone in her eyes as she pulled the ring from the case and slipped it over her right ring finger. "What am I going to do without having you in the other room?"

"Girl, you know you're not getting rid of me that easily," I said, giving her a hug. "I'm just a phone call away. Plus, I'm keeping the spare key."

She laughed, wiping at her eyes. "Birdie, I think you might be the love of my life."

"I *know* you're mine."

72

BIRDIE

Confession: Condoms make great craft supplies.

I got up early Monday morning, because I knew it would take forever to dig through all of my boxes to find the things I wanted to wear to work. It was worth it too, because I found an adorable A-line sequined dress and a pair of strappy silver heels to go with it.

When I'd told Headmaster Bradford I didn't want anyone to dull the kids' sparkle, I meant it. But I realized I'd been hiding my own. Even before Dax broke up with me, I'd kept myself from dreaming of a bright life—one full of passion and love in all areas. Even when I met someone I truly cared for, I had tried to tamp it down.

I was done hiding any part of who I was or how I felt.

With my hair done, makeup on, and disco ball earrings dangling from my ears, I went down the stairs. An old couple lived in the ground-level apartment by the stairs, and I waved at them as they sipped their morning coffee.

"Have a great day," the woman, Coraline, said.

"Same to you." I waved with a smile.

As I got into my car, I heard her husband mutter, "Need to get sunglasses to look at that dress."

I giggled to myself. The outfit was working.

I couldn't wipe the smile from my face the entire way to school. I was early, because I'd have to carry my boxes back in, along with some extra decorative supplies I'd picked up at the dollar store over the weekend.

Today, though, walking into the school felt different. I realized it was just a building—it was the people inside who made it what it was. And after the protest and being offered my job back, I realized there truly were some amazing people here and that I could make a real difference.

I got to work on my bulletin board, hot gluing and sticking beads and sequins to create a shiny display with the quote *Never Let Anyone Dull Your Sparkle*.

Slowly, as I worked, the noise in the hallway grew. Student after student and co-worker after co-worker poked their head into my office, welcoming me back. I thanked each and every one of them with a hug or a high five—whatever they preferred.

After the first bell, another student came into my office: Ollie Bardot.

I immediately went to hug him. According to the news, he'd organized the protest, and I had him to thank for the fact that I was back in my office. "Ollie, I saw what you said on the news... I can't tell you how much that meant to me."

He stepped back, a shy smile on his face. "You and my dad were miserable. I had to do something." He rubbed his arm. "And I—I feel terrible about what Ryde did."

I shook my head. "Ryde's decisions aren't your responsibility. I hope you know I don't blame you at all."

He nodded. "I do."

"Good," I said.

He was quiet for a moment, then he said, "I wanted to thank you—for giving the therapist's information to my dad. It's been really helpful."

"Yeah?" I said, so incredibly happy for him. "That's amazing."

He nodded. "I realized that I don't want to be with someone like Ryde. I broke up with him."

"Wow," I breathed. "That must have been so difficult for you."

His lips turned into a slight smile as he shook his head. "Actually, it was surprisingly easy. Ryde only wants to love me in secret. But I think we all know love doesn't live in the shadows. It happens out loud."

Tears pricked at my eyes, and I nodded. "You're a

smart young man, Ollie. I have no doubt you will continue to do amazing things in your life."

"Thank you, Ms. Melrose."

I smiled and gave him another hug. "You can call me Birdie."

"Okay. I have to get back to class... but I have a suggestion for your board."

"Yeah?" I said, glancing back at the sequins I'd already applied. "What's that?"

He stepped toward the jar of condoms atop my filing cabinets, then pulled one out. "You know there's a silver side of the wrapper."

I grinned. "I like the way you think."

He handed me the condom and said, "I better go."

"You should have your own class," I said. "We have plenty to learn from you."

"Maybe someday." With a wave, he left my office, and I got back to work, using Ollie's idea to spell out the letters with the shiny side of the condom wrappers.

A few minutes later, a knock sounded on the open door. I turned to see Headmaster Bradford eyeing my bulletin board with a wry smile.

"Birdie," he said.

I set my glue gun down, rubbing my hands together to rid them of random strands of glue. "Headmaster. How are you?"

He looked away from the board to me. "Great. We're glad to have you back. However, there is still a protestor in the courtyard. Would you mind going to tell them there's no need? You already have your job back? I'm tired of dealing with them."

I chuckled and patted his shoulder. "Sure thing, boss."

He shook his head. "Come to my office after for a meeting so we can sign your new contract with the updated salary."

"Sure thing." I left my office door open, hearing him exchange a few words with Ralphie—no one could be rude to Ralphie—and continued down the empty hallway.

Who could possibly still be protesting? It seemed like every news channel had reported on the news of my rehiring.

I pushed open the double doors and stood at the top of the stairs in awe.

At the bottom of the stairs, Cohen Bardot held a bright pink sign with letters drawn in thick black marker.

BIRDIE, WILL YOU NOT-DATE ME AGAIN?

73

COHEN

My heart had never beat faster than it was right now.

Birdie stared down at me, her hands covering her mouth. I wished I was closer, that I could see what she was thinking behind her pretty blue eyes.

Her hand gripped the rail as she walked down the stairs on her high silver heels. Her dress was bright too, the sequins reflecting the sun. She looked every bit herself and more. I wanted to take her into my arms. To kiss her. To tell her I'd never seen her look more beautiful.

But soon the space between us was gone, and she stood only feet before me. "Cohen," she breathed, "what are you doing here?"

I lowered the sign, resting it on the ground. "I know you got your job back, but that wasn't the only thing I was upset about."

Her lips quirked as her eyes flickered from the sign to me. "Cohen..."

"Wait," I said. I needed to tell her how I felt. How much she meant to me. But I also needed to tell her how sorry I was. "I was upset when you walked away, but I understand why you did it. I put you in an unfair position, dating me in secret, and I want you to know how sorry I am for not respecting your wishes."

She shook her head, eyes shining. "Cohen, I wanted to date you too. Rules or not, you are exactly the kind of man I wanted to be with."

My heart soared and then sank. "Wanted?" I asked, studying her face. I wanted to remember every single thing about her. The dimple on her chin. The flush along her cheekbones. The curls that fluttered in the soft breeze. This could be the last time we spoke. The last time I saw her as more than Ollie's guidance counselor.

She blinked, sending tears down her cheeks. "Cohen, how could you ever forgive me for leaving you like that? We had such a good thing going, and I ruined it."

"Birdie..." I cupped her cheeks in my hands, wiping away the tears with my thumbs. "You didn't ruin anything."

"What does that mean?" she asked.

"It means if you'll have me, I'm yours."

I'd barely finished the word before she closed the distance and pressed her full lips to mine. It was everything I'd been too afraid to hope for. Everything I wanted.

Everything I *needed*. I slipped my arms around her waist, holding her close.

She tilted her head, kissing me with everything she had.

I got lost in the moment, letting myself savor what it felt like when dreams came true. I smiled against her lips, realizing I still needed my answer, to hear her say it out loud. "Birdie," I breathed.

"Yes?" She pulled back, giving me a perfect view of her beautiful eyes.

"Is that a yes to my question?" I asked.

She glanced at my sign and stepped back, biting her bottom lip. "No, I can't."

Blood rushed through my ears, the ground swayed beneath me, stronger than any California earthquake.

She stepped forward, taking my hands in hers, but I couldn't meet her eyes.

"I can't not-date you, Cohen," she said.

"Why?" I asked, forcing myself to look at her, even if it meant breaking my heart. "The rules are different, I—"

She held a finger to my lips. "I can't not-date you, because love doesn't live in the shadows." She moved her hand to my cheek. "I love you, Cohen Bardot. And it would be an honor to be with you."

My smile was so wide, and I couldn't stop myself from picking her up and spinning her. From dancing with the love of my life. "I love you, Birdie Melrose."

I kissed her long and hard until the air felt hot and I

wanted nothing more than to take her home. But we were at the school. "Can Ollie and I take you out after school? We want to celebrate."

She came closer, pressing her lips to mine again. "Work can wait. I'm busy sparkling."

CHAPTER 74
BIRDIE

Confession: My life looks so different one year later.

I looked around my empty apartment. The last year here had been nothing short of the best year of my life. Although, to be fair, I spent just as much time here as I had at Cohen's place.

A knock sounded on the door, and Henrietta, the property manager and a new friend, came inside with her clipboard. "I can't believe you've only been here a year. It seems like yesterday I was showing you around."

I grinned. "I know exactly what you mean."

She sniffed and said, "I'm happy for you, but I'm going to be sad not to see you every day!"

"Trust me, I'm going to miss you and the office coffee

maker very much. But we'll see each other next week at the housewarming, and we'll get drinks with Mara this weekend. It will be great."

She nodded, glancing back at her clipboard. "Let's get you checked out. You and Cohen have a lot of work to do." Going down the list, she walked around the apartment, checking the fixtures, that everything looked like it did when I'd first moved in.

When we finished with the walk-through, I gave her my keys and a hug. "I'll see you soon, Hen."

"You sure will," she said.

I walked down the three flights of stairs, realizing that was the only thing I wouldn't miss about this place. It had been an incredible home, but I couldn't wait to move in with Cohen and Ollie.

A house had gone on the market a couple months ago, on the same street as Mara's, and the three of us had quickly fallen in love with its charm, as well as its location. It might have been a little soon for us to buy a home together—we weren't even engaged—but Cohen and I both knew what we were to each other. There was no point in waiting.

I got in my car and drove toward my new home. (I still couldn't believe I was buying a house!) It appeared in my windshield, along with Cohen's car parked in the driveway. An overwhelming sense of peace consumed me.

This was *right*. I was exactly where I was meant to be.

I got out and went inside, ready to continue unpacking

and decorating with the love of my life. But I found something else instead.

The living room was already unpacked, but Ralphie's cage sat on the coffee table. "What are you doing here?" I asked him. I thought Cohen and I had agreed to keep him on the corner table on the weekends.

I went to pick up his cage to move him, but then I noticed a card leaning against the cage. It said. *Welcome home.*

I smiled at the words in Cohen's scrawl. At the meaning of the word *home* and how long it had taken me to find it.

I tucked the card carefully back in the envelope, planning to save it in a scrapbook. I wanted to remember everything about today.

But when I looked up, I saw Cohen kneeling in the arch between the living room and the dining area and Ollie standing behind him. Cohen held a red velvet box in his hands.

"Cohen," I breathed, shaking my head. This wasn't happening. It couldn't be.

He smiled up at me as I walked toward him. "Birdie Melrose. This has been the best year of my life. I've never been to an aviary more than we've been. And I've certainly never encountered so much glitter." He chuckled. "But I've also never laughed so often, and I've *never* felt as loved as I do by you."

I folded my hands over my heart. I loved him so much

it could have beat right out of my chest and landed in his palm.

"Will you and Ralphie do me the honor of being my happily ever after?"

Ollie kneeled next to him. "Will you be a part of our family?"

Tears fell down my cheeks, and I looked from Cohen to Ralphie to Ollie, smiling wider than I ever had. "Absolutely."

He slipped the ring onto my finger and took me in his arms.

We were finally, *finally* home.

EPILOGUE
MARA

I stood at the end of the table in Waldo's Diner where we were celebrating Birdie and Cohen's engagement. They didn't serve alcohol, but Grandpa Chester had gotten out a couple bottles of scotch from his office. We were all drinking it on the rocks—aside from Ollie and Birdie's one-year-old niece, of course.

"I'd like to make a toast," I said, quieting the rowdy crowd. All of Cohen's friends had been over the moon about the engagement. And Birdie's family? At this point, I was pretty sure we were just as in love with Cohen as she was.

Everyone held up their glasses, one by one, and I dug deep inside for the right words to say. Even though I was a romance writer and wrote about love all the time, speaking was hard for me. I wanted to make sure I got it right, especially since I couldn't edit myself on paper.

"Birdie is... the best friend a girl can have." Shit. My throat was already getting tight. "And Cohen? If he had a horse, I'd call him prince charming." Everyone around me chuckled. "We all know it hasn't been easy for them—with hard breakups, a divorce, and bull shit rules from schools that are still earning back my trust." Birdie sent me an exasperating smile. "Still, love won. As it always does. I love you two. Congratulations."

I lifted my glass a little higher and drank the rest of my scotch on the rocks, savoring the burn as it went down my throat. It blended with the aching in my heart.

I loved Birdie so much. She was my best friend and had been since we were twenty. Now, I was almost thirty, still single, and still writing smutty romance with no love in sight. But for the first time, I was starting to feel alone.

Henrietta, our new friend and Birdie's old apartment manager put an arm around my shoulders. "That was beautiful, as always."

I grinned at her. "I better get my act together for the wedding, though." They hadn't set a date yet, having just gotten engaged, but judging by the way they looked at each other, it wouldn't take long.

She chuckled. "You know you'll do great. And then you'll catch the bouquet and it'll be your turn."

I laughed out loud. That was the kind of story I wrote about. My real life story? It had all the early heartbreak of a fairytale. It was full of hot sex, sure. Plenty of new experiences too. But happily ever after? That wasn't likely to show up on any of my pages.

Birdie worked her way around her family and gave me a hug. "I love you, girl."

I hugged her back. "I love you too. I'm still pissed at Cohen for stealing you from me."

"You'll forgive him eventually," she replied with a wink. "Especially once you learn how amazing Jonas is."

I rolled my eyes. "I swear if you try to set me up with that accountant one more time, I'll—"

"Fall in love and live happily ever after?" Birdie said.

I took her glass and sipped from it. "I would ruin him. And you don't want me doing that to Cohen's friend. It'll make things awkward at the wedding."

She pulled her glass back and said slyly, "It'll all come together. You'll see."

♥・♥・♥・♥

Continue reading Mara's story in Confessions of A Smutty Romance Author!

Use this QR Code to access Mara's story!

Want to see what Cohen and Birdie's home together looks like? Check it out today!

Use this QR code to see Birdie and Cohen's home!

JOIN THE PARTY

Want to talk about Confessions of Being a High School Guidance Counselor? Join Hoss's Hussies today!

Join here: https://www.facebook.com/groups/hossshussies

AUTHOR'S NOTE

I've always been the kind of person who bucked the rules. That's probably because I'm the oldest of four siblings and I make the rules. Haha. Just kidding. (Although my siblings will probably tell you otherwise.)

But as I grew older, that inclination to push boundaries decreased. I don't know why—maybe more life experience or maybe just being worn down. Either way, when we encounter a system or way of life we don't like, we have a few choices: accept things as they are, change them, or leave it entirely.

This is the question Birdie and Cohen and Ollie were ultimately faced with. Did they want to go along with Emerson Academy's (stupid) rule at the cost of an amazing relationship? Or did they want to fight, and take some lumps along the way.

I love that they ultimately chose to fight—and that Ollie with his young spirit was the one to help them make big changes. In my opinion, love is always worth fighting for. Even if it's hard. Even if people don't understand.

I hope you'll always fight for love in your life. And if you're weary like me, I hope this story gave you some extra vigor. Just like Birdie, you deserve to shine.

ACKNOWLEDGEMENTS

This is my first book as "Kelsie Hoss" but I've written more than twenty as Kelsie Stelting. After years of writing young adult romance, my readers encouraged me to step into adult, and after getting Birdie in my head, I couldn't let go.

I want to thank my readers, from the bottom of my heart, for pushing me as an author. This book was hard and so so fun to write. I hope you absolutely loved it.

Thanks to my mom for reading my book and not giving me too much guff for writing "spicy."

And thank you to my siblings for always being my loudest cheering section. I love you all so much.

Thanks to Tricia Harden, my editor. One of my favorite parts of the writing process is seeing her comments in the edited document. They make me smile and encourage me to be better.

I'd also like to thank my cover designer, Najla Qamber, for bringing such a beautiful design forth for this cover. It is so gorgeous!

And thank you, dear reader, for picking up this book and reading it through! With each page you read, you were helping a dream come true. <3

ABOUT THE AUTHOR

Kelsie Hoss writes sexy romantic comedies with plus size leads. Her favorite dessert is ice cream, her favorite food is chocolate chip pancakes, and… now she's hungry.

You can find her enjoying one of the aforementioned treats, soaking up some sunshine like an emotional house plant, or loving on her three sweet boys.

Her alter ego, Kelsie Stelting, writes sweet, body positive romance for young adults. You can learn more (and even grab some special merch) at kelsiehoss.com.

facebook.com/authorkelsiehoss
instagram.com/kelsiehoss